SUMMER LOVING

OCEAN SHORES #2

BARBARA FREETHY

Fog City Publishing

PRAISE FOR BARBARA FREETHY

"A fabulous, page-turning combination of romance and intrigue. Fans of Nora Roberts and Elizabeth Lowell will love this book." — *NYT Bestselling Author Kristin Hannah on Golden Lies*

"Freethy has a gift for creating complex, appealing characters and emotionally involving, often suspenseful, sometimes magical stories." — *Library Journal on Suddenly One Summer*

"Barbara Freethy is a master storyteller with a gift for spinning tales about ordinary people in extraordinary situations and drawing readers into their lives." — *Romance Reviews Today*

"Freethy is at the top of her form. Fans of Nora Roberts will find a similar tone here, framed in Freethy's own spare, elegant style." — *Contra Costa Times on Summer Secrets*

"Freethy hits the ground running as she kicks off another winning romantic suspense series...Freethy is at her prime with a superb combo of engaging characters and gripping plot." — *Publishers' Weekly on Silent Run*

"PERILOUS TRUST is a non-stop thriller that seamlessly melds jaw-dropping suspense with sizzling romance. Readers will be breathless in anticipation as this fast-paced and enthralling love story evolves and goes in unforeseeable directions." — *USA Today HEA Blog*

"I love the Callaways! Heartwarming romance, intriguing suspense and sexy alpha heroes. What more could you want?" — *NYT Bestselling Author Bella Andre*

PRAISE FOR BARBARA FREETHY

"Gifted author Barbara Freethy creates an irresistible tale of family secrets, riveting adventure and heart-touching romance." *NYT Bestselling Author Susan Wiggs on Summer Secrets*

"Freethy skillfully keeps the reader on the hook , and her tantalizing and believable tale has it all -- romance, adventure and mystery." *Booklist (Starred Review) on Summer Secrets*

"A warm, moving story of the power of love." *NYT Bestselling Author Debbie Macomber on Daniel's Gift*

"Freethy's zesty storytelling will keep readers hooked, and the sisters' loving but prickly interactions will make anyone with a sibling smile." *Publishers Weekly on Summer Secrets*

"Freethy has a gift for creating complex, appealing characters and emotionally involving, often suspenseful, sometimes magical stories." — *Library Journal on Suddenly One Summer*

"Tragedy haunts her, regrets shadow him and passion lures them into a mystery as dangerous as their feelings for each other. Freethy captivates with a sensuous game of tainted hearts and tempting romance. My Wildest Dream is a hotbed of intriguing storytelling. Brodie and Chelsea are sure to get under your skin." I*sha C – Goodreads*

"I have just finished CAN'T FIGHT THE MOONLIGHT and WOW such an emotional story. Absolutely loved this book...and can't wait for the next one!" *Booklovers Anonymous*

CHAPTER ONE

Maverick's Bar and Grill was crowded when Gabe Herrera arrived just after ten o'clock on Friday night. After the day he'd had, he needed a drink, and Maverick's was his go-to bar. Located on a bluff overlooking the ocean in Oceanside, California, it was only a few blocks from his apartment at Ocean Shores, and he knew just about everyone who worked at Maverick's, including his roommate, Max Donovan, and the owners of the bar, Brad and Tyler Morrison.

He was almost to the door when he heard his name called. He turned to see his nineteen-year-old sister, Christina, hurrying toward him, her long black hair flying out behind her. His first thought was that her dress was too short and her heels too high, but she wasn't a little girl anymore, and he needed to keep those thoughts to himself. He just felt protective. At thirty-one, he was twelve years older than Christina, and after their father had died eight years ago, he'd had to step into his dad's shoes and help watch over his three younger siblings, all of whom seemed to be in some sort of crisis at the moment.

"What are you doing here, Christina? Is everything all right?"

"Mama wants to kick me out of the house," she replied in dramatic fashion.

He let out a quick breath, happy her trip to see him was just about another fight between Christina and his mother. "There's no way that's true. She wouldn't kick you out."

She gave him a hurt and angry look. "I wouldn't lie."

"Why would she say that?" he asked. "What did you do?"

"I didn't come home last night. It was late, and I stayed at Eric's apartment. I meant to send her a text, but I forgot."

"So, she gave you the speech about if you want to live with her, you have to follow her rules."

"I'm nineteen, Gabe. I'm an adult. If I was away at the university where I wanted to be, she wouldn't even know what I'm doing, but I stayed home and went to community college to save money, and now I'm being punished."

"You're not being punished, you're being loved."

"I'm being smothered."

"She worries about you, Christina. And you're going away to school in September. It's June. You have three months to get through. Just go home by midnight and you'll be fine. Or don't forget to text Mom if you'll be late, so she won't worry."

"It won't be fine. I want to live my own life the way you do, the way everyone else in the family does. I hate being the youngest."

Her whining made him smile. She might be nineteen, but sometimes, she still sounded like she was nine.

"Our house is also like a childcare center since Laura moved in," Christina added. "And guess who she's always looking for when she needs a babysitter?"

"I had to babysit you when I was a teenager," he reminded her.

"Hardly ever," she retorted. "I need you to help me, Gabe."

"I can't convince Mama to bend any rules for you." He knew that for a fact because Christina was not the first one of his siblings to ask him to do that.

"Then maybe you could lend me some money," she suggested, giving him a pleading look. "I can move in with my friends for the summer. Kim got a place near the beach. There are two bedrooms, and there will be four of us in the apartment. It will be pretty cheap."

He frowned at her request. "I don't know, Christina. I have a lot going on."

"But your business is so successful, and it's really not that much money. I just need an extra three hundred dollars a month for three months. That's a total of nine hundred dollars. I can cover the rest with my job. I'll pay you back, I promise."

"It's bad timing, Christina. Lucas asked me for cash today, too. His car broke down, and he can't get to work without it. Can't you just hang in at home for a few more months?"

"I'm going crazy, Gabe. It's not just Laura and her kids or Abuela's health issues; it's also Mom. It's the anniversary of Dad's death this week, and she's so sad; she's crying all the time. When she's not crying, she's angry. I cannot be in that house anymore. I've been the one living with her the past eight years while the rest of you went off to do your own thing. I need a break. It's not like I won't visit her and Abuela; I just need my own space."

There was truth in her statement, and he felt bad he hadn't realized the burden she'd carried. "All right. I'll help you with the apartment."

She immediately threw her arms around his neck and gave him a hug. "Thank you, thank you," she said. "You're saving my life."

"I'll give you three hundred a month, but you have to come up with the rest yourself."

"I will. I'll tell Kim I'm in."

"And about Eric..."

She rolled her eyes. "Don't go all big brother on me."

"So, I can be a big brother when you need money, but no other time?" he asked dryly.

"Fine. Say whatever you have to say."

"Don't let him call the shots. You're young. Live your life, not his."

"Well, of course. What else would I do? I'm not looking for anything serious," Christina said. "We're young. We're having fun. I'll talk to you soon."

As Christina jogged across the parking lot, he sighed. He was a sucker for his family, but he couldn't help it. He was the oldest, and if they needed help, he was there.

Turning toward the door, he headed into Maverick's and made his way through the crowd to the bar where Max was mixing drinks. Max had black hair and striking blue eyes, and the ladies were often lined up at his end of the bar. But Max was more than a bartender; he was an aspiring screenwriter, and two weeks ago, he'd gotten an option picked up on one of his screenplays and was heavy into rewrites. Even now, he could see the distraction in Max's eyes. He might be serving up cocktails, but his mind was in the apocalyptic thriller he couldn't wait to bring to the screen and finally get his big break.

He'd met Max three years ago when Max's roommate had moved out, and he needed someone to split the rent in his two-bedroom, two-bath apartment at Ocean Shores. While he hadn't been looking for a roommate, the extra space and the lower rent was enough to convince him to grab the deal and not look back.

He was pouring all of his money into his food truck, and he didn't much care where he slept. Living with Max had turned out to be good for a lot more reasons than saving money. He'd become part of the Ocean Shores community, where he'd made a ton of friends and found a second family. Not that he needed a second family. He had his hands full with his first one. But his second family wasn't continually coming to him looking for a handout, and that he appreciated.

As a stool emptied at the bar, he slid into the seat. A moment later, Max put a whiskey in front of him.

"How was your night?" Max asked.

"Busy and long," he said, taking a sip of his whiskey. "Business has picked up since I changed locations, but the truck is old and it's starting to break down. I don't know how long I can keep it operating. Nor do I know how long I want to. Working in that small space is starting to get to me."

Max gave him an understanding look. "You'll be in your own restaurant one day. You're too stubborn not to get what you want."

"I hope you're right."

"I am. By the way, Michael dropped by. Your brother said he just got accepted into law school, and he needs to talk to you about his tuition. I told him where you were parking your truck these days. Did he find you?"

"No, he didn't. Law school, huh?" He wanted to feel happy for his younger brother, Michael, but all he could think about was how he was going to help Michael with tuition, pay for Lucas to get a new car, and subsidize Christina's rent. "I don't know why my family thinks I'm made of money."

"Maybe because you don't share your problems with your family," Max said pointedly.

That was true. But there was no point in sharing. While his siblings might come to him for help, he could only rely on himself. "How are you doing, Max? How are the rewrites going?"

"Not well. I ran into a plot problem today that I can't quite figure out. I'm going to work on it tonight when I get out of here."

"I'll stay out of your way."

"I wouldn't notice if you were there. I barely know what's going on here. My mind just wants to get back into my story."

"I thought you were going to take some time off."

"He is," Brad Morrison said as he stepped up to the bar next to Max. Brad was a friendly, outgoing guy in his early thirties with sandy blond hair and brown eyes. He owned Maverick's with his brother Tyler. "Starting now," Brad added. "Dave and I can cover for you the rest of the night, and for the next week, too, if you want to take some shifts off and work on your screenplay."

"That would be great," Max said. "I just need a few days."

"You've got 'em. Go."

"I'm not going to argue with you," Max said. "See you at home, Gabe."

"Good luck with your plot twist," he said. He smiled at Brad as Max left. "You're a generous boss."

"Max is more of a friend than an employee, and I want this movie to get made."

"So do I. Max has been working hard on his craft for a long time."

"Speaking of working hard for a long time, how's the new location going?"

"Surprisingly great. My regulars have found me, and there's more parking by the park. There's also more foot traffic in the area, so it was a good move."

"But it's not the restaurant you wanted. How is that place doing?"

"Looks pretty dead to me," he said.

"They should have hired you."

"Well, they didn't. Anyway, we don't need to talk about that."

"I hear you. You should drink, relax, have some fun. There are a lot of pretty women here tonight."

He grinned back at him. "You're still allowed to notice the pretty women?" Brad had gotten married in March to Serena, a pretty brunette who also worked at Maverick's, and they both lived at Ocean Shores.

"He can look but not touch," Serena said as she joined her husband at the bar. "How are you, Gabe? I haven't seen you around the building lately."

"I've been working a lot."

"Well, I hope we can catch up some time." Serena turned to her husband. "Can I grab you for a second?"

"Always," Brad said, giving her a wicked look.

Serena laughed and shook her head. "Not for fun. The guy who booked the back patio wants to talk to you."

"Again? He has complained three times already."

"I don't think he's having the best night. The woman he's throwing the party for seems to be interested in someone else."

"Well, that makes me feel sorry for him. See you later, Gabe. Have some fun tonight. You look like you could use it."

As Brad left, Serena poured him another whiskey. He'd no sooner gotten his drink when a group of women crowded in behind him.

"Would you mind sliding down?" one of the women asked. "We're having a bachelorette party, and we want to sit together. There's a seat down there."

"No problem." He was happy to get away from the heavy cloud of perfume that now surrounded him. Plus, the empty seat at the other end of the bar was next to a stunningly pretty blonde, whose green-eyed gaze sent a jolt through his body when he sat down.

"Hello," he said, unable to stop staring at her. She looked a little familiar, but there was no way he'd met her before. He wouldn't have forgotten her eyes, which held an expression mixed with too many emotions for him to decipher. Then she turned her gaze back to the shot in front of her, picked up the glass, and downed it.

"Tequila?" he asked as she set the glass on the table with a shiver.

She nodded. "Yes. My friend bought it for me."

"Your friend?" He was really hoping it wasn't a male friend.

She tipped her head toward a dark-haired woman who was making out with a guy at a nearby table. He didn't recognize either one of them. "She looks like she's found another friend."

"She did. I should probably just go."

"Or," he said, not wanting the conversation to end. "I could buy you another drink."

She hesitated, giving him a pointed look. "I'm not interested in hooking up."

"I just offered to buy you a drink."

"Because you want to hook up."

"I just want to talk to you. Another tequila shot or do you want to switch it up?"

She hesitated. "All right. I'll take a margarita, and then I'll be done."

He motioned to the bartender working this end of the bar and ordered her a margarita. Then he said, "What's your name?"

She shook her head. "Let's not do that. Let's not exchange names or talk about our jobs or where we went to school. It's so boring."

He couldn't really argue with that. He'd gotten bored with first-date conversation a long time ago. "Okay. What do you do for fun when you're not shooting tequila?"

"I don't think I remember," she said slowly. "It's been a while since I thought about fun."

"Think about it now."

"I like to play the piano," she said after a moment.

Her answer surprised him. He'd thought she'd say working out or yoga. "Are you good?"

"I'm average."

"How often do you play?"

"Lately, almost never. I haven't played since I moved here a few months ago."

"Where did you come from? Or is that on the list of taboo questions?"

"San Francisco."

"A lot colder there."

"That's true." She paused as they got their drinks. "I like the warm evenings around here."

"Let's make a toast," he said, lifting his glass.

"To what?"

"How about—escape? For the next hour, we have no worries, no problems, no family."

She picked up her margarita glass. "I could definitely drink to no family."

"Me, too," he agreed as they clinked glasses. He felt a little guilty as he shared in the toast. He did love his family. They were just a lot.

"I like this song," she said suddenly as she swayed in her seat to the beat of a Jason Mraz song. "Music has always been an escape for me."

"Not just tequila then."

"I almost never drink this much," she said, slurring her words a little. "But I feel good. What about you?"

"Getting better by the minute. I also like music. And I enjoy surfing, too. Or is that too much information about me?"

She gave him a guilty smile. "I was rude when I said I didn't want to know anything about you, wasn't I?"

He shrugged. "I get it. You probably get hit on all the time."

"It's not that. When I ask someone a question, I know they're going to ask me a question, and I'm just tired of myself. It's been a long month, and I want to get away from everything for a night. Is that okay? If not, I'm sure one of the bachelorettes would love to talk to you."

"I'm good here," he said, finding himself becoming more and more intrigued by her. "We don't have to get personal. How about three questions, three answers, and if we like what we hear, we keep talking?"

"All right," she said warily. "But you already asked a question, so you only have two more."

"You're a big rule follower, aren't you?"

"Is that your question?" she asked with a tipsy smile.

"No," he said quickly. "I can't waste my question on that." He thought for a moment, trying to think of something that wouldn't be boring. "What's your most embarrassing moment?"

"What if I don't have an embarrassing moment?"

"Then I'll know you're a liar. And that was one question for you."

"You got me," she said. "Okay, let's see. I've had quite a few embarrassing moments, actually. I was an awkward kid." She gave him a self-deprecating smile. "I had railroad tracks of braces on my teeth until I was a freshman in high school, and in the ninth grade, I had a huge crush on Mick Vimiglio. We were at the Halloween fair together, and it was going well. I was sure he was going to kiss me at some point. But before that could happen, he bought us caramel apples." She paused, catching his eye. "That's right, caramel apples."

"Bad idea."

She nodded. "I didn't want to say no, so I bit into the apple. My braces got stuck on the caramel, and there was apple juice and caramel dripping from my mouth. I couldn't get the apple off my braces. It was just horrible."

He laughed at the expression on her face, her words creating a very unfortunate picture. "I'm sorry for laughing, but that sounds awful. Did Mick give you a second chance?"

"God, no. Everyone was laughing at me. Mick was never going to date a girl who was that embarrassing."

"I think it was his loss. Look at your teeth now. They're perfect."

"They better be. I went through a lot of pain to get them. Your turn, same question."

"Mine involves a kiss scenario, too. I was in the tenth grade, at a homecoming dance. I'd been seeing this girl Emma for a few weeks, but she was ignoring me at the dance. I got annoyed and went out to the parking lot to drink beer with one of my friends whose older brother had hooked us up."

"That sounds like a bad idea, too."

"It got worse. After chugging two beers, we went back to the dance. I marched up to Emma, pulled her around and planted a kiss on her lips. Only, it wasn't Emma. It was a girl who looked like her. She punched me in the eye. My friends thought it was hilarious. Emma thought I was an idiot."

"You were an idiot," she agreed.

"In my defense—"

"You have a defense?" she challenged.

He grinned. "You're right. I have no defense. I was hanging around with stupid friends with stupid ideas, but I was the one who acted on them."

"Did you and Emma stay together?"

"Nope. Is that your third question?"

She frowned. "It wasn't, actually. It was a follow-up question. That's allowed."

"So, we do have rules for this conversation. And that wasn't a question, either," he said hastily. "It was an observation."

"I like rules because I don't like to mess up. Unfortunately, that still seems to happen even when I think I'm doing everything right."

"We all screw up. It's called being human."

"That's not what they call it in my family," she said darkly as she sipped her margarita.

"What do they call it?" he asked curiously.

"Disappointing, unacceptable, not what *we* do." She took another drink.

"I'm beginning to see why you wanted to toast to no family."

"Yes, so let's stop talking about them."

"Then it's your turn for a question."

"Is it hot in here?" she said, fanning her face.

"It's warm. I'm assuming that wasn't your real question."

"It wasn't." She set down her drink. "What's your favorite food, the one thing you'd want to eat before you die?"

"That's a little dark." He realized there was an undertone of darkness behind a lot of things she said. She was clearly having some sort of drama in her life, which meant he should probably get up and go, because she had trouble written all over her. But she was so pretty. He couldn't stop looking at her, and he couldn't stop talking to her. At least, not yet.

"Are you going to answer my question?" she asked.

"I'm thinking. Last meal, huh? That's a tough one. I like to eat. I have a lot of favorite foods."

"This has to be a special meal. Will it be a decadent dessert, a spicy stew, a melt-in-your mouth steak, or would it be fries and a cheeseburger?"

"You're making me hungry."

"And you're stalling."

"I would hate to have to choose, but if I had to pick one meal, I'd pick hallacas."

She gave him a confused look. "What are hallacas?"

"You've never heard of one of the most popular dishes in Venezuela?"

"I have not."

"My abuela, my grandmother, makes them every Christmas. A hallaca is like a tamale but better. The filling is made from chicken, pork, and beef, along with corn masa, then it's wrapped in banana leaves and the leaves are tied with twine, preferably red, if it's Christmas. The hallacas look like presents, and they taste like heaven." He paused. "My abuela was sick last Christmas. It was the first year she didn't make them. It didn't feel like Christmas without her bustling around the kitchen making her favorite dish."

She stared back at him. "Is she better now?"

"Yes. She swears she'll be back on her feet and making hallacas come December."

"Was your grandmother born in Venezuela?"

"In Caracas. My grandparents came to the US when my father and his siblings were very young."

"Have you ever been there?"

"I went when I was eighteen. It was a wonderful trip. I enjoyed seeing where my grandparents came from. They grew up in poverty, but their dreams took them to the US. Their journey has always inspired me to try harder. My abuelo, my grandfather, died about ten years ago. I still miss him."

"It sounds like you were close to your grandparents."

"I'm close to everyone in my family." He cleared his throat. "But we aren't talking about family tonight. What about you? What's your choice for a last meal?"

She didn't hesitate for a second. "The perfect roast chicken with mashed potatoes and roasted baby carrots."

"Really? That sounds dull for a last meal. No spice."

She frowned. "It's not dull. It's simple perfection. Why doesn't anyone understand simple can be great?"

He had a feeling she was talking about more than her choice of a last meal. He sipped his whiskey. "Then roast chicken it is. Hopefully, neither of us is dying soon."

The music grew suddenly louder as the bachelorette party started an impromptu dance party in the middle of the bar.

"That looks fun," she said with a wistful look in her eyes. "They're so carefree, just living in the moment."

"Well, so are we." He got up and held out his hand. "Let's join them."

"This isn't a dancing kind of bar."

"It is now."

"I'm not a good dancer," she protested.

"You don't have to be good. You just have to move. Come on, beautiful stranger. Dance with me."

Her gaze flickered with hesitancy, but then she said, "Okay," and she slid her hand into his.

The heat between them almost knocked him off his feet.

She must have felt the same jolt because she tried to jerk her hand away, but he held on tight and pulled her into the laughing, dancing group of bachelorettes. Others in the bar joined in, too, and suddenly it was a full-on dance party.

At first, she was a little stiff and restrained, but as the music played on, she let go. It was an amazing thing to watch, like a tight flower bud opening up to the sunshine. Her blonde hair swung around her beautiful face, and she moved her body in a way that made him want to get as close as he could.

One song led to two, then three, and with each beat of the music, she seemed to relax even more, freeing herself from whatever had made her feel so wary, so unhappy. All the shadows were gone as she danced and smiled and laughed until the impromptu dance party finally slowed down.

Hot and sweaty, they moved outside with the crowd to get some air. He wasn't ready to let her go, so he pulled her toward the bluff overlooking the sea on the pretense of getting more of the breeze. But once there, he took her into his arms, craving her lips, her touch, her body with every breath he took.

And she was right there with him, kissing him back with the same enthusiastic fervor.

Everything around them faded into nothing. He couldn't hear the cars in the lot or the people chattering as they waited for their rides. All he could hear was the roaring sound of the blood in his veins as he kissed the beautiful stranger, whose name he still didn't know. But names were the last thing he wanted to share now.

He just wanted her.

And then his phone started buzzing in his pocket. He ignored it the first two times, but finally, he pulled away. "I'm sorry. Someone is trying to call me." He saw Michael's name flashing on the screen. "It's my brother."

"You should talk to him," she said breathlessly. "I should go anyway."

"Wait. Just wait a second. I'll tell him I'll call him back."

"I don't think so." She pulled away from him, taking two steps back.

He felt a cold chill. "Are you sure I can't take you home?"

She stared back at him for a long minute. "You already had your three questions."

"But if we were having fun, there could be more than three, remember?"

"I can't." She shook her head. "I'm sorry."

His phone started buzzing again. "Damn."

"Answer your phone. I'm going to call for a ride."

She walked away, pulling out her phone as she did so. "Wait," he said.

She flung him a smile. "I had fun. Goodnight."

"I don't want to say goodnight."

"You just did," she said as she moved toward the line of people waiting for rides.

The incessant buzzing of his phone finally drew his attention away from her. He answered the call.

"What the hell do you want, Michael?"

"I've been trying to get a hold of you, Gabe. I got into law school. Can you believe it?"

He heard the amazement and happiness in his brother's voice and felt bad for answering the phone so abruptly. "Congratulations. I want to talk about this, but can I call you back?"

"Okay, but I really need to talk to you about the tuition. I have some idea on how I can cover everything, but I might need help."

"We'll talk about it," he promised. "I'll call you."

He ended his call and ran toward the line waiting for ride shares. He was almost there when he saw her get into a car and slam the door. The car pulled away a moment later. His beautiful stranger was gone, and he didn't even know her name.

CHAPTER TWO

"You look like hell," Drea Scott told Madison Baldwin when she walked into La Marée restaurant Saturday afternoon.

Madison frowned at Drea, who wore a simple black dress, her brown hair pulled back in a French braid, her brown eyes sparkling with humor. Drea appeared to be bright-eyed and clear-headed after her night at Maverick's, while she had a hammer pounding against her right temple.

"My headache is your fault," she said pointedly. "I told you tequila shots were a bad idea."

"I only bought you the first shot. The second one was your idea, and I don't know what happened after you started chatting up that sexy guy at the bar. What was his name?"

"I don't know."

Drea's gaze widened in surprise. "Seriously? You didn't get a name?"

"I didn't want his name because I didn't want to give him my name."

"Why not?"

"I wanted to have fun and not talk about myself or my job. I just wanted to be a woman in a bar, which, by the way, was also your idea. Remember? But you bailed on me twenty minutes after we got there. That was not cool, Drea."

"I know." Drea flashed her a guilty look. "But I've been crushing on Marcus for weeks, and I couldn't believe it when he showed up at Maverick's. In fact, I couldn't believe I'd never been there before. Thank goodness, my friend, Lexie, from yoga told me about it. There were a lot of attractive men. I may have to rethink living in Encinitas when my lease comes up. There are a lot more fun places to go to in Oceanside. Anyway, I am sorry for not hanging out with you. But when Marcus told me he'd broken up with the woman he was dating, I had to grab my opportunity."

"You grabbed a lot more than opportunity," she said dryly.

Drea laughed. "Guilty. But you told me to go for it. Don't you remember?"

She vaguely remembered having said something like that. "So, are you two a thing now?"

"I don't know about that, but we had a lot of fun last night and this morning."

"You're moving fast."

"It's been a long time, Madison."

"I know." She was happy for Drea. Her friend had been in a dating slump the past year since she'd caught her ex cheating on her. "I hope it works out."

"We're a long way from working out; I just want to keep seeing him. What about the guy you were with? Will you see him again?"

"No," she said flatly.

"Really? He looked interested from what I saw."

"I don't even know his name, and I don't have time to date. I only went with you last night because the bookings were down, and I was depressed and frustrated. I needed to blow off some steam. But now I need to focus. This restaurant is hanging on by a thread. And if it fails, it's on me. This is my first and maybe my last opportunity to run my own restaurant. I have to make it a success."

"You will," Drea said with confidence. "We've only been open a month. It's early days. And you've been running on empty for a few weeks. When the pressure gets too high, sometimes you need to let off a little steam. I still think it was good you went to the bar last night. And as for your mysterious, good-looking stranger, he probably goes to Maverick's all the time. You could always go back to the bar."

"Did you not just hear me say I have to concentrate on this restaurant? And besides that, I need to find a more permanent place to live. There are so many things on my to-do list, I can't add any more."

Drea let out a sigh. "I hear you."

"Good. How's tonight looking?" she asked with some trepidation, hoping for positive news, but steeling herself for bad.

The smile on Drea's face faded. "Two parties just canceled."

"Why? Why is no one coming here? This place is amazing. Isn't it?"

She shook her head in bewilderment as she looked around the beautiful restaurant that she and the owner, Larry Shaw, had created. It was sophisticated and luxurious, with glittering crystal lights discreetly placed above and between expensive paintings.

Square tables filled the dining room, with a row of semi-circular booths upholstered in deep- blue fabric, offering intimate and cozy seating. The back of the dining room was all windows, offering a view of a garden patio filled with shrubbery and a fresh herb garden that she utilized every day in her menu.

The other side of the room boasted a sleek, marble-topped bar with glass shelves lined with an impressive selection of wines and spirits. Behind the bar was an enormous gleaming mirror adding depth and sparkle to the room.

Everything was top of the line, and perhaps a little over the top, she secretly admitted. Larry had embellished every simple idea she'd had, so while it wasn't her vision exactly, it was still very pretty. It was certainly a place diners should want to come.

She'd called the first two weeks a soft opening, encouraging her staff to bring in their friends and family members and using a publicity firm to market the restaurant on social media. While comments had been positive, they'd seen little increase in business.

She hadn't expected instant success, but she also hadn't anticipated such a slow pace of growth. She had to find a way to get more customers into the restaurant or Larry would lose confidence in her. She could already tell by his daily calls that he was starting to wonder if he'd made the right choice in hiring her, and she couldn't let him question that, because part of the reason he had hired her was because he was good friends with her father.

It was the one and only time in her life she'd accepted a favor from her dad, and now she had two people she couldn't let down —three, if she included herself.

"Everything looks good, and the food is phenomenal. It will get better," Drea said, with an optimistic note in her voice. "It will just take time."

She wanted to believe Drea. Her front-of-house manager had been working in restaurants for almost fifteen years. She'd actually met Drea eight years ago at a restaurant in New York City. She'd been a sous chef then, and Drea, a waitress. For two years, they'd been great friends, until Drea had moved back to Southern California to help her divorced sister take care of her kids.

Despite the distance between them, they'd always kept in touch, and when she'd been hired to run Larry's new restaurant, her first call had been to Drea. She was good with customers and knew exactly how to handle the waitstaff. Plus, she was a great cheerleader to have, and her unflagging cheerful attitude definitely helped her keep her head up.

"It will get better," she agreed. "We just need to find a way to draw more customers in."

"I was thinking about that, Madison." Drea pulled a piece of paper from the shelf underneath her countertop. "You might want to consider this."

"What's that?" she asked warily as Drea handed her the flyer. She shook her head as soon as she read the headline for the *San Diego Cook-Off*. "No. I don't do competitions like this."

"It would be a great way to get local buzz and interest in you. Everyone who watches these competitions wants to go to the restaurants of the competitors. You'll become a local celebrity."

"I don't want to be a celebrity. I want to be a chef."

"Can't you be both?"

"Even if I was interested, I don't have time." She handed the flyer back to Drea.

"You might have to make time. You need something to jump-start this place. You shouldn't dismiss the opportunity so easily. I've watched this competition before. It's very well-run. The media shows up at every round, and it's televised as part of a series of cooking competitions on the Culinary Network. It's also livestreamed on the Internet. It has a far bigger reach than you might imagine. And while we're not in the heart of San Diego, we're an easy drive for someone who wants to have a fine-dining experience by an incredibly talented new chef in the area."

Drea made a good argument, but she inwardly shuddered at the thought of putting her skills on display in a competition. She wasn't good at competing. She did not like cameras or people watching her every move. On the other hand, it probably would help drive business to the restaurant. "I'll think about it," she said. "But now, I need to get to work."

"One last thing, Madison. My friend, Lexie, said there's an open apartment in her building. It's right on the beach, and it's not far from here. It sounds perfect. I know you're eager to get out of that residence hotel."

"I am. That sounds good."

"I'll text you Lexie's number. She said to call her tomorrow, and she can show it to you. Her aunt manages the building."

"Thanks. It would be a relief to settle in somewhere, and I never seem to find time to look at anything. Although, the way business is going, maybe I shouldn't make a move yet," she added, feeling a weight of fear she couldn't seem to shake. Her initial optimism had definitely taken a hit the past several weeks.

The phone rang. "Maybe this is a new reservation," Drea said with a smile.

"I sure hope so."

As Drea took the call, she left the dining room and entered the kitchen, instantly feeling better. Kitchens had always been her safe space, and this one was perfect in every way. It was a chef's dream. Larry had spared no expense in setting it up, never questioning her expertise on what was needed in the kitchen. But it was too clean and too quiet. She wanted to feel the heat of the stoves, hear the quiet, efficient chatter of her staff, and smell the food cooking. But with the limited number of reservations on the books, none of which were coming in for an hour, there wasn't much to do at the moment.

Her chef de cuisine, Elliott Vemeer, a classically trained French chef, was sitting on a stool checking his phone, while one of her prep cooks was chopping carrots at a very slow pace. Her other prep cook wasn't even in the kitchen. He was probably outside taking a cigarette break.

Her sous chef was flirting with her pastry chef, which seemed to be happening more and more often. She wondered what was going on there and how it might affect their relationship in the kitchen going forward, but she didn't have the energy or the time to worry about that right now.

Clearing her throat, she said, "Hello, everyone. Let's get ready for a great dinner service. We may not have a packed house, but we want everything that leaves this kitchen to be perfect. Let's get to work."

Her words were met with polite smiles and at least the

appearance of energy as Elliott got off his stool and put his phone away and her sous chef returned to his station while her pastry chef turned her attention to the cake she was making.

She told herself it was all good, but she was faking it as much as they were. It wasn't all good, and she didn't know what to do about it.

———

Around seven thirty on Saturday night, Drea came into the kitchen with a worried look on her face.

"What's wrong?" Madison asked immediately. "You're not bringing back a plate, so..."

"It's not the food. Larry just walked into the restaurant with your father."

"What?" she asked in shock. Her father lived in San Francisco, and the owner of the restaurant, Larry Shaw, spent most of his time in Los Angeles. Neither of them was supposed to be in the restaurant tonight.

But she should have seen this coming. She'd had disturbing conversations with both of them over the last few days, with each expressing doubts about her running the restaurant. Her father, Philip Baldwin, had wanted to remind her that if she let Larry down, she was letting him down. She was tarnishing his reputation because he'd recommended that Larry take a chance on her.

Larry was obsessed with the numbers. He had a lot of money on the line, and he was not a patient man. She'd told both of them she just needed time. Each had agreed that made sense, but here they were.

"They just sat down," Drea continued. "Larry wants you to come out and say hello."

"I'll be right there." She took off her chef's coat and walked out of the kitchen.

When she got into the dining room, she paused by the bar.

Larry and her father were talking to their server about wine, so it gave her a minute to compose herself. She needed to be calm and to speak articulately. They were not her enemy. Larry was her boss and Philip was her father, and they both wanted her to succeed. It helped her to reframe the upcoming conversation in those terms. But she still delayed, telling herself it would be better to talk to them after they got some wine.

Larry Shaw was a short, stocky man with a square face and thinning brown hair. Her father, Philip Baldwin, was his opposite: tall and lean, with silver hair that brought out his green eyes. She'd gotten her green eyes from her dad, probably the only thing she'd gotten from him. They were as different as two people could be.

But Larry and Philip were very much the same person, both extremely successful businessmen, who based their success on the size of their bank accounts and their prestige on the private clubs they belonged to. They weren't completely shallow, though; they were both philanthropists, and they supported nonprofits and entrepreneurs trying to make a difference in the world. That was one thing she liked about both of them.

Larry was also a little softer than her father, so he was easier to talk to. Larry liked to joke and laugh, while her father rarely found anything funny. He was a man who kept a very tight rein on his emotions, which made it impossible, at least for her, to get close to him.

As the server came over to the bar, she realized her time was up. She walked over to their table and forced a smile on her face.

"Hello, this is a surprise," she said.

Her father immediately stood up and kissed her on the cheek. It was a cool, barely there kiss, but his manners were always impeccable.

"We had a meeting in LA today," Larry said. "Philip wanted to see the restaurant, so we drove down. I didn't expect it to be this quiet so early on a Saturday night."

"There's a line down the street for a food truck," her father said, tipping his head toward the front window. "We could barely get in the door. This is disappointing."

In her head, she didn't hear the word "*this*"; she heard "*you*". *You are disappointing.* It was a phrase that had been used to describe his feelings toward her since she was a little girl.

As she followed his gaze to the crowd on the sidewalk, she felt another wave of frustration. She'd sent Elliott to talk to the food truck owner last week, asking him to move his truck and his line, but he'd refused, showing Elliott his permit.

"What do you think of the dining room?" Larry asked her dad as Philip took his seat.

"It's very nice," her father said. "I just wish it was more crowded."

"So do I." Larry sent her a pointed look.

"We've only been open a month. It's going to take time. But we're getting good reviews every day. Are you going to have dinner?"

"Yes," Larry said. "I'll have the duck."

She nodded. The duck was his favorite dish and one he had insisted she showcase. "What about you, Dad?"

Her father looked at the menu, then said, "I'll go with the steak. Make sure it's medium rare."

"Perfect," she said, ignoring his request. She always served her steaks medium rare. "What about appetizers and dessert?"

"Why don't you send us a variety?" Larry suggested.

"Will do."

She headed back to the kitchen. "Listen up, everyone," she said sharply. "Larry is here with my father, and we're going to give them the meal of their lives."

For the next hour she cooked, making sure she tasted everything before it left the kitchen. She tried not to think about her father or Larry, just the food. That was where she could shine.

Their plates continually came back clean, so she felt like the meal was going well. After the dessert was delivered to their table, she gave them a few minutes and then took off her chef's jacket and reentered the dining room.

Larry and her father were the only two people left in the room, which gave her a sinking feeling in the pit of her stomach. But she pushed past that and approached their table with a smile.

"How did you enjoy your meal?" she asked.

"It was wonderful," Larry replied. "You can definitely cook, Madison. We just need more people to know that."

"I'm glad you liked your food." Her questioning gaze moved toward her father.

"It was good," Philip said. His words brought a momentary flash of happiness, until he added, "But clearly you have problems here that go beyond the food."

"Those problems are being addressed."

"I hope that's true. I need to get to the airport. I have a late-night flight to San Francisco." He got to his feet. "Your mother wants to come down two weeks from now. Hopefully, things will look better by then." He turned to Larry, giving him a brief smile. "We'll talk soon. Thanks again for supporting Madison."

"Happy to do so," Larry replied.

She didn't like the exchange between them, the idea that Larry was still doing her father a favor by keeping her on. But with the situation she was currently in, she didn't have any ammunition with which to fight that belief.

"Why don't you sit down?" Larry said as her father left.

She took the seat next to him. "I know the numbers have been slower than anticipated, but I believe it will change. I will make it change."

"I hope so. Your food is wonderful, Madison."

"Thank you."

"But I'm a businessman. If my investments don't turn a profit in a short amount of time, I move on."

"I understand, but four weeks isn't enough time for any restaurant. There's always some massaging of the menu, the prices, everything..."

"I agree. But there is a limit to my patience. I'll give you four more weeks. That will be two months in business. If you can't show a significant amount of growth by then, I'm going to bring in someone who can."

"You won't have to do that," she said, infusing as much confidence as she could into her statement.

"I hope that's true. But I don't live by words, only results. You're a talented chef, but I need someone who can run a restaurant, who can bring in a crowd. I respect your father a great deal, and I want to do right by you, so I'll give you more time. Your success is in your hands, Madison. Don't tell me what you can do...show me."

"I will," she promised. "I won't let you down. Can I get you anything else?"

"No. I need to get going."

"Are you staying in town tonight?"

"Yes, but I'll be leaving early in the morning." He gave her a small smile as he set down his napkin. "I know you probably didn't appreciate our pop-in visit, but your father and I wanted to see the restaurant the way any customer would see it. I didn't want you to do anything special because we were coming."

"I understand." She got up and walked Larry to the door.

As he stepped outside, he had to navigate his way through a thick line of people waiting to get tacos from the food truck parked down the street. She could see his expression tighten as he looked at the crowd, probably wondering why a food truck could draw so many customers while La Marée could not.

There was really no comparison in food quality or pricing. It was a completely different customer base. But it was frustrating to see so many people willing to wait in line for tacos when they were standing right outside her beautiful restaurant. The line was not only blocking her front door but also prohibiting anyone from driving by to see her signage.

On the other hand, the line made it difficult to argue that this street didn't get foot traffic.

Drea came up next to her. "Do we still have jobs?" she asked.

"For the time being, but Larry wants to see a lot of progress by the end of two months—four weeks from now."

"That's not much time. Any thoughts on how we're going to turn things around?"

"I have one thought. I need to get this damn line to go in the other direction. It's blocking our door."

"There's no one trying to get in our door," Drea pointed out.

"Well, they couldn't if they wanted to."

"I don't think there's anything you can do. The owner of the truck has a permit. His truck is parked however many yards away from us it has to be."

"But the line is a hazard. I'm going to talk to whoever's in charge. I'm going to get this line moved."

"Okay, but then what?"

The line wasn't her biggest problem, but at the moment, it was the only problem that seemed solvable. "I don't know. But I'm going to start there."

She moved down the block as fast as she could, which wasn't that fast as she had to weave her way through the line. When she got to the bright-orange truck, she saw two windows, one for purchasing and one for picking up food. There was a young man in one window and a woman in the other.

The large menu board was filled with colorful photos of tacos, enchiladas, and a special of the day. There were all kinds of boastful words, like "world's best" and "Southern California's hottest", and she had to admit there was a delicious smell emanating through the air.

But she didn't care about any of that. Bypassing the line, she went up to the back door of the truck and peeked her head in. "Hello?"

A man stepped away from the grill to give her a questioning look. "Yes?"

"Are you the owner?"

"No. He's not here."

"When will he be back? I have a restaurant down the street, and your line is blocking my entrance."

"He'll be back soon," the man said, turning his attention to the grill.

"Actually, he's back now," a voice said from behind her.

She whirled around in surprise, shocked even more by the man standing in front of her, the man with thick, wavy brown hair, dark-brown eyes, and a sexy mouth that he knew how to use really well.

This was the man she'd made out with last night in the parking lot of Maverick's, the one she'd never thought she'd see again.

"Well, if it isn't my beautiful stranger," he drawled. "You found me."

"I wasn't looking for you. I was looking for the owner of this truck."

"That's me. Gabe Herrera. And you are?"

"I'm the chef at La Marée."

Now he was the one with shock running through his dark-eyed gaze. "You're the chef there?"

"Yes. I'm Madison Baldwin." She cleared her throat. "Your line is blocking my door. I was hoping you would get someone to move it in the other direction."

"I just walked by your restaurant. It's closed."

"Well, yes. It's closed now, but this is happening all the time, even when the restaurant is open, and it's hurting my business."

"My line for tacos is hurting your fancy restaurant?" he drawled, an unmistakable note of sarcasm in his voice. "How could that possibly be? According to the owner, he was bringing in a chef so good, his restaurant would be overflowing with customers."

"When did you speak to Larry?" she asked warily.

"When he bought the space. I heard he was an investor looking for a chef to build a restaurant, so I offered to bring him my business, but he said he was only interested in fine dining."

"Well, that was his choice. He's the owner."

"And you were his pick. Now you're struggling. Interesting."

"I didn't say I was struggling. I said your line is blocking my door. I'd appreciate if you'd move it, starting tomorrow, if not tonight."

He gave her a long look. "I don't have the manpower to keep track of my line. Sorry."

"Really? That's all you're going to say? I thought you were..." Her words faded away as she realized she didn't know what she thought. She knew he was fun and friendly and a great kisser, but she knew nothing else about him.

"You thought I was what?" he prodded.

"A nice guy."

"I am a nice guy. But I have two people working the windows and one person cooking. I don't have anyone else to monitor a line. Why don't you put a cone in front of your door or something?"

"A bright-red cone? That's not going to go with my vibe."

He shrugged. "That's your choice."

She stared back at him. "You're doing it on purpose, aren't you? You're mad you didn't get to put your restaurant in that space. That's why you're parked down the street, why you're blocking the door, isn't it?"

"I can't say I didn't want to show your boss how much business I could bring in," he admitted. "But I also like this street. And I have a permit. You're just going to have to deal with my line. Or I'll have to deal with yours."

Except she didn't have a line, which annoyed her, and the smug look on his very attractive face didn't help. "Did you know who I was when we met last night?"

"No," he said, shaking his head. "I had no idea who you were.

But now that I think about it, your question regarding my choice for a last meal makes a lot more sense. Of course you'd want the perfect roast chicken. No spice for you. Just bland, sophisticated perfection."

"Have you eaten my food?"

"I have not," he admitted.

"Then you have no idea how good my food is."

"And you have no idea how good my food is. Although, this line should give you some indication."

"We're not competing in the same ballpark. You serve tacos for five dollars."

"The best tacos in the world," he told her. "You should try one. I'll even give it to you for free."

"No, thank you."

"Too good for tacos?" he challenged.

She shook her head, wondering how her hot, mysterious stranger had turned into this guy. "I don't know why I ever kissed you last night. You're cocky and obnoxious and boastful. If you have to tell people your food is the world's best, it's probably not."

"And you're pretentious. Acting like the only food worth eating has to be expensive and sophisticated, put together with tweezers, and have very little flavor."

"You're jealous because I got the restaurant, and you didn't."

"Well, I heard you got it because your father is friends with the owner."

She really hated that he knew that. "That's not why I got it. I'm a damn good chef."

"Didn't you just tell me that someone who has to boast about being the best probably isn't? If you're that good, then why is your restaurant half-full every night?"

"This isn't over," she vowed. "I'm going to get your line to move."

"I don't think my line is your problem," he returned. "But feel free to do whatever you need to do."

"Oh, I will," she said. She practically ran down the street, rage propelling every step.

She flew into the restaurant and slammed the door behind her.

Drea looked at her in surprise. "What the hell happened? You look like you're about to explode."

"It was him," she said. "The owner of the food truck. He was the guy in the bar last night, the one I made out with in the parking lot. The one I thought was sexy and fun and kind and... Well, he is none of those things. He's an ass."

"I take it he doesn't want to move his line."

"No. He wants to put me out of business."

"What are you talking about?"

"He spoke to Larry when Larry first bought this building. He wanted to be the chef here. He wanted to make his tacos inside this restaurant. That's why he's parked down the street. He wants to show Larry he made a huge mistake in hiring me." She paced around the room. "But that's not going to happen. I can't let him win. I need to beat him down, Drea. He thinks he can compete with me. He serves food out of a truck."

"What are you going to do?"

"I don't know, but I have to do something."

Drea pulled out the flyer. "Then do this cooking competition. You just said you wanted to beat him. Look at the list of chefs and the restaurants already entered."

She took the flyer, her gaze running down the page to find Chef Gabe Herrera from Picante Express. Gabe was signed up for the competition, along with at least twenty other chefs, some of whom were from restaurants she knew about, others she had never heard of.

"There's a twenty-five-thousand-dollar prize for the winning chef," Drea continued. "And as I mentioned before, the competition will be covered by the local media and food critics from around the country. Each round will be livestreamed on the Internet and broadcast on a show called *Chef Battles* on the Culi-

nary Network. It's a cooking show featuring various competitions from around the country. You want people to know who
you are, and this can't possibly hurt." Drea paused. "Unless
you're afraid you'll lose?"

"I'm not going to lose," she vowed.

"Does that mean you're going to enter?"

CHAPTER THREE

Gabe went for a six-mile run on Sunday morning, needing to burn off the conflicting emotions that had kept him up all night and hopefully get the image of Madison Baldwin out of his mind. He couldn't believe the beautiful blonde from the bar, the one who kissed like a dream, had turned out to be his worst enemy. He also couldn't believe she'd had the nerve to tell him to move his line away from her door when her restaurant was closed, and she barely had any customers anyway.

He'd been watching her restaurant ever since it opened, still feeling burned that Larry Shaw had given the space to his friend's daughter. When he'd talked to Madison's executive chef last week about his permit, the guy had been a pretentious asshole. And Madison had given off the same air of entitlement when she'd given his food truck a look of disgust and asked him to move his line.

He'd worked hard to get that line. What had she done? Used her father to get her own restaurant. Maybe she was a good chef; he had no idea. None of his friends had gone to the restaurant, mostly because he'd talked shit about the fact that he should have gotten that job instead of her, so he had no idea whether her food was good or not.

What he did know was that the restaurant was struggling, and that gave him some satisfaction. He'd wanted Larry Shaw to see he could bring a crowd, and he'd done that, which was why Madison wanted him to move his line away from her door so his success would be less obvious.

He wouldn't do that. He'd moved his truck from the parking lot at Maverick's for the explicit reason of proving he could take his customers anywhere, and he would continue to sell from that location until La Marée failed.

Frowning, he felt guilty about wanting any restaurant to fail. And it wasn't like Shaw was going to suddenly wake up and hand him the keys to La Marée and tell him to do whatever he wanted with it. Clearly, Shaw had wanted a fine-dining restaurant in that location, and he was not that kind of chef.

Putting aside his reasons for moving his truck down the street from La Marée, his new location was actually better for him than the Maverick's parking lot. He didn't have to compete with their burgers and fish and chips.

La Marée didn't take his customers away because his customers would probably never eat there. The truth was that he was no competition for Madison, and she was no competition for him. He might have told her that last night if she hadn't started immediately attacking him.

He couldn't believe she was the same woman he'd danced with at Maverick's. That woman had a vulnerability behind her drinking bravado. That woman had been friendly and fun.

But he'd seen none of that friendly fun or vulnerability last night.

He slowed his pace down to a walk as he headed into the courtyard of the Ocean Shores apartment building where he lived. It was almost eleven now and a very warm June day, so there were already sunbathers at the pool, including Kaia Mercer, an attractive redhead who worked as a paramedic, and her brother, Ben, who had dark hair and eyes and had recently transferred to the Oceanside Police Department and moved in a few doors down from his sister. Ben had once been in a band, and he often seemed to be with his guitar, which he was now strumming softly while Kaia spoke to Emmalyn McGuire, a pretty and fair blonde, who was floating on a blow-up unicorn in the pool.

"Hey, Gabe," Kaia said as he walked toward them. "You look sweaty."

"Just finished a run," he said, thinking the pool looked inviting.

"I hit up your food truck last night," Ben said as he stopped playing. "I didn't see you there, but I had a burrito supreme, and it was very good. Kaia has been raving about your food for a while, and for once in her life, she was right."

"I've been right lots of times," Kaia told her brother.

"I'm glad you enjoyed the burrito," he said. "How's the new job going?"

"Still feeling my way," Ben replied. "I like who I'm working with, and it's a nice change to be stationed by the beach instead of downtown Los Angeles."

"You'll never want to leave."

"That's what Kaia keeps telling me," Ben said with a laugh. "By the way, I hear you're in a softball league with Max."

"I am. The season just finished, but there's a summer league starting in July. You interested in playing?"

"Absolutely. I used to pitch when I was in high school."

"We can always use a pitcher. I'll let you know when sign-ups open." He turned to give Emmalyn a smile. "Where did you get the unicorn?"

"Ava gave it to me. One of Liam's distributors dropped off a bunch of blow-up floaties for the Beach Shack, and she thought we could use some here. Are you coming in for a swim?"

"Maybe later."

"Well, I'm planning to be here all day," Emmalyn said. "School is out for the summer, and I am so ready for it."

He laughed. Emmalyn was a kindergarten teacher, and he

could only imagine how much she needed a break. "I bet you're more excited than your students."

"That's probably true, but it won't be a summer-long break; I'm teaching summer school, and that starts in two weeks. Until then, this is where you'll find me." She paused. "How's Max doing with his rewrites? I've seen your living room lights on late at night."

"He's been working a lot. He has to turn something in early next week."

"I really hope his movie gets made. He deserves it."

"I agree." He paused as he saw two women walking down the stairs toward the courtyard, and one of them was Madison. He was shocked. *Why was she here? Why was she with Lexie? If she knew Lexie, why hadn't she known he owned the food truck that was driving her crazy?* Nothing was adding up.

He heard Lexie tell Madison she wanted to introduce her to some of her friends, and then they were heading in their direction. As they drew near, Madison's step faltered as her gaze connected with his. She looked as shocked as he felt.

"Hi, everyone. We have a new tenant," Lexie said. "This is Madison Baldwin. She's going to be renting 16B."

No way! She was renting the apartment right around the corner from him?

Lexie introduced Madison to Kaia, Ben, and Emmalyn, leaving him for last. While the others had all given her a warm greeting and welcome to the building, he could find absolutely no words, and neither could Madison. Finally, he said, "We've met."

"Yes," Madison said shortly.

"You're moving in here?"

"I am," Madison replied. "I didn't know you lived here."

"Maybe you should change your mind then."

"Why would she do that?" Lexie asked in surprise. "What's going on?"

"Gabe doesn't like me because I'm running the restaurant he wanted to run," Madison said evenly.

"And Madison doesn't like me because my food truck line is so long, it's blocking the entrance to her restaurant," he returned, his gaze meeting hers.

"At least you admit it," Madison said. "Even if you refuse to do anything about it."

As anger sizzled between them, mixed with other emotions he didn't want to identify, he noticed the hushed interest in the group by the pool. He cleared his throat. "Well, welcome to the building."

"I'm sure you don't mean that, but whatever," she said.

"Whatever," he echoed, walking past her. He took the stairs two at a time, his pulse racing way too fast. He could not believe Madison was moving in here. Ocean Shores was his home, his haven, a space where he always felt good. Maybe she would change her mind now that she knew he was here. He'd seen the disdain in her eyes when she'd looked at his food truck. She thought she was above him.

As he entered his apartment and slammed the door behind him, Max looked up from his computer, giving him a questioning look. "What's wrong? You look like you want to punch someone."

He ran a hand through his hair. "I just met the woman who's moving into 16B."

"And?" Max asked. "Did she do something to piss you off?"

"She's the chef of La Marée."

Max's eyes widened. "The one who got into it with you last night?"

"Yes."

"I did not see that coming."

"Neither did I."

"Maybe you should talk to Josie or Lexie before she signs the lease."

"It's a done deal. She's signing it now." He paced around the room, the peaceful, happy feeling from his run having quickly vanished. And it wasn't just because Madison rubbed him the wrong way; it was also because she'd rubbed him the right way before he'd known who she was.

He still couldn't sync the woman he'd met at Maverick's who'd just wanted to drink and dance and make out, with the self-righteous chef from La Marée. It bothered him that he hadn't seen who she really was at Maverick's. But clearly, she had not been herself that night. The woman who wanted him to move his line away from her empty restaurant—that was the real Madison Baldwin, not the sexy, flirty blonde whose kiss he couldn't quite forget, but really needed to.

"Do you want to get some breakfast?" Max asked, distracting him from his thoughts. "I could use a break from my computer. Pancakes at Daisy's?"

He probably needed another run more than pancakes, but seeing the stressed expression on his friend's face reminded him that he wasn't the only one with problems. "Sure. But let me take a shower first."

"I'll be ready when you are."

He nodded, then went into the bathroom and turned on the shower, keeping the temperature cool because he was definitely feeling overheated.

————

"Is Gabe living here going to be a problem?" Lexie asked as she showed Madison the laundry room.

Her pulse was still pounding after seeing Gabe and realizing he lived at Ocean Shores. She'd had no idea. And if she had, she wouldn't have even looked at the apartment. But now that she'd seen it and met some of the residents, she didn't want to say no. She'd been living out of a residence hotel for two months, and she wanted a place that was hers, where she could move her furniture in, where she could set up her life. And this place was perfect. It was right by the beach, and she'd loved the apartment.

Although, after her conversation with Larry last night, was she wise to sign a lease? What if she didn't make good on her promise to increase business at La Marée? What if she was out of a job in four weeks?

But she couldn't keep living in a hotel. And she had to have confidence in herself. Maybe this was a step in the right direction. And it wasn't like she'd have to see Gabe.

That thought brought a question to her mind. "Where is Gabe's apartment?"

"It's around the corner from yours. He's in 12B."

"Oh, that close, huh?"

"You two don't like each other?"

"I don't really know him," she said, not wanting to think about or mention the night they'd kissed as two strangers who were very attracted to each other.

"Gabe is a great guy. I know there's some problem with his food truck and your restaurant, but hopefully you can work that out."

"I'm not sure we can. Gabe told me he wanted to work for my boss, but I got the job instead of him. That's why he parked his truck down the street from my restaurant, so my boss would see how busy his truck is. That doesn't sound like a great guy."

"Gabe has been looking to get into a restaurant for several years," Lexie said slowly. "I know he was very interested in that space and disappointed when he didn't get the job, but I'm sure he doesn't blame you for that. You're not the owner, right?"

"No, I'm not, and I had no idea he'd talked to the owner or that anyone else was in contention until last night when he told me."

"Gabe is passionate, but he is a good person," Lexie said. "He's very well-liked around here. We have a lot of tenant events: barbecues, happy hours, and more. If you think the two of you being in the same building will be a problem, then maybe you'll want to reconsider renting the apartment."

She probably should reconsider, but she didn't want to. "I want the apartment. I'm sure you're right that once Gabe and I get to know each other, we'll be able to work things out."

"Okay, good," Lexie said with relief. "Drea told me you're an amazing person, and I know Gabe is as well. I have to believe two amazing people will find a way to get along."

"It will work out," she said, not sure that was true, but she wouldn't let Gabe stop her from getting the perfect apartment or losing her perfect restaurant.

"Great. I'll introduce you to Aunt Josie now. She's the official manager, and we'll sign the paperwork and give you the keys. How soon will you move in?"

"Is tomorrow okay?"

"Eager to get out of that hotel, are you?"

"You can't imagine. It's so sterile and impersonal."

"Well, Ocean Shores is anything but that."

"The restaurant is closed on Mondays, so it's a good day for me to rent a truck and get my stuff out of storage."

"If you need help with manpower, I have people I can recommend. They help with a lot of moves in and out of Ocean Shores."

"That would be great. You're making this so easy, Lexie."

"We do whatever we can to help. You're going to love living here, Madison."

"I hope so," she said. "I'm ready to settle in somewhere."

"I can't wait to try your restaurant."

"I'd love to have you. Let me know what day you'd like to come, and Drea and I will make sure you get a good table and the best service."

"I'll let you know."

As she followed Lexie out of the laundry room and back into the courtyard, she saw several more people had joined the group by the pool. There was a lot of conversation and easy laughter, and she could feel the warm, friendly vibe.

She didn't know if that vibe would include her if Gabe made it a point to ostracize her from the group, but she'd deal with that if it happened. She'd had a lot of practice. She'd been the outsider many times in her life, including her own family.

She couldn't really imagine what it would feel like to be on the inside of a group, part of familiar teasing jokes and banter. But she needed an apartment more than she needed a group, so she was going to sign the lease, get the keys, and move in before she changed her mind.

CHAPTER FOUR

"I can't believe you put your apartment together so fast," Drea said as she walked around Madison's apartment early Monday evening.

She tucked a loose strand of hair from her ponytail behind her ear as she looked happily around her living room, proud of what she'd accomplished. She didn't have a lot of furniture, but the pieces she'd acquired during her somewhat gypsy life of cooking in restaurants around the country gave her comfort and a feeling of home.

"I had a lot of help," she said. "The movers Lexie recommended were fast and efficient. I couldn't believe they could come on less than twenty-four hours' notice, but Lexie made it happen. She's great, by the way. I'm so happy you introduced me to her."

Drea flopped down on the sofa. "She is really sweet and a very talented photographer. You might want to hire her to take some professional photos of you in the kitchen at La Marée. I know the PR company took some, but I don't think they were that good. Maybe we could build a social media story about you."

"That's a good idea, but we don't have money in the budget for more photos. Plus, I need to think about what will move the needle in terms of profitability, and I don't think that photos of me will do that."

"I understand." Drea paused. "Anyway, this apartment building feels fun. There were some hot guys around the pool. I should have taken this place for myself."

"You had first shot at it."

"But I also have a lease for six more months," she said with a sigh.

"Something might be open when you're done with your lease. In the meantime, you can spend all the time you want here."

"I'm going to take you up on that." Drea reached into her bag and pulled out the flyer that Madison was starting to hate. "The deadline is tonight at midnight. Thinking time is over. You're a great cook. You could win this competition and make a name for yourself with the local foodies and critics. Not to mention all the cash you could win."

"I know," she said with a groan. "I just don't want to do it."

"Wouldn't it feel good to beat your food truck nemesis?"

Her lips tightened at the mention of Gabe. She hadn't seen him during her trips back and forth to the moving truck, which she'd been extremely happy about, but it was only a matter of time before their paths would cross again. She'd made sure of that by moving into his building.

"That would feel good," she admitted.

"Then sign up."

"I don't know. It's not the cooking that worries me; it's the cameras, the audience, and the judgment. The producers will try to create drama."

"Of course they will, but you can handle it."

She wasn't as sure of that as Drea seemed to be, but she was running out of excuses.

"Where's your computer?" Drea asked. "I'm not leaving until you submit your application. You just said you need to do something that will make a real difference, and this is your best option, so stop being so stubborn and sign up."

Drea was right. She got up from the couch and grabbed her computer, then came back and set it on the coffee table. "Okay, let's do this."

It took about twenty minutes to fill out the form, a little longer than it should have, because she wanted to read everything carefully to make sure she knew what she was getting into, while Drea kept urging her to just say yes to everything and hit Submit.

But she refused to go too fast. Skipping important instructions because they seemed too long to read had gotten her into trouble before. In the end, she couldn't find any real reason not to enter, so she sent in her entry. She just hoped there would be enough chefs in the competition that she wouldn't have to deal with Gabe.

"You won't be sorry," Drea said.

"If I am, I'm blaming you."

Drea laughed. "Put it on the list."

She grinned back at her. "It's getting to be a long list."

"Well, I have to go, so we'll discuss the list later," Drea said as she got to her feet. "I'm meeting Marcus tonight."

"Really? That's still going?"

"It is," Drea replied with a happy smile.

"Have fun." After Drea left, she looked around her apartment, feeling a sense of relief that she finally had a home again, and while it was sparsely furnished, it felt relaxing with her plush light-gray couch, oversized armchair, and her white coffee table, already decorated with a vase of flowers that Drea had brought by.

Under the window, she'd set her television on a long white table with a shelf for books. She wasn't a reader, but she'd put something on the shelf at some point to make it look less bare. In the corner of her living room, she'd set up a keyboard with a small stool in front of it. It wasn't the piano she would like to have one day, but for now it would let her play her stress away, which meant she'd probably be playing a lot in the next few weeks.

As her gaze moved to the small dining area next to the open kitchen, she thought about picking up some colorful placements for her round, white table, and she definitely needed to get some food for the refrigerator. Dinner she usually grabbed at the restaurant, but she needed breakfast and lunch items.

Her doorbell suddenly rang, and she jumped up, wondering if Drea had forgotten something. But when she opened the door, there was a blonde woman with pale, freckled skin, and warm, friendly eyes in the hallway. She had a basket of wildflowers in her hand.

"I'm Emmalyn McGuire," she said. "We met yesterday at the pool. I was on the unicorn."

"I remember."

"These are for you—a welcome to the building."

"That's very thoughtful. Thank you."

"I was going to make you cookies. That's what I usually do, but Lexie said you're a fancy chef, so I decided to stick with flowers."

"Well, I'm not a pastry chef, so I also appreciate homemade cookies. But these are beautiful."

"Do you need any help unpacking?" Emmalyn asked.

"Uh, no, I think I'm set. Do you want to come in for a minute?" she asked hesitantly, a little taken aback by Emmalyn's friendliness. She was used to living in buildings where neighbors didn't mingle.

"Sure, for a minute. I won't keep you," Emmalyn said as she moved into the room. "Wow. You've done a lot. It took me a month to hang all my pictures. Not that I have art this nice."

"They're just pieces I've collected along my travels. I love art. It inspires my cooking and my plating."

"That's cool. I don't know much about art. At least anything beyond kindergarten art. I'm a teacher. We do a lot of drawing and painting in my classroom, but it's mostly blobs, not pretty scenes like this. Have you been to Paris?" Emmalyn asked, pointing to a painting on her wall of a Paris street scene.

"Yes, I studied cooking there for over a year. It was one of the best years of my life."

"Paris seems like a magical place. I'd like to go there," she said with a little sigh. "Maybe someday."

There was a wistful yearning in Emmalyn's eyes as her gaze lingered on the picture. Then she shrugged off whatever emotion was gripping her and put a smile on her face as she turned back to her. "I heard there's a rivalry between you and Gabe."

"Only on his side," she returned. "I don't feel like we're in competition at all. Our menus are very different."

"Have you tried his food? It's amazing."

"I haven't had the chance."

"Well, I'm sure you will get one. He usually parks the truck in the lot once a month so we can all partake. We have a lot of events here. Josie, the manager, likes everyone to feel like they're part of a big family. Some people take a little more warming up to the idea than others, of course. But I hope you won't be one of them."

"I'm looking forward to meeting everyone." As she finished speaking, her doorbell rang again. She opened the door to Lexie and a strikingly good-looking man with black hair and bright-blue eyes. She'd seen him Friday night at Maverick's. He'd been behind the bar.

"We brought you some housewarming gifts," Lexie said, handing her a bowl of fresh berries while the man held out a bottle of wine. "This is Max Donovan. He's a screenwriter. He lives down the hall."

"I think you served me a drink Friday night," she said.

"I did," he said with a nod. "I also work at Maverick's, and full disclosure, I share an apartment with Gabe."

She wasn't thrilled to hear that, wondering what Gabe had said about her, but she wasn't sure she wanted to ask that question. "Please come in."

They brought their gifts into the apartment and set them down on her small dining table.

"Don't worry, Madison," Max added. "I make up my own mind about people. Welcome to the building."

"Thanks," she said, relieved by his words. "I really appreciate this. You are all being so friendly and thoughtful."

Lexie shrugged. "That's how we are at Ocean Shores. We want everyone to feel like this is home.

"I'm already starting to feel that way."

"Great. We'll let you settle in," Lexie said. "But I'm sure we'll see you soon."

"I'm sure," she said as she walked them to the door.

As they left, she felt very good about her decision to move into Ocean Shores. Gabe might dislike her intensely, but so far, the other people she'd met, including his roommate, seemed inclined to form their own opinions.

As she moved back to the table to grab the bowl of fruit and put it in the fridge, her phone buzzed. The number wasn't one she recognized, but it was the local area code, so she answered.

"Hello?"

"Is this Madison Baldwin?"

"Yes. Who's this?"

"Alina Devereaux from the *San Diego Cook-Off.*"

"Oh. I just submitted my application," she said, her nerves tightening.

"And we just read it," Alina said. "The entries close at midnight tonight, so you got in just under the wire. We'd like to invite you to participate. Your credentials are quite impressive."

"Thank you. That's great," she said, still feeling mixed emotions about the competition.

"We're having all the contestants come in for a lunch meeting at the Lazure Hotel on Thursday at noon. We know most of you are busy in the evenings at your restaurants, so the

competition events will be held during the day, including the
kickoff on Thursday. We'll give you all the details then."

Thursday was three days away. Everything was happening
fast. Maybe that was a good thing. She didn't have time to waste
to build her restaurant base, so if she was going to do this thing,
she might as well do it now. "I'll be there."

———

Monday night, Gabe stopped by his mother's house. He
needed to talk to her about his sister, Christina, moving out of
the house and into her own apartment and try to calm things
down between them. He also wanted to check on his
grandmother.

When he arrived, the two-story house was in its usual state
of chaos. His cousin, Laura, had moved in with his mother two
months ago when her husband was deployed, and she had three
kids between the ages of four and ten. There were toys and kids
everywhere. The TV was blaring in one room and music was
coming from another. He was beginning to realize why Christina
was so eager to move out.

"Gabe," Laura said as she came down the stairs. She was a
short, curvy brunette with a tired smile.

"How are you doing?" he asked.

"Not bad," she said, her voice tense. "But I haven't heard
from Brett in a couple of days, and that makes me nervous. I tell
myself he's okay, he's just busy, but sometimes it's difficult to
believe that."

He frowned at her words. "I'm sorry to hear that. Can you
reach out to anyone?"

"I talked to one of the other wives, and she hadn't heard
anything, either. I'm sure it's all fine." She cast a quick look over
her shoulder. "Your mother and Christina have not been getting
along lately. There have been a lot of slammed doors in this
house. My four-year-old is thinking that's the only way you close

a door," she said lightly as her four-year-old girl ran up to him, raising her arms to be picked up.

He happily complied, smiling into Allison's angel face. "How's my girl?"

"Do you want to see my new horse?" she asked.

"I do, but first I have to talk to my mother."

"She's crying in the kitchen," Allison said. "I gave her my doll to hug, but it didn't help."

"Then I better see what I can do," he said, setting her down. "Then I'll come see your horse."

As he headed into the kitchen, he steeled himself for what was to come. His mother was a strong woman, but also someone with deep emotions, and the loss of his father still haunted her, even after eight years. When he opened the door, he was relieved to see her standing by the stove.

She turned and a smile slowly spread across her face. Her eyes and nose were red, but she'd obviously pulled herself together. She set down the spoon she was using and walked over to give him a hug.

Her arms around him always felt good, but today he could feel her fragility more than he normally could.

"I didn't know you were coming by," she said as she released him. "You'll stay for dinner, yes? No food truck tonight?"

"Not tonight. I can stay. I want to talk to you about Christina."

Her expression hardened. "She knows my rules. She needs to follow them."

"It's hard for her here with Laura and her kids, you and Abuela... The house is a little crowded, no?"

"The house is filled with family and love. And Christina is barely in her room, so I don't see how sharing it with a small ten-year-old girl is such an issue."

"She wants to move out and live with girlfriends until she leaves for school in September."

His mother stared at him with mixed emotions in her dark

eyes. "Well, I suppose that's her choice. If she wants to leave us, then that's what she should do."

"She doesn't want to leave you or Abuela. She just wants more freedom. She's nineteen."

"I know. Christina reminds me of that every day. But I've always had the same rules—rules to protect my children and keep this family together, and they've worked well." She paused. "Are you helping her, Gabe?"

"She asked me for a small amount to help her make rent each month," he admitted. "I agreed, but I told her I thought she should stay here until she leaves for school. I'm wondering if you two can't compromise."

"You're as soft as your father when it comes to Christina. She could always wrap him around her little finger. As for compromise, I won't change my rules for her. They're not that strict. They're based on respect. Staying out all night without telling me...that is not respectful."

"I understand that. And she is sorry."

"Is she? She didn't tell me that. If she wants to leave, she can leave."

"I don't think she wants to go until she makes things right with you."

"Well, she can't have everything she wants," his mother said tartly. "At any rate, I'm glad you came over, even if it was to fight your sister's battle."

"That wasn't the only reason. I wanted to see you and Abuela. How is she?"

"Better. But this week has been a bit of a setback with the anniversary of your father's death. We're both feeling his loss more strongly."

"I miss him, too," he mumbled.

"I know. You look so much like him...tall, lean, strong." She dabbed at her eyes, then she turned back to the stove. "You should say hello to your abuela."

He wrapped his arms around her stiff back and gave her a

hug, then left the kitchen and walked down the hall. His abuela was sitting by the window, knitting yet another baby blanket. She made one after another, distributing them through the neighborhood and to the local hospitals. The arthritis in her hands had made her a little slower in recent years, but she still kept at it.

When he entered her room, a light immediately brightened her eyes, and a smile lifted her lips. "Gabe. Mijo. Come."

He walked over to her and kissed her cheek. "It's nice to see you." He sat down on the corner of the bed across from her chair. "You look like you're almost done with that blanket."

"Just a few more rows to go." She set her knitting aside. "Your mother told me you're in a cooking competition starting this week."

"Yes. The *San Diego Cook-Off*. It will be filmed for a show on the Culinary Network and there may be some local press, but what I'm most excited about is the possibility of winning the grand prize, which is twenty-five thousand dollars."

"Oh, my, that would be wonderful. You could put it in the savings fund for your own restaurant."

He didn't want to tell her that his restaurant fund was being constantly depleted by the demands of his family, so he said nothing.

"I'm so proud of you," she added. "Your grandfather would be, too. We always hoped your father would become a chef, but he was far more interested in the land, and your Aunt Marie was only ever interested in fashion. Thankfully, you followed in our footsteps."

He'd always been inspired by his grandparents' journey from Venezuela to the US and their struggle to open their own restaurant in San Diego. It had taken them twenty years to do that, and it had been a small café with only six tables, but there had often been a line down the street. After his grandfather passed away, his grandmother had given up the restaurant, since neither his aunt nor his father had been interested in taking it over.

His father was too busy building his organic farm collective, where multiple farmers planted and grew vegetables and herbs that were sold to restaurants around the area. He'd wanted to grow food, not cook it. While Gabe had appreciated his father's green thumb, he'd only been interesting the cooking.

"I think Abuelo would have been prouder if he'd seen me open a restaurant," he said.

She shook her head. "That's not true. He would have loved your food truck, and the way you make good food available for so many people."

"I could do more in a bigger kitchen."

"I know," she said with sympathy. "I often wished for a bigger kitchen, too. But you'll get where you need to be. I believe in you."

"Thank you. That means a lot."

"When does the competition start? Can we watch you?"

"I don't know all the details yet. There's a meeting on Thursday to go over the schedule."

"Do you know any of the other chefs you'll be competing against?"

"A few of them. They're good."

"But you're better."

He laughed. "You said that; I didn't."

She gave him a knowing smile. "You were thinking it."

"I'm good, but I'll be competing with chefs with more culinary training than I've had. I haven't studied in Europe. I haven't run my own restaurant," he added. "I'm probably a long shot to win."

"Long shots are the best. When they pay off, they pay off big. And sometimes talent can't be taught. You have it, or you don't."

"I think you're prejudiced."

"Perhaps. I can't wait to see them give you that prize check. I want to be there when it happens."

"I'll make sure you get a front-row seat. Now tell me what's happening on your shows," he said. His grandmother spent most of the day watching telenovelas, and she was always happy to share. For the next hour, he listened to the scandalous tales, a little disturbed that his almost ninety-year-old grandmother was talking about adultery and sex so easily. He was actually relieved when his mother called them for dinner.

The meal was loud, noisy, and messy, with his mother, grand-mother, cousin, and three little kids. Christina did not show up for dinner, which seemed to annoy his mother even more. He wanted to wring his little sister's neck. He was okay with helping her, but she needed to respect the rules while she was here, and they'd grown up knowing if they weren't going to be home for dinner, they needed to call.

After the meal, he helped his mother clean up. She didn't seem interested in talking, and since he didn't know what to say to make anything better, he kept quiet. When he was done, he gave her a hug and told her he'd see her soon.

As he left the house, he got a text from the *San Diego Cook-Off* confirming the Thursday lunch schedule and a final list of competitors. He scanned the list, his heart stopping when he saw the name of the last entry—Madison Baldwin.

What the hell was going on?

Every time he turned around, he was tripping over her. Well, it was fine. He'd beat her and that would give her boss another reason to be sorry he hadn't hired him in the first place instead of some rich girl whose father had basically bought her a restaurant.

She might have some skills. She had a fancy pedigree, but that might have been bought and paid for, too. And her restau-rant wasn't exactly overflowing. She probably thought the competition would give her publicity, help bring in the customers, turn things around. But she'd have to beat him to do that, and he wouldn't let that happen.

CHAPTER FIVE

On Thursday, Madison parked in the lot at the Lazure Hotel in San Diego, feeling a great deal of trepidation about what lay ahead. She took one last look at her face in the mirror. She'd taken extra care with her makeup and left her blonde hair down instead of up in her usual ponytail. They wouldn't be cooking today, so she'd put on a sleeveless summer dress and high-heeled sandals. She wished she had more of a tan, but since moving to the beach, she'd spent most of her days inside her restaurant. Taking a deep breath, she got out of her car and headed into the hotel.

The lunch was being held in the ballroom, with a buffet and a bar set up for the fifty or so people in the room. She had no idea how many of them were competitors and how many were involved in running the competition, but she hoped she wouldn't have to beat this many people to win the prize.

Feeling a little awkward, she got in line at the bar, thinking a drink might help with her nerves.

And then she heard a husky male voice in her ear. "Going for tequila today?" he asked.

She turned her head to give Gabe a polite smile. She'd only seen him from afar since she'd moved into Ocean Shores on

Monday and had tried to convince herself he was not as attractive as she remembered. But she was wrong. His dark, wavy hair, brown eyes, tan skin, and full lips sent a shiver down her spine, making her flash back on the kisses they'd shared, on the way her body had felt pressed up against his.

She swallowed hard, trying to remember what he'd just asked, since he still had an expectant look in his eyes. "I'm just getting wine," she said.

He nodded. "That seems more appropriate for this version of you."

"What does that mean?" she asked warily.

"You seem a lot more uptight, rigid, and distant than you did last Friday night."

"I don't want to talk about that night."

"We had a connection."

"Because we didn't know who each other was. Now that we do, everything is different."

"Everything?" he questioned.

His gaze bored into hers, sweeping her face and dropping to her lips, making her palms sweat. She had the terrible feeling he knew exactly how she was feeling. "Yes," she said tightly, barely able to get the word out. Thankfully, the line moved forward, and she turned to the bartender with relief. "I'd like a glass of chardonnay, please."

After getting her wine, she moved quickly away from Gabe. As she neared the round tables, she realized there was assigned seating, and she found her name at a table of six. She hung her bag around the back of her chair, noting that there was a woman next to her by the name of Lyssa Osorio and a man on the other side of her, Cliff Meecham.

She stood awkwardly by her chair, not sure if she should sit or wait for others to join her at the table. She should probably mingle, but she didn't know one person in this room except for Gabe, and he was the last person she wanted to speak to.

Finally, two men and a woman approached her table. The tall

imposing man, who looked more like an athlete than a chef, introduced himself as Cliff Meecham, executive chef at the Bella Vista in San Diego. The second shorter, blond man was Art Boswell, who was a chef de cuisine at the Bankers Club in Mission Viejo. The dark-haired woman in her forties said she was Lyssa Osorio from Conti, an Italian restaurant in Del Mar.

After introductions, they settled around the table, with the two seats across from her finally filled by a woman named Renee Tennant, a tall, willowy redhead, who was the chef at a French bistro, and, of course, Gabe Herrera.

She couldn't believe how often their paths crossed. She averted her gaze from his, turning to the front of the room as an attractive blonde woman stepped up to a microphone, asking for everyone's attention. She introduced herself as Francine Gilmore, the host for the competition. Then she waved her hand toward the table next to her and asked each of the three main judges to stand as she called their name: Tim Hunt, food columnist for the *San Diego Tribune*, Maryann Carpaggio, the owner chef of Pasta Mia, a renowned restaurant in San Diego, and finally Hank Richmond, the owner of the Valerian Restaurant Group, which owned two restaurants in San Diego and a half dozen more around the country.

She was more than a little impressed and intimidated by the judging panel. And her stress only increased when Francine mentioned there would be additional judges for each round of the competition. In fact, every word that came out of Francine's mouth made her feel more uncomfortable. She wanted to flee, but she couldn't run. She needed to bring customers into her restaurant, and if she could get the attention of these judges, especially the food columnist, that could certainly help.

"I hope you've had a chance to get acquainted with your tablemates," Francine continued. "We've randomly divided you into four teams of six for round one. Your team will prepare three dishes. Each dish will have a protein and a sauce. You'll pick your proteins and sauces from the baskets on your tables.

It's up to you to decide what protein to pair with which sauce. You'll have the next hour during lunch to talk to your partner, and you'll have two hours tomorrow afternoon to prep before cooking lunch on Saturday for not only this established panel of judges, but also for another twenty excited foodies from the public, who have won the opportunity to be a part of the competition. Their votes, combined with the judges' votes, will decide the top two teams and the twelve individuals moving on to round two."

Her jaw dropped at that piece of information, shocked that the competition would be cut in half after round one.

"We encourage you to work together and help each other shine," Francine added. "Good luck and happy cooking."

She wasn't happy about anything she'd just heard, especially the part about working with the other five people at her table.

"Well, it looks like we should pick for proteins and sauces," Lyssa said, as she reached for the basket on the table. "Does it matter who goes first?"

"Go for it," Gabe said. "But let's not look at our picks until we've all got one."

"Perfect," Lyssa said as she pulled out a thick, folded piece of paper and handed the basket to her.

She made her selection, then passed the basket along. Once that was done, they unfolded their papers to find their assignment. She had drawn one of the three sauces, a roasted bone marrow jus. As everyone revealed their picks, her heart sank again. The three proteins included scallops, lamb, and duck. And the perfect protein pairing for her would be the lamb, which was Gabe's pick. Although, she could do something with the duck. But before she could say anything, the other chefs were already matching up, and Gabe's dark eyes met hers across the table.

"Looks like it's you and me," he said.

"I was hoping to match with the duck," she replied.

"The red wine and blackberry sauce is better for the duck," Cliff interjected.

"I would agree," Art said with a nod. "It's the perfect combo."

"Okay. I can work with the lamb," she said. And she could work with the lamb; it was Gabe she was worried about.

This first challenge was to make a refined dish worthy of a Michelin-starred restaurant, and she was partnering with the guy who ran a food truck. That sounded snobby even in her own head, but it was also reality. He was probably great at his kind of food, but did he even know how to butcher and cook lamb?

"Why don't I switch seats with you, Gabe?" Lyssa said. "I want to sit next to Renee so we can plot our meal over lunch."

"Sure." He brought his beer and smirking smile to the seat next to hers. "Looks like we're going to be working together."

"We all need to work together," Cliff said, latching onto Gabe's words. "This is a team competition, and we'll succeed or fail as a team. Let's run our ideas past each other, make sure our dishes are as tight as they can be." He paused. "But first, let's hit the buffet table. I don't know about you, but I'm hungry. Then we can start working."

As they got in line at the buffet table, she wished she'd given in to her earlier instinct to bail on this whole competition. But as she looked around the room at all the talented chefs and culinary critics, she knew this could be a great opportunity to make a name for herself in the community. But she would have to win to do that. Losing would hurt worse than never having shown up.

———

Madison was going to be a pain in the ass.

Gabe knew that with every fiber of his being. He could not have gotten matched with a worse partner. She probably believed she could produce a Michelin-star-worthy meal since she'd just opened a fine-dining restaurant. In fact, he was sure she thought he'd be a ball and chain around her foot, dragging her down to the bottom, when she wanted to soar to the top. But that wouldn't happen.

He hadn't entered this competition to lose. He needed the prize money, and he needed the connections. As the competition went on, the eyes of the local culinary world and beyond would be on them, and there could be other restaurant owners who were looking for a talented chef to bring their unique style and flair to their restaurant space. That could be him.

Secretly, he had to admit that he wasn't thrilled with the challenge. This wasn't the food he cooked. But part of the challenge was stepping outside his comfort zone, and this was an opportunity to show he was a much better chef than anyone might think, especially the woman who was paired with him.

Their team talked in general terms as they ate lunch, with chefs throwing out random ideas for their dishes, but no one quite settling in to exactly what they wanted to do.

Madison had nothing to say, which he found somewhat curious. He didn't know if it was because she was new to the Southern California restaurant scene and didn't know anyone, if she felt like she was above all the other chefs, or if she was just a shy person.

He hadn't found her shy the first night they'd met at Maverick's, but that woman had been so completely different from the woman he'd seen since then. Maybe it was the tequila that had changed her personality. If that was the case, it was too bad because he'd liked that version of her.

When they were done eating, they focused on their partners to speak more specifically about the sauce and protein pairings, and Madison was forced to actually look at him.

"What are you thinking?" he asked.

"I'm thinking that I'm going to make the best roasted bone marrow jus anyone has ever tasted."

"Good. I intend to make the best roasted herb rack of lamb anyone has ever tasted. But we need to work together to complement each other."

"Have you ever made lamb before?" she asked with a doubtful look in her eyes.

"Yes. A few times."

"Do you know how to butcher the meat?"

"I know how to order a rack of lamb from the butcher," he said, irritated with her obvious belief that he had no idea what he was doing.

She frowned at his comment. "This isn't a joke to me. I want to win."

"I want to win, too," he returned. "So, maybe drop the *I'm better than you* attitude."

"I never said I was better than you."

"It's clear you believe that."

"Well, you have to admit that this first round in the competition is more closely aligned with the kind of food I make than the kind of food you make."

"You have no idea how good of a chef I am, but that's okay. You'll find out."

"You're very cocky," she said.

"You're calling me cocky?" he challenged. "Maybe you should look in the mirror, Madison."

She licked her lips, giving him a guilty look. "Obviously, we've gotten off to a bad start."

"Actually, our start was good. Everything after that has been bad."

A wash of red moved through her face at his words, and that heat in her cheeks reminded him of the woman he'd kissed outside of Maverick's.

"That wasn't me at Maverick's. That was the tequila," she said. "And I don't want to talk about that night. Let's discuss the food. We need to think about the entire plate. I'd like to do butternut squash purée with butter and a hint of nutmeg. It would enrich the meat."

"Braised vegetables," he countered. "Baby turnips, carrots,

tender, flavorful and colorful. And I want to do a mint chimichurri for the lamb."

"That will clash with my sauce," she protested.

"It will enhance it," he argued.

"It won't," she said flatly.

"What are you two arguing about?" Cliff interrupted.

It was then he realized that the rest of the table was staring at them. "I'd like to do a mint chimichurri for the lamb," he said.

"Which will clash with my sauce," Madison quickly added.

"Actually, I think that sounds good," Renee put in. "It could provide a fresh and herbaceous contrast to the richness of the jus."

"You can always see how it goes and if it doesn't work, leave it off," Art suggested.

Madison bit down on her lip. "We can talk about it," she said tightly.

Clearly, she wanted to appear to be a team player, but he didn't think he'd heard the end of it. And he had a feeling that if they didn't find some harmony, their dish would reflect that.

Before he could say anything further, Francine returned to the microphone to announce that their time was up. Tomorrow they would meet at the local market at noon. They would have a half hour to shop and two hours to prep for the lunch on Saturday.

After she wished them luck, Madison got to her feet. "I have to get to my restaurant," she said. "I'll see you all tomorrow."

"I'll walk out with you," he said quickly, following her out of the ballroom.

She didn't say a word until they were in the parking lot. "What do you want?" she asked, turning on him with anger in her green eyes. "Why are you dogging my steps? I said I would see you tomorrow."

"We need to talk, Madison. We have to figure out a way to get along. The tension between us is going to hurt our food."

She stared back at him with conflict in her eyes. "I don't see how a partnership between us can possibly work."

"We have to make it work, unless you want to lose in the first round."

"It can't be all your way," she said. "I don't like the mint chimichurri idea."

"I don't like the squash purée. And they certainly don't go together."

Her lips tightened. "I can't spend the rest of the day arguing with you. I have to get to work."

"So do I. Why don't we both think about the dish, and we'll meet tomorrow and come up with a compromise?"

"A compromise won't win. The dish has to sing. It has to be special, memorable, fantastic. It can't be a mishmash of ideas."

"Well, it has to represent both of us, so what's the alternative?" he challenged. "I'm not going to let you make whatever you want, and you're not going to let me do that, either."

"I really hate this whole thing."

"Why did you even enter? What do you need twenty-five thousand for? You've got your own restaurant with money behind you. You don't need this competition. You already have everything you need to be successful." As he threw out the question, he realized he already knew the answer. "It's because the restaurant is failing, isn't it? You're looking for attention, recognition, word of mouth. That's it."

"And you're not looking for all those things?" she challenged.

"I'm mostly looking for the cash. You've seen my line. I have plenty of word of mouth and a growing base of customers. But I want more than a food truck, and I don't have a rich father to find me a rich friend to invest in my business."

She turned pale at his words. "You don't know anything."

"Are you telling me it's not true? Larry Shaw told me he had an obligation to hire you because he was good friends with your father."

"They have a relationship. But I have a lot of experience, and

I am fully qualified to run the restaurant." She blew out a breath. "I don't need to explain myself to you."

He could see not just anger but pain in her eyes now, and he felt guilty for his harsh words. "I'm sorry," he said. "I shouldn't have said that about your father. I went too far."

"Whatever." She opened her car door. "I have to go. I'll see you tomorrow."

He stepped back as she slammed the door in his face and then sped out of her spot. As he walked to his car, he felt bad about what he'd said to her. He'd made as many assumptions about her as she'd made about him.

Tomorrow, he was going to have to find a way to smooth things over with her. Otherwise, they were going to lose, and he couldn't let that happen.

CHAPTER SIX

Madison drove to the market on Friday with a sick feeling in the pit of her stomach. And that had more to do with Gabe than it did with the competition. His harsh words had been hard to hear, because they were words that had run around in her own head ever since she'd asked her father to talk to Larry. She had wanted to get her own restaurant on merit, not on a relationship with her father, but she'd been trying for ten years to make that happen, and she'd finally broken down and asked for the favor.

Now accepting that favor made her feel like an imposter. And maybe she was. The restaurant wasn't thriving, and she couldn't blame anyone but herself. She'd thought about quitting the competition, but that wouldn't get her anywhere. She couldn't run away and hide. She couldn't let Gabe be right about her. She couldn't let her own doubts take hold. She had to prove to everyone that she was good enough. And she would do that... starting now.

With that mental pep talk, she parked her car and joined her fellow competitors at the front of the market. She didn't avoid Gabe. She walked right up to him and gave him a determined smile. "Are you ready?"

His return look was wary. "I am. What about you?"

"I've thought about the dish. I think we should go with your suggestion of the braised baby vegetables. I'm not sold on the mint chimichurri, but you can make it, and then we'll decide. I also want to do some crispy shallots. It will add flavor and crunch to the meat and the vegetables. Any comments?"

"Just one. I want to apologize for what I said to you yesterday."

"I've already forgotten that conversation." She paused. "Along with other things we have said to each other. I'm only interested in moving forward."

"I'd like that as well," he said with relief in his gaze. "So, I'll head to the meat counter."

"And I'll start with the produce."

As the clock hit noon, they rushed into the store. She felt more decisive now that she'd committed herself to a dish and a course of action. She also felt slightly better that Gabe had apologized again. He probably still believed what he'd said, but, clearly, he knew they needed to work together and tearing each other down wouldn't accomplish that.

She probably owed him an apology as well for looking down on his food truck, but she didn't want to keep bringing up the past and hoped that they could just move on. At the end of the day, they both wanted to win. And they weren't going to get out of the first round unless they stopped fighting with each other. Once this round was over, hopefully, they would be going against each other and not have to work together. That would be easier to handle.

The thirty minutes of shopping went fast, and she continued plotting her plan of attack for her jus on the short drive back to the kitchen at the Lazure Hotel, where they would be prepping today and cooking tomorrow.

It was crowded in the kitchen with twenty-four chefs, but she and Gabe found a workspace in one corner of the kitchen and went over their strategy for their plate.

While she'd taken the lead at the market, Gabe was ready to

take charge now, and as much as that rubbed her the wrong way, she kept her mouth shut and tried to think of him like any other chef.

It was easier when they stopped talking and started working. While she felt confined in the small space, Gabe didn't seem bothered at all, but why would he? He worked in a truck every night. This little corner was probably as much room as he ever had, which actually made her respect him a bit more because he was far more efficient and contained than she was.

He also seemed comfortable handling the rack of lamb, and that gave her confidence. She liked his use of herbs, and he was impressed with how many ingredients she was using to make her sauce. As they prepped, the tension eased between them. Or maybe it was just that cooking relaxed both of them. Whatever the reason, she was happy not to spend the entire afternoon at war.

They spent some time talking with the other four people on their team, but not a lot. Everyone in the group was an accomplished chef. She'd done some research the night before on her fellow competitors, and she was much more appreciative of her teammates now that she knew how much experience they had. She wasn't sure they felt the same way about her.

While she ran a fine-dining restaurant now, it was very recent, and before that she'd never been in charge, although she had been cooking for a long time. Gabe was also on the bottom of the chain of experience, having only run a food truck. But while the other chefs had given them a few suggestions, everyone was more worried about their own dishes than anyone else's.

The two hours passed quickly, and soon it was time to wrap up what they'd done and pack it away for tomorrow. As they left the kitchen and then the hotel, she blew out a breath, relieved to be out of the hot kitchen.

"That was fast," Gabe commented, as they neared her vehicle.

"Yes, but we got done what we needed to get done," she said, feeling tired after the pressure of the time limit. "Now I get to prep for dinner service."

"Me, too. Busy day for both of us."

"In some ways, it's just getting started."

"That's true." Pausing, he added, "I think we have a winning dish, Madison."

"Don't jinx it. We still have to cook and put it all together tomorrow."

"It's going to be great. What did you think about the other two dishes from our team?"

She was surprised he was even remotely interested in her opinion. "I think Art and Cliff may be taking too simple of an approach, but if they pull it off, then the beauty will be in the simplicity. The opposite for Renee and Lyssa. They have a lot of ingredients. I'm worried they're going to dull the flavors by having too many things on the plate. But there's still time for editing, and I'm sure they'll do that."

"I agree." He appeared a little surprised by that fact. "Look at that, we're on the same page."

She gave him a brief but wary smile, not quite trusting the truce they'd engineered. "I guess miracles can happen," she said lightly.

"I don't think it took a miracle, but okay." He smiled back at her in a way that sent a shiver down her spine.

This was the guy she'd met at Maverick's, the one who was attractive, sexy, and charming. She really didn't want to remember that guy.

"By the way," Gabe added. "I asked one of my staff to set up some cones to direct my line down the other side of the side-walk. You shouldn't have a problem tonight."

She was shocked to hear that. "Why did you do that?"

"Because you asked me to."

"That wasn't your response when I asked."

"I had time to think about it."

She didn't know if he'd realized he was in the wrong, or if he didn't believe blocking her doorway would matter if no one was trying to get in her restaurant. Either way, she should just be happy about it. "Thank you."

He nodded. "I'll see you tomorrow. Bring your A game."

"I always do."

———

Saturday came faster than Madison would have liked. When she entered the kitchen at the Lazure Hotel just before noon, her nerves tightened as the reality of what she was about to do hit home. She wasn't just cooking for a panel of judges; the competition would be shown on *Chef Battles* and livestreamed on the Internet. Whatever mistakes she made would be highlighted and publicized forever, and that was a disturbing thought.

There had been only one lone photographer in the kitchen yesterday, and that guy had been so quiet she hadn't really noticed him, but now there were three cameras and several bright lights set up in the kitchen. She felt like she was on a movie set, not in a kitchen.

"You ready for this?" Gabe asked as he came up next to her, looking handsome in his white chef's coat, his dark eyes brimming with excitement and energy.

"I'm not sure. I wasn't expecting all the cameras in the kitchen."

"Forget about who's watching and cook the way you know how to cook."

As much as she hated to give him credit for anything, he was right. She had to find a way to just keep her head down and concentrate on her sauce and their plate.

The other four members of their team came over, and they discussed their game plan for serving their dishes, and then they broke into their pairings and started to cook.

Today, only two groups would cook at one time. They were in the second group, so the kitchen was already hot. While there were half the number of chefs in the kitchen as there had been during prep time, there were still twelve people to work around, along with the cameras and the lights. But she focused on her food and tried to ignore everything else. Halfway through their cook time, one judge came through the kitchen to check on their dishes. As he approached her and Gabe, the cameras moved in closer, and she almost sliced off her finger in her distraction.

Gabe put a calming hand on her arm as Hank Richmond, the owner of the Valerian Restaurant Group, asked them what they were making. She wanted to answer the question, but she couldn't seem to find the words, and Gabe jumped in with his effortless charm and ready smile, confidently telling the judge that their lamb dish would be the best he had ever tasted.

Hank loved Gabe's cockiness and bantered back and forth while she gave them both a tight smile. When the judge asked her about her sauce, she stuttered out a few of the ingredients, knowing she wasn't in any way doing her sauce justice, but she was better at showing than telling.

Finally, Hank moved on to the next team, and she blew out a breath.

"Way to not sell your sauce," Gabe said dryly.

"I...I'm not good with cameras or public speaking."

"Clearly. Thankfully, your sauce tastes great."

"Do you think so?" she couldn't help asking, needing the reassurance.

"Yes. Now it's time for you to taste my mint chimichurri."

She had agreed to let him make it and decide at the last minute. "Okay, but it doesn't feel like we need it. I'm comfortable with what we have. It's risky to add another element."

"What we have is good, but we're looking for great. We need to play to win, not to avoid losing, Madison."

"I am playing to win."

"Then taste my chimichurri."

"Fine. I'll taste it." She dipped a spoon into his chimichurri and was shockingly surprised by the flavor. "It is good," she said grudgingly. "But we need to put together our plate and taste it with everything else."

"Then let's do that."

They spent the next ten minutes assembling a plate and then tasting each element separately and together. She didn't want to admit it, but he was right. A small drizzle of chimichurri enhanced the meat and her sauce. She played it safe in life, but not with food. That was the one area where she took risks.

"Well?" Gabe asked.

"We'll put it on the plate," she said decisively. "But I'm plating. I'm good at that."

"You are good at it," he admitted. "I'll follow your lead."

They finished plating just as the timer went off. Then they followed their servers into the dining room.

There was one round table of judges featuring the individuals who had been introduced the day before. And then there were four other tables with six people at each table, who had been selected in an online lottery to participate as the public judging in the competition. Their scores, along with the judges, whose opinions would be more heavily weighted, would determine the two teams moving on to the next round.

They stopped by the judges' table where there were more cameras and more lights, and beads of sweat broke out across her forehead. Francine asked them to explain their dish, and she found herself completely tongue-tied. Gabe jumped in once more with an easy smile to talk about his lamb and her sauce. Fortunately, he did justice to both.

When they returned to the kitchen, he held up his hand to give her a high five, and she couldn't help but slap his hand, feeling immensely relieved that at least one part of this day was over. But they still had to get through the judging. She prayed that they would make it to the next round, that all this would not have been for nothing.

"Our dish was great, Madison," Gabe said, excitement in his gaze. "We're going to win."

"I hope so, but it's not up to us."

"How did it go?" Renee asked as she and Lyssa were third up, with Cliff and Art heading next into the dining room.

"It went great," Gabe said confidently.

Renee nodded in approval. "Good. Do you mind helping us plate?"

"No, of course not," he said as they stepped up to help their team.

After their final team dishes had left the kitchen, their team exited onto a nearby patio where the other teams were already sipping champagne, wine, and beer, celebrating the end of round one. All twenty-four chefs appeared exhausted, exhilarated, and nervous.

Madison certainly felt all those emotions and more. There was a small part of her that wouldn't mind if this was all over. But the bigger part of her wanted to win. She sat down at a group of outdoor sofas and chatted with Renee and Lyssa while they were waiting for the judging. They seemed very confident in the dish they'd put out, so hopefully that was a good sign, because it wasn't just about her and Gabe. They needed their entire team to do well, or they'd be cut.

After about thirty minutes, they were called back into the ballroom in front of the judges. The tables had been cleared and there was an expectant hush in the room as both the contestants and the public participants waited eagerly to hear who had won.

She felt an enormous wave of anxiety that made her feel a little unsteady on her feet. As her hand brushed against Gabe's, she had to forcibly stop herself from curling her fingers around his. She couldn't lean on him. She had to stand on her own two feet. She just needed them to get on with it because she didn't want to pass out in front of everyone.

Francine spoke first. "Chefs, thank you for a wonderful meal. We truly enjoyed our lunch. There were some very exciting pairings. Good job, everyone. While you're all talented chefs, we will be picking our two favorite teams, based on our guests." She waved her hand toward the crowd. "And the opinion of our talented group of judges. In addition to moving on to the second round, the top pairing from our top two teams will also each enjoy a one-hundred-dollar gift certificate to dine at Pasta Mia. Without further ado..." Francine paused dramatically, then said, "Our favorite team was team two."

Her heart jumped. They were in team two, weren't they?

Gabe grabbed her hand and gave it a squeeze. "We did it," he murmured.

She couldn't quite believe it, but then everyone on her team was hugging each other. When they settled down, Francine continued. "Our top pairing on team two was the lamb dish from Chef Gabe Herrera and Chef Madison Baldwin. Photos of their dish and their recipe will be posted on our website."

She was stunned to hear their dish had been the favorite dish on the team. And more congratulations came their way.

Francine went on to announce that team three would also be moving to the second round, and there were more cheers and hugs of congratulations, as another pair of chefs was singled out for having the favorite dish on that team.

"Unfortunately, that means team one and team four will be leaving us today," Francine added with a regretful smile. "Thank you so much for joining us this week, for giving us a great meal. You're all incredibly talented, and this was a very tough and close decision. You can now say your goodbyes to your fellow chefs and leave the ballroom."

It took several minutes for the other two teams to hug their fellow contestants and then exit the room. Once they were down to the twelve chefs continuing in the competition, Francine gave further instructions.

"Congratulations again. We'd like our favorite pairings from each team to return to the kitchen where your dishes will be photographed along with you, and Emilia Everett, a food columnist for the website *Eating with Emilia,* who will be interviewing you for her blog. For the rest of you, the second round will take place on Monday at noon. You'll find out what your challenge is then. It will be an individual challenge, so you'll be working on your own. Enjoy your day off tomorrow."

When Francine finished speaking, the lights dimmed, and the cameras stopped whirring.

Madison blew out a breath of relief. She and Gabe had won the best dish of the day for their team. She'd known it was good, but she'd been afraid to believe it was that good.

As the crowd in the ballroom dispersed, she and Gabe returned to the kitchen with the two winning chefs from the other team. The production staff had created a background for the photo shoot with the banner from the competition hanging over a stainless-steel counter where the two winning dishes were displayed.

They did several shots with all four of them, and then more shots with each pair. It was a blinding session of photos, and she had no idea how she looked in any of them.

When they were finished with the photo shoot, they spoke to Emilia Everett, a forty-something redhead, who seemed quite taken with Gabe, directing most of her questions to him. Madison found it irritating to take a back seat to Gabe, but she wasn't great at interviews, and at the end of the day, she would still get great exposure on the food blog. Emilia's site got a tremendous amount of traffic, especially in Southern California, so hopefully that would bring more people into her restaurant.

Finally, everything was done, and they made their way out of the kitchen and the hotel.

As they headed to the parking lot, Gabe said, "I think we should celebrate."

"I have to go to work."

"Right this second? It's only three."

"And dinner service starts at five thirty, so yes. Maybe you should have asked your groupie journalist to help you celebrate."

He smiled. "You sound jealous."

"I'm annoyed you took over an interview about our dish. You do remember we made it together, right? Because it didn't sound like it."

"I never made it sound like I did it alone," he protested. "And you were free to speak up whenever you wanted. Why didn't you?"

"I couldn't get a word in."

"You didn't try that hard."

"Oh, forget it," she said wearily. "We're done working as a team, so we can go back to being what we really are—rivals."

"If that's the way you want it," he said. "But can we postpone that until tomorrow?"

"Why wait?"

"Because we had a victory, and we should enjoy it. We have to celebrate the wins when they come, right?"

"My father would say you don't celebrate until the end, and we're not at the end."

"We're at the end of round one. Let me buy you a drink."

"I can't drink now. I have too much to do tonight."

"How about a coffee and a cookie?"

"A cookie?" she echoed, surprised by the suggestion.

"There's a café down the block with the best coffee and cookies. I know because my sister, Christina, is addicted to chocolate chip cookies, and we have spent many a day looking for the very best one." He paused, giving her a wheedling smile. "What do you think? Coffee and a cookie? We can brag to each other about how good our dish was compared to everyone else's, which will feel really good after the last hour of pretending to be modest."

She laughed in spite of herself. "That was you being modest?"

He grinned. "I was trying."

"How far away is this place?"

"Two blocks. We can walk. Tomorrow we can go back to being enemies."

"All right," she said, giving in to what was probably a dangerous impulse. But she wanted to celebrate, and she could use a coffee—maybe even a cookie.

CHAPTER SEVEN

It felt good to be out of the kitchen and walking along the beach, Gabe thought. It felt even better to have Madison by his side. She was a prickly mix of contradictions, and from now on they would be on opposite sides, but he wasn't ready to be her rival again, not yet anyway. It had been a stressful day, and he would never admit it to anyone else, but he'd felt a little out of his depth in a group of chefs with far more culinary training than he had. He was a self-made chef, but he'd come out on top today, with some help from his partner. And that was a big win.

Madison didn't seem to have anything to say, but he could feel her earlier tension dissipating with every step. She'd been on edge all day. And her nerves had gotten worse when they'd gotten into the competition portion of the event. That's why he'd spoken for both of them. He'd had the feeling she couldn't get a word out. He didn't know why she was so nervous because she had created the perfect sauce pairing for his perfect lamb. And she should have been proud to tell the judges all about her sauce.

He frowned, feeling like there was something he didn't know about her, something he wanted to know. On the other hand, their truce was only temporary, so maybe he should just enjoy the moment because it wouldn't last long.

When they arrived at the café, there was a short line, but it gave them a moment to pick out what they wanted to eat. After getting their cookies and coffees, they sat down at a table by the window, overlooking the beach walk, where a kaleidoscope of people from every nationality and all ages passed by.

San Diego was busier than Oceanside where they lived and worked, but it still had the same beachy vibe, at least along the ocean.

Madison took a sip of her coffee first and then tried the oatmeal chocolate chip cookie she'd ordered.

He watched as she savored her first bite. "Well?" he asked. "Did I lie?"

She swallowed and gave him a smile. "No. This is an excellent cookie."

"Told you. It's on Christina's top five list. She wasn't sure about the addition of oatmeal at first, but then she was thirteen at the time and oatmeal sounded healthier than what she was looking for."

"How old is she now?"

"Nineteen."

"You're a lot older than her, aren't you?"

"I'm thirty-one, so yes. I'm twelve years older. She's the youngest of my three siblings. I have two brothers as well, also younger. I'm the oldest."

"I can see you being the oldest of four," she said with a nod. "You have a take-charge attitude about you."

"So do you. Are you the oldest in your family?"

"No. I'm the middle child. My brother, Carter, is thirty-two. He's a lawyer in New York. He just made partner this year. My sister, Vivienne, is twenty-seven. She graduated last year with an MBA and is working at my father's tech company. I'm thirty, and by my family's standards, the underachiever."

"How is that possible? You're running your own restaurant."

"Well, that has given me some credibility," she admitted. "But cooking isn't high on the list of skills or talents my father values. He is interested to see if I can make the restaurant a success. That, I believe, would finally impress him."

He didn't want to get into her father and his relationship to her restaurant since that was a touchy subject, so he stuck with her siblings. "Are you close to your brother and sister?"

"Not really. They're closer to each other than they are to me. I was always kind of the odd one out in the family."

"You definitely sound like the middle child now," he said with a smile.

"That's what I am. Are you close to your siblings?"

"Sometimes too close. My father died eight years ago, and since then, my siblings come to me when they have problems. I also seem to be their bank as well as their brother."

"Does their bank pay out frequently?" she asked lightly.

"More often than it should."

"What about your mom? Why don't they go to her?"

"They don't want to put a burden on her. My mother works in the business my father started, and she spends a lot of time trying to keep his legacy alive. She also takes care of my grand-mother and one of my cousins, who moved in with her three children while her husband is deployed. So, she's busy."

"It sounds like a lot."

"It is a lot, but family is important to her and to me, so we all do what we need to do." He paused, wanting to talk less about himself and more about her. "When did you start cooking? I know you went to school in Paris and worked in restaurants for the past ten years, because that was in your bio, but I don't know when you first decided to cook."

"I don't know that I ever decided...I just loved being in the kitchen. It was my happy place. We had a nanny who also cooked when I was really young, and shredding lettuce or grating cheese always felt relaxing to me. The kitchen is where I went to escape, to feel like I was good at something, because I definitely wasn't good at school. I was a horrible student."

"That doesn't seem possible. You're very focused and detail oriented."

"Only in the kitchen. Who taught you to cook?"

"My abuela—my grandmother," he said. "She and my grandfather were both chefs and had a restaurant in Venezuela before they immigrated to the US. They took several career steps backward when they first arrived. They had to start at the bottom, but they were just happy to be in a kitchen. Eventually, after working at several restaurants, they were able to open their own small café. All of our family celebrations were held there, and from the time I was about eight, I helped in the kitchen."

"Is the restaurant still around? You said your grandmother had been ill, right?"

"The restaurant closed after my grandfather died ten years ago. But she still cooks a lot for the family."

"Like the hallacas at Christmas."

"Yes. I forgot I told you about that. Who made the perfect roast chicken? Your nanny? Your mother?"

"No. It was Yvette Dumond, a cooking teacher I had in Paris. She made it for me one night and told me that the true talent of a chef was being able to turn something very ordinary into something extraordinary. And it was out of this world. I've never been able to replicate it, but one day I hope I will."

"Really? You haven't mastered a roast chicken?"

"I can make a good roast chicken, don't get me wrong. But the one I tasted at her house was magical. I can't seem to find the same flavor, and she's passed away, so I can't ask her what I'm missing. I just have to figure it out one day."

"Maybe it was the person who made the chicken who was magical or the moment in time," he suggested. "You were in Paris. You were learning how to be a chef. That must have been amazing."

"It was, and you're right, it was probably partly her and partly Paris, but it was also the chicken."

He smiled. "Well, I hope one day to taste this magical chicken."

"When I get it right, maybe I will let you do that. If only to prove that it exists." She paused. "I will say that Yvette was a big inspiration for me. My mother encouraged my cooking, but she wasn't a cook herself, and my father thought it was a nice hobby but not a career path. When I got to Paris, and I met Yvette, she took me under her wing. She didn't have any children, and we were kindred spirits in the kitchen. Not that I consider myself even close to her level as a chef, but I hope one day I will be."

"You set high standards for yourself. I've seen that firsthand in the kitchen."

"I do," she admitted. "I've always felt a need to prove that cooking can be more than a hobby. That sounds silly, but it's true."

He nodded, beginning to understand her better. "I get that."

"Anyway, this cookie and coffee have definitely revived me. All those lights, cameras, and people—they were a lot."

"They were. And it will probably get worse as we move along in the competition. Are you ready for the next round?"

"No. But I wasn't ready for this round, and somehow I made it through."

"With a little help."

She tipped her head, meeting his gaze. "True. You were a better partner than I anticipated." She raised her cup of coffee. "Shall we toast to us?"

"The best cooking duo in the competition? Definitely," he said, clinking his cup against hers. "You know what put us in the top, don't you?"

"I'm sure you're going to say it was the chimichurri," she said with a knowing smile.

"I told you it would be good. I'm glad you weren't too stubborn to give it a try."

"I'm glad it was as tasty as you promised it would be." She set down her mug. "What do you think the next challenge will be?"

"I have no idea. They said it would be an individual challenge, so we won't have to work together. That should be a relief for you."

"And you," she said.

He left that comment alone as he sipped his coffee. Then he said, "How do you like living at Ocean Shores?"

"I haven't spent a lot of time there this week, but everyone is very friendly. I met your roommate, Max, a few days ago. He came by with Lexie. He said he wasn't going to let your poor opinion of me influence him."

He smiled at that comment. "That sounds like Max. He's always Switzerland. He never gets in the middle of a fight."

"He was nice. So were Emmalyn and Kaia, who also dropped by. I met Brad and Serena and Liam and Ava yesterday. I guess Serena and Ava are sisters."

"They are. Ava actually fell in love with Liam when they both ended up cat-sitting for Serena and Brad when they were on their honeymoon. Ava is an investment analyst and Liam runs a sporting goods store called the Beach Shack."

"He mentioned that and also that he used to be a professional surfer. I guess a lot of people around here surf. Do you?"

"It's one of my favorite things to do. How about you?"

"Not yet, but Liam told me he runs a surf school out of his store, so maybe I'll take a lesson sometime."

"I could take you out."

"I think you and I are spending enough time together," she said with a pointed smile. "Anyway, I am impressed with how welcoming everyone is at Ocean Shores. How long have you lived there?"

"Almost three years. It was supposed to be temporary. A water leak damaged my last apartment, and someone told me Max had a spare bedroom. I wasn't looking for a roommate, but we got along well, and one week led to a month, then a year, and so on. We both have big plans for our futures and saving money by sharing an apartment has been good for us."

"He sold a screenplay, right?"

"Yes, and he's busy rewriting it now so that it will hopefully get made into a movie. This could be the break he's been waiting for."

"When will he find out?"

"Could be a few months. From what I've seen, nothing in Hollywood moves quickly." He paused, knowing he should probably continue with this casual, not very personal conversation, but he couldn't seem to stop himself from wanting to go deeper. "Can I ask you a question?"

She gave him a wary look. "Can I stop you?"

"What was Friday night about?"

"What do you mean?"

"You don't seem anything like the woman I met at the bar."

"I was drunk."

"Not that drunk. But you were definitely feeling a vibe I haven't seen since."

"It was the tequila. I'm never that chatty or really even that fun," she admitted.

He smiled at that. "You were definitely fun. Quite the dancer. And quite the kisser."

A pretty flush swept her cheeks. "That wasn't me."

"It looked a lot like you."

"I mean it wasn't how I usually act. And it was Drea's fault. She took me there. She ordered that first shot of tequila."

"Drea is the friend who ditched you?"

"Yes. She runs the front of the house at La Marée. We actually met each other years ago when we worked at a restaurant together in New York. Anyway, she's working for me now, and she's probably the only real friend I have in this town. She told me I needed to blow off steam, and she was very persuasive. There has been a lot of stress in my life the last couple of months. Opening a restaurant is a tremendous amount of work."

"I wouldn't know," he said shortly, her words reminding him that it should have been his restaurant to open.

She stiffened. "I'm sure you will one day. There must be other restaurants in this area you could work for."

"None that are willing to give autonomy to me as a head chef. I want to put my imprint on a restaurant, not just cook for someone else."

Understanding flashed through her eyes. "I understand completely. I hope it happens for you."

"I'm going to make it happen. No one else will do it for me. I don't have...connections."

"You're making connections through this competition. Who's to say you won't find an investor through that? I'm sure that thought crossed your mind when you entered. Because twenty-five thousand dollars is a fantastic prize, but you're going to need more to open your own place."

"I'm aware of that, and I'm eager to make as many connections as possible on my way to the grand prize."

"You'll have to get past me to win."

"Right back at you. But we don't have to worry about beating each other until we get to the finals. Until then, we can be allies, friends."

She gave him a long, thoughtful look. "I don't think so, Gabe."

"Why not?"

"I work better alone."

"You didn't today. You were half of a perfect pair."

"But we each had our own space."

"We'll continue to have our own space. I'm just saying we don't have to be enemies."

"We don't have to be anything," she returned.

His gaze met hers, and while it was probably a bad idea, he couldn't stop himself from voicing the thought in his head. "We're going to be something, Madison. We're living in the same building, working on the same street, and I haven't forgotten what it felt like to kiss you."

"Really? Because I barely remember that."

He saw the truth in her eyes. "You're a terrible liar. We made a connection that night."

"Maybe. But that connection broke the next day when we finally exchanged names. When you figured out I was the one who got your restaurant."

"And you realized I was the one with the annoying food truck line," he finished.

"Yes. And I don't want to talk about our kiss again. It didn't mean anything. I'm sure you've kissed plenty of women after a night of drinking. Why are you trying to make this into something?"

"Why are you trying to pretend it was nothing?" he challenged, not liking how she was downplaying something that he couldn't forget.

"Because it was nothing. And it won't happen again. We're competing against each other for a prize we both want. That's probably not going to end well." She got to her feet. "I need to get to the restaurant. Thanks for introducing me to this place. I'm sure I will be back, especially with the competition happening just a few blocks away."

He nodded as he stood up and followed her out the door. She was right. They couldn't be friends or even allies. They were both after the same prize. He'd just gotten distracted for a few minutes because he'd found himself liking her, wanting to get to know her better. She was a puzzle he couldn't quite figure out. But that puzzle was standing in his way of getting what he wanted. He needed to stop thinking about Madison and focus on what really mattered—winning the competition. He needed the money, not just for himself, but for the people who needed his help, and he couldn't forget that.

CHAPTER EIGHT

It was the busiest Saturday night Madison had had since opening La Marée, but dinner service didn't go as perfectly as she'd hoped. She didn't know if it was because her staff wasn't used to handling so many orders at once, or if she was just exhausted from the competition, but some of her dishes felt flat, and while no one was complaining, a few plates came back with the meals only partially eaten, and that never boded well. Drea assured her that the diners were leaving happy. She hoped that was true, but as she parked at Ocean Shores just after eleven o'clock, she realized she was too hot and tired to worry about it.

As she left her car, the cool breeze felt insanely good. Despite the late hour, it was still in the low seventies, and she had a feeling her apartment would be steaming hot.

When she entered the courtyard, the tiki lights were on, and there were four people sitting at a table by the pool: Emmalyn, Kaia, Max, and Lexie.

"Hey, Madison," Emmalyn said, waving her over.

"Hi," she said as she joined them. "What are you all doing?"

"Cooling off," Kaia said. "It's very hot inside my apartment, and I don't know if you've noticed, but the window air conditioners aren't great."

"I haven't been in my apartment yet."

"Sit," Emmalyn said, patting the empty chair next to her.

"How was your night?" Lexie asked.

"Busier than usual."

"Gabe said you two won the first round," Max said, a curious gleam in his eyes. "Congratulations."

"Thanks."

"We need to go to your restaurant," Kaia said.

"I agree," Lexie put in. "My friend Drea works with Madison, and she has been telling me about the restaurant in yoga class. Let's all go one night."

"I'd love to have you," she said.

"We'll find a night," Lexie said with a nod.

"Are you hungry, Madison?" Emmalyn asked. "That's probably a silly question. You must eat at your restaurant every night."

"Actually, I ate nothing tonight, aside from tasting dishes here and there."

"Then stay. Gabe should be here any second with our food."

"Gabe's bringing you food?"

"From the truck," Lexie said. "And he always brings a ton. Have you had Gabe's food yet?"

"I've only tasted the lamb he made today," she admitted.

"Then you have to stay."

The last thing she wanted to do was taste Gabe's food and spend more time with him, but he was already walking into the courtyard with a large box in his hands. She didn't want to alienate her new friends and neighbors by refusing to partake in Gabe's tacos or for them to think there was some war going on between them that would affect the vibe at the building.

"Hello, Madison," Gabe said, when he saw her. "I didn't realize you were in on this order."

"I just got here. I'm not really that hungry."

"Yes, she is," Kaia said. "And I know you brought plenty, Gabe."

"I did." He gave her a smile. "Join us." He set the box on the table and started handing out containers filled with tacos, burritos, enchiladas, a taco salad, and chicken quesadillas. When he handed her a container, he said, "Do you like fish tacos?"

"Sure. Thanks."

She knew Gabe could cook. She'd seen that during the competition earlier today, and his truck always had a line. There had to be a reason for that, but she was still surprised by the spicy flavor of the fish and the shredded salad that enhanced that flavor and added an extra bite.

She hadn't thought she was that hungry, but she finished the taco in a few bites, very aware of Gabe's questioning gaze.

"Well?" he asked.

"You know it's good."

"Still, it's nice to hear, especially from a fellow chef."

She realized it wasn't only Gabe who was waiting for her answer. "It's probably the best fish taco I've ever had," she admitted.

A smile spread across his face. "I did not think you were going to say that."

"Well, it's the truth."

"I agree," Emmalyn said. "Don't I always tell you that your fish tacos are the best?"

"Everything is the best," Kaia added. "Thanks for our midnight snack, Gabe. You always come through."

"What have you all been doing tonight?" Gabe asked.

"I was working," Max said. "And I need to get back to it now. I just took a break because the apartment got too hot."

"I was working, too," Kaia put in. "I just finished my shift an hour ago."

"Lexie and I were not working. We went to that movie, *Racing Against Time*," Emmalyn said. "It was not very good."

"Way too many car chases," Lexie agreed.

"Car chases are awesome," Gabe said.

"Not when they go on forever," Lexie retorted.

"I agree with Lexie," Max said. "Even though I haven't seen the movie. But sometimes car chases just cover lazy writing."

"Well, you would know," Gabe said.

"Speaking of writing..." Max got to his feet. "I need to get back to it."

"It's so late," Lexie said. "Why don't you do it in the morning?"

"Actually, your car chase comment just gave me an idea."

Lexie shook her head. "You and your ideas. Go. Write it down before you forget. I'm going to go to bed."

"Me, too," Kaia said as she collected the trash. "I'll throw this away upstairs."

Madison was surprised at how fast everyone disappeared, leaving her and Gabe alone at the table.

"I should probably go upstairs as well," she said.

"Are you in a rush? I don't know about you, Madison, but I've been standing in a small space by a hot stove all night. I could use some fresh air." He got up and stretched out on a lounger. "These are pretty comfortable."

She had to admit he looked comfortable, and she was still hot.

She got up and laid down on the lounger next to him. "It feels nice out here," she said. "Although the lights are a little bright."

"They'll go out in a few minutes. They're set to turn off at midnight." He paused. "How was your night?"

"Busier than I expected. Some guests at the Lazure Hotel booked my restaurant after hearing about our win today. It was the best Saturday night we've had," she said, then instantly kicked herself for letting him know how bad things had been. "Of course, I expected things to improve as people heard about La Marée."

"I had some hotel guests, too, at the food truck."

"An unexpected bonus from our win. I didn't realize they were broadcasting the competition on the hotel channel. I'm kind of glad I didn't know that. It would have made me even more nervous."

"Why were you so nervous?" he asked, a curious note in his voice. "You're an excellent chef, and you know that. I could see the confidence when you were cooking, but in between times, you look petrified."

"I'm not used to cameras in the kitchen, people wanting to interview me. I don't think fast on my feet, and I prefer not to be in a position where I have to do that."

"From what I've seen, you think fast enough to keep up with some food columnist's questions." He paused. "It feels like there's something else you're not saying."

As she thought about his words, the lights in the courtyard suddenly went out, plunging them in dark shadows, with a starry sky overhead. She stared up at the stars for a long minute, happy that there were no more lights to deal with.

There was another reason for her anxiety, one she didn't like to share, so she wouldn't. It wasn't Gabe's business. And she couldn't show a weakness to a rival competitor; that would be stupid.

"You're not going to tell me, are you?" he asked. "It's okay. You're entitled to your secrets."

"I didn't say I had secrets."

"Everyone has secrets."

"Even you?" She turned her head to look at him. His face was half-lit from the bright moon overhead, but she couldn't see his eyes.

"Didn't I just say everyone?" he asked.

"What secrets do you have?"

He turned to look at her. "You want me to tell you, but you don't want to tell me. That's not fair."

"You're right. Forget I asked."

There was quiet for a minute, broken only by the sound of the crashing waves on the nearby beach. Then he said, "I know something about my father my siblings don't know."

She was surprised by his words. "Something bad?" she ventured.

"I found two love letters after his death. They were written to my father by a woman who was not my mother. The letters were dated about six months before my parents were married. I have no idea if he answered the letters, but it was apparent that there was something between them. I found that odd because my parents were engaged at the time that the letters were sent."

"Do you think your mother knew about this other woman?"

"I don't know. The letters were tucked away in a box in the attic. I'm not sure why he never threw them away."

"Did you tell your mother?"

"God, no. She was devastated after his death. I couldn't hurt her with speculation about some old love affair that ended before their marriage. At least, I hope it ended."

"Do you have reason to doubt that it didn't?"

"No. None. I believe he was faithful. It was just strange to think about him loving someone who wasn't my mother."

"Maybe he didn't love her. But even if he did, people don't always marry the first person they love."

"You're right. I just wish I'd never read the letters. The information weighs on me sometimes. I wonder if my siblings have a right to know."

"They don't," she said sharply. "Everyone has a right to a private life. Just because you die doesn't mean your secrets have to come out."

"That's true."

"But I am sorry you're carrying the burden."

"It's not really a burden. Like you said, he married my mother, and they had from all appearances, a happy, loving marriage. It's just been on my mind more this week because it's the anniversary of his death tomorrow."

"I understand. For what it's worth, I think you made the right decision to keep the information to yourself. What did you do with the letters?"

"I still have them. But I should throw them away. I don't know why I haven't done it already."

"You'll know when the time is right." She was surprised at how deep their conversation had gotten so fast. Maybe it was the darkness that surrounded them, the weariness of the day catching up, allowing Gabe to let down his guard, allowing her to let him. "Were you close to your dad?"

"Yes. He wasn't a man of many words, whereas I had lots of words and lots of questions. He always said I drove him crazy with my questions."

"You do like to dig into things," she commented.

"So did my father. But his digging always involved a shovel."

"How did he get into organic farming?"

"He started working for a gardener when he was sixteen. In his twenties, he became obsessed with organic gardening and grew produce that my grandparents could use in their cooking and later in their restaurant. From there, he took his small business and made it even bigger when he cultivated some acres behind a church and used that land to grow food for the church's free meal service. Eventually, he got other farmers to start plots on that land. After a few years, it grew into an organic garden collective, and it was a tremendous success. Eventually, my father found an investor who helped the group get more land, and while they kept a garden at the church, they moved to a bigger space on the outskirts of San Diego. Now, they have fresh markets there several days a week."

"Where is it? It sounds amazing."

"About ten miles from here."

"I'd love to go there and pick up fresh produce for the restaurant." She paused. "Unless...is it still there? You said your father passed away."

"It's still there. His legacy lives on, thanks to my mother. She's determined to keep it going."

"Did you ever work there?"

"No, I don't love growing vegetables; I just want to cook them."

"I've always wanted to have a vegetable garden, but I've been living in apartments for the past ten years."

"Me, too."

"Did I taste some of the collective's vegetables in my fish taco tonight?"

"You did," he said. "I go there Sundays and Wednesdays to stock up."

"What time do you go tomorrow?"

"I usually get out there around eleven."

"Could you tell me where it is? I'd like to go."

"Why don't you come with me?" he suggested.

She hesitated, wondering if she should keep spending time with a man she was competing against.

"Afraid of getting too close to the enemy, Madison?" he teased. "Like I said earlier, we don't have to be enemies; we can be allies. Tomorrow, I can show you which gardener has the best vegetables. I have valuable connections."

"I thought you were against using connections to get ahead."

He let out a sigh. "I came on too strong when we first met. I shouldn't have come down on you for using your connections. It's the way the world works."

"I really didn't want to use a connection to get my own restaurant. I've been on my own for a long time, and working as hard as I could, but nothing was happening for me, so when this opportunity came up, I took it, even though I really didn't want to take a favor from my dad. His goodwill always comes with his opinions."

"I get it. I probably would have done the same thing if I'd been in your position." He paused. "How is it going now that you've been in business a month?"

"I'm pretty sure you know it's not going well. Tonight was busier, which was good, but I didn't feel like the kitchen staff was in sync. We've been working so slowly the past few weeks, with lots of time to perfect our dishes, and tonight when we had to speed up, it felt off. Or maybe it was just me. It's been a long day of cooking."

"It has," he agreed.

"I'll work it out. I'm not going to fail. I can't. Even if you'd like me to."

"It was easier to want you to fail before I met you," he said, surprising her with his words.

"I didn't think you'd actually admit to that."

"I'm not proud of my petty, jealous feelings," he said dryly. "I've never been in the business of revenge before. I just wanted that space so badly. And I thought Larry Shaw was going to give it to me. We had a few conversations before he mentioned he was hiring you. The disappointment was a little soul-crushing."

"I had no idea Larry had talked to anyone else. I understand how you felt. I've lost jobs before that I've really wanted. But your food truck is doing so well, I can't believe someone else won't take a chance on you."

"I don't have the pedigree a lot of restaurant owners are looking for. Not like you. I didn't study in France. I've never even been to Europe."

"You should go to Europe, especially to Paris. The food there is amazing. It's exquisite."

"I'm not sure Paris would love me. No one has ever called my food exquisite."

"I haven't heard that about my food either," she admitted. Looking up at the stars, she added, "Sometimes, I don't know if I'm good enough to be the chef I need to be. I want my restaurant to be talked about, to win awards. I want my food to be in magazines and for foodies to come to my dining room and take photos and tell everyone about La Marée." She paused, feeling a little embarrassed for having revealed so much. "I guess every chef wants that."

"I don't want that. I don't care about foodies taking photos and putting them on the Internet. I don't care about awards. I want to have a place where people come to celebrate the important moments in their lives. I want my food to be part of their memories, their joy."

His heartfelt words touched her, and she was a little embarrassed that his goals were more altruistic than hers. But maybe they weren't really that different. They both wanted to leave an impression on their customers, to make them happy, to give them the best meal they'd ever had.

"What made you want to go into fine dining?" Gabe asked.

"It was all I knew. Whenever my parents took us out to dinner, it was always to a fancy gourmet restaurant, and I loved the experience. Every plate was a work of art. The service was structured and formal. And my father was so proud to introduce us to the food he loved. When we were in those restaurants sharing a meal, for a few hours I felt like I belonged in my family. My father and I were on the same page, and that rarely happened."

"It sounds like you two have a complicated relationship."

"He's a hard man to please, but his heart is in the right place. He wants his children to achieve great things, and that's a good goal, right?"

"I suppose," Gabe said as he let out a yawn. "I'm so tired; I could sleep right here."

She felt remarkably comfortable, too, but she knew she had to get up and go to bed. She'd already let down her guard with Gabe far too much, and while he seemed more like a friend than an enemy now, she needed to be careful his friendship wasn't part of some strategy to win.

"I'm going upstairs," she said, swinging her feet to the ground.

"I didn't mean to end the conversation," he said, stifling another yawn. "Sorry."

"Don't apologize. We're both exhausted. I need to go to bed."

"Me, too. I'll meet you down here at ten thirty tomorrow," he said. "You'll love the market."

She hesitated. "Maybe we're spending too much time together, Gabe."

He smiled. "Stop worrying about me, Madison. I don't have an ulterior motive."

"I'm sure if you did, you wouldn't admit it."

"You're a very suspicious person."

"I prefer to think of myself as carefully cautious."

"Except when you're drinking tequila," he said.

She didn't bother to reply because they both knew the answer to that.

CHAPTER NINE

Gabe waited for Madison in the courtyard on Sunday morning. He had mixed feelings about their conversation last night. He'd opened up to her about his father and the love letters, something he'd told no one else. He didn't know why he had, except it had been on his mind all week, and it had been surprisingly easy to talk to her while sitting in the dark under the stars.

They actually had a lot in common. They were both obsessed with food and being chefs and running their own restaurants. They were competing for the same prize, both dreaming of what that prize could do for them.

He hoped the competition would not only bring him the cash he needed to invest in his business, but also give him the connections he needed. He might not have a rich father with rich friends, but all he needed was someone who wanted to invest in him, which meant he had to prove he was as good as every pedigreed chef out there. But Madison and ten other chefs were standing in his way. He would have to beat all of them to get the prize. And it would probably be easier to beat Madison if he stopped talking to her, spending time with her, hearing about her dreams, sharing confidences.

He shifted his weight, checking his watch. She was five

minutes late. He hoped she wasn't going to bail, but he probably shouldn't be surprised if she did. She had a tendency to put her walls back up as soon as she realized she'd let them down.

"Hey, Gabe," Liam said, interrupting his thoughts.

He smiled at Liam and Ava, who had just entered the courtyard, each holding a cup of coffee. They both looked relaxed and happy in shorts, T-shirts, and flip-flops. Ava had become a much more chill person since she'd moved to Ocean Shores. "Good morning. How's it going?"

"Great," Liam returned. "And congratulations. We heard you won the first round of the competition and are moving on."

"That's right."

"We also heard our newest tenant was your partner," Liam added.

"She was. Madison made the perfect sauce for my perfect lamb."

"Sounds like the perfect match," Liam said with a gleam in his eyes. "But isn't this the chef who runs the restaurant you were hoping to get?"

"Yep," he said shortly, beginning to tire of that old story. "But that's behind me. I'm focusing on the present. Madison and I were able to work together well in the first round, but we'll have to go against each other in the next one."

"I'm sure you'd like to beat her, considering she beat you out for the restaurant," Liam said.

He shrugged. "I need to beat everyone, not just her. Maybe we'll be battling at the end if we keep winning. We'll see what happens." He paused as Madison came down the stairs wearing a thin-strapped blue sundress, her blonde hair falling around her shoulders, her legs bare, with a pair of sandals on her feet. She was so pretty, his gut clenched at the sight of her.

"Battling, huh?" Liam murmured quietly as Ava said hello to Madison. "I think you've already lost that war, Gabe."

"Can't afford to lose it," he said cryptically.

Liam gave him a speculative look, then said hello to Madison.

Madison turned to him with an apology in her eyes. "Sorry I'm late, Gabe. I couldn't find my tote bags after moving, but they were buried in my closet." She held up the two canvas bags in her hand.

"No problem."

"Where are you two off to?" Ava asked.

"To get some fresh produce at a farmers' market," he replied.

"Is that for the competition? Are you already doing your next challenge?"

"No, we're buying for our businesses. We should probably go. We'll see you two later."

"Later," Liam echoed as they walked away. He was very aware of the curious eyes following their exit, but he couldn't worry about it. Gossip was rampant at Ocean Shores, but it was usually good-natured. And it didn't matter what anyone else thought. He knew what was happening with Madison, and that was nothing. Because that's the way she wanted it and the way he wanted it, too.

Well, at least some of the time.

And as he opened his car door for her, he silently admitted it didn't quite feel like nothing.

———

What the hell was she doing? The question went around in Madison's head as Gabe drove her to the garden collective. She told herself she just wanted to see this fabulous market he'd told her about, but that answer didn't ring true because she could have gone on her own. Instead, she'd chosen to go with him and spend more time with him, for reasons she refused to acknowledge. She knew she was getting too caught up in this man, but there never seemed to be a good time to pull away.

"You're not much of a talker, are you, Madison?" Gabe said, interrupting her thoughts.

"What?" she asked, glancing over at him, realizing she'd been distracted for at least a few minutes.

"You're not very chatty."

It wasn't the first time she'd heard that. "I speak when I have something to say."

"Okay," he said evenly. "Then tell me something about yourself I don't know."

"You know very little about me," she pointed out.

He gave her a dry smile. "Well, you are the woman who refused to even exchange names the first time we met. Why was that, anyway?"

"I told you at the time I just didn't want to have another boring conversation about where we went to school or what our favorite colors are."

"My first conversations with a woman are usually more interesting than that."

"Well, my first conversations with men I meet at bars are not."

"Why don't you tell me about your mom?" he suggested, ignoring her comment.

"Why?" she asked, feeling a little wary at the personal question.

"You've mentioned your father and your overachieving siblings. I'm curious about your mother. What's your relationship with her?"

"It's good."

He gave her a pointed look. "You can do better than that."

"Why do you care what my mother is like?"

"It's called getting to know you."

"We don't have to get to know each other."

"But we can, right? There's traffic. We have time..." His voice drifted away.

She let out a sigh, realizing that it was either talk or sit in the growing tension between them. "Fine. My mother is creative. She likes to decorate. I think she wanted to be an interior designer when she was younger, but she married my dad when she was twenty-three. Then she had three kids and a busy husband, so she ended up taking care of all of us. When we got older, she started volunteering a lot, and she helped her friends decorate their houses." She paused. "My mom is very kind and sweet. She loves us a lot."

"But..." He shot her a look. "There's a but, right?"

He was more intuitive than she would have thought. "There's not a *but*. She was a good mom. I just sometimes wished she'd stood up for herself a little more," she admitted.

"For herself or for you?"

"Both. She likes to keep everyone happy, and when my father isn't happy, no one is happy. So, she plays peacemaker. Because my dad and I are often at odds, she had to do that a lot between us, and sometimes it felt like she could have said more in my defense. But that's probably the twelve-year-old girl in me talking. In retrospect, she did encourage me to pursue cooking, which was my passion. And last year, she was the one who encouraged my father to talk to Larry about getting me into the restaurant. He was resistant at first. When his name is on the line, he likes to have control, even if it's just about recommending his daughter to his friend. I wouldn't have even accepted his help if I hadn't just lost my job because the executive chef brought in a good friend and couldn't use both of us. I'd been working hard toward the goal of having my own restaurant and getting nowhere so I couldn't say no to my father helping me, even though I knew it would put him in the middle of my business."

"Does he have a say in the business?"

"No. But he's in Larry's ear all the time. And my father doesn't want me to embarrass him by letting Larry down, so I have pressure from both of them. I have to make the restaurant work. Larry wants to see results in the next four weeks."

"Or what?"

"I didn't want to ask. I can't fail, though. That's not an

option." She cleared her throat. "But I'm sure the last people you want to hear about are my father and Larry. Why don't you tell me more about the collective we're going to?"

"There are about a dozen farmers now. Some work there full-time, others grow their produce elsewhere and then bring it to the market. My mother does a lot of the administrative work and keeps in touch with everyone. She knows every farmer and what they're growing and how they're doing."

"Did she garden, too?"

"No. Never. She was a teacher for a long time, but when my dad died there was a void, and she filled it so that the collective would keep going. She now spends most of her time there. We may run into her today. She's usually there on Sunday mornings, since it's the busiest day for the market." He paused as he turned into a crowded parking lot. "And we're here."

"Along with a lot of other people," Madison commented. "I don't know if there's any parking."

"Don't worry. I've got this."

The market was behind a large fenced-in area with a wide gate and banner announcing the times of the open-air markets. Beyond the market, she could see extensive fields where the vegetables and herbs were grown, and excitement ran through her at the idea of picking up some really fresh produce right out of the field.

Gabe bypassed the public lot, turning down a small alleyway and parking in a reserved spot.

"Special privileges?" she asked.

"Yes. It's one of the few legacies I've inherited from my parents, a family parking spot."

He was being sarcastic but not bitter, and she appreciated the difference. Despite his lack of privilege, he seemed to really love his family.

She grabbed her tote bags and followed him out of the car as he popped the trunk. He had two large coolers in the back and a couple of canvas shopping bags.

"We'll shop and then put our bags in the coolers," he said. "Keep everything fresh until we get home."

"That's a good idea."

He grabbed his bags, then shut the trunk, and they walked through a side gate and into the market, where a festive air of food and community enveloped her. There were two long rows of booths, but at this end of the market there was also live music and tables set near a coffee and pastry booth.

"This is much bigger than I expected," she said.

"It grows every year. My mother hasn't just kept the collective going, she's actually increased the number of participants. Are you looking for anything particular today?"

"I'm looking for nothing and everything," she said, feeling a little giddy with excitement.

He smiled. "You look like a kid in a candy store."

"That's exactly how I feel. I love getting the freshest ingredients. It makes such a difference."

"So do I, and I have to warn you, I like to go slow and look at everything."

"That's exactly what I want to do." She was eager to explore the market with someone who had the same interest and joy as she did. The few times she'd taken a date to an open-air market she'd been forced to rush through it because her date got bored within five minutes. But Gabe was different. He was as happy as she was to take the time to really study the vegetables, to talk to the farmers, and pick out the best of the best.

As they made their way down the line of booths, they munched on samples so fresh the flavors exploded on her tongue. She bought way too much of everything, her tote bags full before they'd reached the last booth. But Gabe still had a little room in his, so she filled his bags to the brim as well.

When they were finally done, they decided to grab a coffee, but before they could get in line, an older woman with dark hair and eyes approached them.

"Gabe," the woman said, throwing her arms around Gabe. "I

wasn't sure if you were coming today. You were very vague about your plans when I spoke to you."

"I wasn't sure I'd be able to come with the competition going on."

"We are so excited you won the first round. And with this lovely woman, too." She sent Madison a beaming smile. "I'm Gabe's mother. Theresa Herrera. I must say the photos online this morning did not do you justice."

"Online photos?" she echoed.

"Yes. They posted them this morning: photos of you and Gabe and your wonderful meal. We are so proud of both of you. You must both come to the house for lunch," Theresa continued. "I want to hear all about the competition, and how you put those ingredients together."

"Oh, I don't know," she began. "I'm sure Gabe can tell you everything."

"Actually, I still don't know all the ingredients you put in your jus," Gabe said.

She gave him a questioning look. "Are you sure?"

"My mother doesn't take no for an answer."

"He's right, I don't. And it's not just for me," Theresa said. "Ana, my mother-in-law, Gabe's grandmother, wants to know all about your sauce. She's the original cook in the family, where Gabe got some of his inspiration. Please join us."

Theresa was so friendly and determined, it was impossible to say no. "Okay, I'll come."

"That's wonderful. I'll meet you both at the house," Theresa said with a happy smile.

As his mother left, she turned to Gabe. "Are you really okay with this?"

"Sure. Why not?"

"It's your family, your mother, and your grandmother."

"I'm aware of who will be at lunch," he said with a smile.

"They think we're partners, but I'm the person standing

between you and your dream. I didn't just get the restaurant you wanted; I'm competing against you."

"Again, I'm aware of all that."

She tilted her head to the right as she gave him a thoughtful look. "Why are you suddenly being nice to me? Why do you want me to meet your family? Do you have a hidden agenda?"

He grinned. "One thing you should know about me, Madison, is that I never have a hidden agenda. If I have an agenda at all, it's in plain sight. It's like when I parked my truck down the street from your restaurant. It was not hidden at all."

"Larry did notice your line when he stopped by last week. You got his attention."

He tipped his head in acknowledgment. "I'm glad. I wanted him to see how strong my customer base is. But it was somewhat of a petty move."

"Somewhat?" she echoed.

"Okay. It was a petty move," he admitted. "But it turned out to also be a good business decision. My customer base has increased since I moved out of the parking lot at Maverick's. It's easier to park at the new location and I'm not competing with Maverick's fish and chips and burgers."

"Just my restaurant," she said dryly.

"Well, if people want to eat at your restaurant, I doubt they'd stand in line at my food truck and vice versa. I think we can coexist, don't you?"

"Yes. But I'm still standing between you and twenty-five thousand dollars."

"And I'm standing between you and that prize as well," he returned. "Having lunch together won't change that. Today we'll be friends. Tomorrow we'll be competitors."

She couldn't help wondering what they'd be the day after that...

CHAPTER TEN

Gabe's mother's house was overflowing with people. Madison's head spun as Gabe introduced her to his grandmother, his cousin, Laura, and her three kids, his sister, Christina, and his brother, Lucas, who had brought along a guy named Gary, who'd apparently once lived next door.

There was noise everywhere between the kids yelling and squealing, a television blaring sports in the living room, and another showing cartoons in the family room. She was thankful when they entered the kitchen, but it wasn't that quiet there, either. Christina, who was helping her mother make a salad, also seemed to be fighting with her. Gabe's grandmother, Ana, seemed to be getting annoyed by their argument as she worked on a sauce at the stove.

As Christina's voice rose in protest about some rule of the house, Ana set down her spoon and turned. "Enough," she said in a firm voice. "My food does not need this chaos. Please take your argument somewhere else."

"We're done," Theresa said.

"We're not done," Christina complained. "Nothing has been resolved."

"Fine. Come with me." Theresa waved her daughter toward the door leading to the backyard patio.

As they left, Ana let out a breath and said, "The two of them are driving me mad."

"Well, Christina will be moving out soon," Gabe said. "That should quiet things down."

"I heard you're helping her," Ana said. "Your mother is not happy about it. She wants Christina to stay home until she goes to school in September."

"It will be more peaceful around here if Christina lives with her girlfriends, and I'm just helping her with a little extra cash. She's going to pay for most of the rent on her own."

"You're a pushover," Ana said, a knowing gleam in her eyes. "But also, a very generous brother."

"They each need space. And if they don't get it soon, they're going to say things they regret."

"I suspect you're right," Ana agreed, her gaze moving to her. "But we must be boring Madison with this family talk. I want to know more about the sauce you made for Gabe's lamb."

"She threw about a thousand ingredients into it," Gabe said.

"Not a thousand, but quite a few," she admitted as she told Ana how she'd put the sauce together.

Ana nodded approvingly as she finished. "You picked the perfect ingredients to blend and to go with Gabe's lamb. The mint chimichurri was an excellent touch."

"That was all Gabe," she said, ignoring his pointed grin.

"I thought as much," Ana said. "My grandson knows how to cook even better than I do."

"That would be impossible," Gabe said. "I might have added the mint chimichurri, but Madison really sold our dish with her plating skills. It was beautiful."

"I saw the photos," Ana said. "The plate is so important, isn't it?"

"I think so," she agreed.

The kitchen door opened, and Christina said, "Gabe, could

you come out here, please?" Her voice held more than a little frustration.

"Really? You two need me?" Gabe asked reluctantly. "Can't you figure things out on your own?"

"We need you," Christina said firmly.

"Fine. I'll be right back."

As he left, Ana smiled. "Gabe can't say no to his family. It's his best and his worst trait. Sometimes, his siblings need to work things out without him. But since his father died, he's been put into that role. And it fits him well. Gabe is a fixer. If something is broken, he tries to fix it. Unfortunately, he can't fix the fact that this family lost an important person—my son, Gabe's father and Theresa's husband."

"I was sorry to hear about that," she said.

"Thank you. Gabe tries to make the loss less horrible for everyone. I give him a lot of credit for that." She paused. "Sometimes, Theresa gets upset when Gabe overrides her with his siblings, but she can't have it both ways. She relied on him a lot after my son died, and this is where we are now."

She was impressed by how much Gabe cared about his family and how willing he was to stand up for his siblings. Neither her brother nor her sister had ever stood up for her. She couldn't imagine what it would be like to have a defender, a protector, like Gabe.

"Did you learn to cook from your parents or grandparents?" Ana asked.

"No. I had a nanny who taught me the basics when I was very young, and then I taught myself until I went to cooking school."

"Your family must be proud of how much you've accomplished at such a young age."

"I guess," she said, not really sure that was true. But it felt like the appropriate answer.

"I hope you and Gabe can make it to the end together."

"I hope so, too. What are you making?"

"An enchilada sauce," Ana said with a dismissive wave of her hand. "Nothing special."

"May I taste it?"

"Of course." Ana reached into a drawer, pulled out a spoon, and handed it to her.

She spooned up the simmering sauce, let it cool for a second, then tasted it. The flavors packed a punch. "Now I know where Gabe gets his taste for bold seasoning. It's very good."

"Thank you. I like heat."

"So do I," she admitted, even though Gabe would never believe that. Clearing her throat, she added, "Gabe told me the hallacas you make at Christmas are his favorite food."

A proud smile spread across her tired face. "They are my favorite, too. He keeps asking me for my secret recipe. But I haven't given it to him yet. I'm not quite ready to turn that dish over to him. I suppose that sounds silly. It's just that I learned how to make them from my mother, and it's always been my tribute to her every Christmas. I missed making them last year, so I probably should teach Gabe before...well, I should teach him soon."

She didn't know what health issues Ana was facing, but she hoped they weren't dire enough to force her to give up her cooking any time soon.

"What can I do to make this sauce better?" Ana asked her.

"I think it's perfect as it is."

"You're a talented chef. What would you do to make it more special?"

"I really don't believe it needs anything," she said, feeling very put on the spot. She didn't want to offend Ana. She was such a lovely person.

Thankfully, Gabe came back into the kitchen, his assessing gaze sweeping from one to the other. "What's going on?"

"I thought Madison might be able to add something to improve my sauce," Ana said.

"But I can't think of anything," she quickly put in.

Ana shook her head. "I'm sure it's not perfect. And Gabe said you are a genius at sauces."

"You called me a genius?" she asked in surprise.

"I don't think I used that exact word," he murmured.

"Don't be shy, Madison. Talk to me about this sauce. What would you add?" Ana asked again.

"Well, if I had to add something, it would be more smoked paprika," she said.

Ana laughed. "That's what Gabe always says."

She looked at him. "Really?"

"Yes, but Abuela doesn't listen to me." He paused as his grandmother reached for the smoked paprika. "Apparently, she listens to you."

"Because I'm a genius," she murmured with a smile.

He grinned. "You're not going to let me forget that, are you?"

"Nope."

"I figured."

The back door opened again, and a subdued Christina entered first, her mother following. Whatever had been going on between them seemed to be over.

As Christina and Theresa helped Ana with lunch, Gabe walked her outside to the patio, where a beautiful flower garden and a fountain provided a soothing backdrop to the table and chairs.

"This is lovely," she said. "Very calm."

"An escape from the house," he said dryly.

"It is a little loud inside, but happy, too. It's a good noise."

"It is. It got too quiet after my father died. My brother, Michael, and I were out of the house by then, but Lucas and Christina were here, and so was my grandmother. She had moved in after my grandfather passed away and then, two years later, she had to bury her son. It was a difficult time."

"It must have been."

"I think my mother took Laura and her kids in, not just because they're family and that's what family does, but because she wanted the house to feel happy again. Of course, she didn't consult Christina, who is now sharing her bedroom with a ten-year-old."

"I understand why she wants to move out."

"I believe she and my mother have finally made a truce about that. They've been arguing a lot this year, and that's one reason I wanted to help Christina. I don't want a war between them, and Christina made me realize she's been the one here for the last eight years since my father died. She's had to deal with keeping spirits up while her siblings were off living their lives. It's her turn."

"So the bank of Gabe paid out."

"Just a partial amount to help her cover her rent. She's working full-time this summer at a clothing boutique in town. She's making some money, just not enough."

She was beginning to see how generous Gabe was. Not a lot of guys would be that concerned with helping their nineteen-year-old sister. But he was not like a lot of guys. And that was part of her problem with him. The more time they spent together, the more she liked him.

"Anyway," he continued. "Christina moving out will free up some space in the house. It's always felt crowded to me. Growing up, because Christina was the only girl, she got her own bedroom, while me and my brothers shared a room with bunk beds. It was always loud and smelled like sweat most of the time. On the other hand, it was probably good training for me to work in a small space that is also hot and sweaty."

"But doesn't smell like socks," she said with a laugh.

He grinned at her. "Definitely not."

"When did you get your food truck?"

"Four years ago. I got a deal on the truck because it needed some paint and some repairs. I thought it would be a great way to get out on my own and build my brand, even if it was just in a truck."

"That makes sense."

"It wasn't what I thought it would be. I had bigger plans of serving more complex dishes, but the reality of cooking in the truck forced me to focus on more straightforward items where everyone knows what they are, and I can just try to make them as good as I can make them. But I miss cooking a wider variety of dishes, which I used to do when I worked in restaurants. I have to admit when the competition started yesterday, I had a momentary doubt that I might have forgotten how to cook like I used to."

She raised a brow. "You were nervous? I never would have guessed."

"Well, I have a better poker face than you do, Madison."

"True. What other restaurants have you worked in?" she asked, curious about his background.

"I've worked in a variety of restaurants, from pizzerias and diners to a vegetarian restaurant and even a Japanese teppanyaki steakhouse. That was fun. I got to cook and perform and meet people from all over the world. But it was also limiting in what I could cook, and I got bored with the knife tricks."

"You have knife tricks? I'll have to remember that, in case I see one flying in my direction," she joked.

"What about you? Where have you worked?"

"I've worked for high-end restaurants most of my career, except a few months in Paris when I worked in a very small, casual café that served rustic dishes. I haven't thrown any knives, although there were a few chefs that made me want to."

"Had some bad bosses, did you?"

"More than a couple. And it wasn't like they were tough because they wanted to make me better. They were just assholes. Talented but complete jerks. And they didn't respect female chefs. I told myself I was just paying my dues, but..." She gave a helpless shake of her head. "It never felt like I was getting very far. However, I also had a couple of superb chefs that I worked for along the way, chefs I could learn from. One was Diane Couvier. I don't know if you've heard of her. She has a Michelin-starred French restaurant in New York, and she was incredible. I never would have left that restaurant, but she got sick, and she had to shut it down. That was a sad day, but I'm so grateful for how much I learned from her. She was the one who really taught me how to plate, too, beyond what I'd learned in school."

"It sounds like you're going to kill it in a fine-dining or plating challenge."

"I might have an advantage there. But we'll see what the judges come up with. I don't want to think about that now. It will just stress me out."

"Then don't think about it." He got to his feet. "Lunch is probably ready. Let's see what you think of a typical Herrera Sunday lunch."

———

Lunch with Gabe's family was more fun than Madison would have imagined. She was warmly welcomed by everyone at the table. The conversation flew fast and furiously with inside jokes, friendly teasing, and a lot of laughter. Christina and her mother seemed to get along better now that they'd resolved their issues. Lucas was a quiet guy with a dry sense of humor and seemed to be more of a spectator than a participant, although she couldn't blame him. Between the kids and the adults, there were many people talking at once.

The food was also delicious, a mix of Mexican and Venezuelan dishes. Everything was hot, spicy, and flavorful and filled her stomach and her heart. Love and care had gone into every dish. Ana seemed tired during the meal, but she was also eager to talk to Madison about cooking, and they had a long discussion about the different kinds of peppers before lunch eventually ended.

After leaving the house, Gabe drove her to La Marée so she could drop off the produce she'd picked up at the market. She wanted to use some of it in her dinner service, and her prep cooks could get started while she went back to her apartment to change clothes.

She was happy that Gabe had the foresight to bring along coolers because her bags were cool and her vegetables crisp.

When they walked into the restaurant, she watched Gabe, wondering what he'd think of the interior. His gaze swept the furnishings, the expression on his face hard to read. "What do you think?" she asked.

"It's beautiful," he murmured, nodding in approval. "Very sophisticated with a feeling of luxury and calm. You did a great job putting this together."

"Larry's designer had a lot of input. It's a little fancier and formal than I would have gone for, but I had to make compromises." She paused as Drea walked out of the kitchen, looking at them in surprise.

"Hello," Drea said, her gaze moving to Gabe. "You're the food truck guy, right?"

"That would be me. Gabe Herrera." He held out his hand.

"Drea Scott," she replied, shaking his hand.

"Nice to meet you, Drea."

"You, too. I saw you at Maverick's a few nights ago."

"I saw you, too," Gabe returned with a grin. "You were a little busy."

Madison cleared her throat, not wanting Drea to point out that Gabe had gotten just as *busy* with her. "We should take the produce into the kitchen."

"What produce?" Drea questioned. "What are you two doing together? Are you cooking something for the competition?"

"No. Gabe took me to a farmers' market. I picked up some amazing produce. I'm just going to put it in the kitchen and then I'll go home, change, and come back."

"Okay." Drea gave her a pointed look that suggested she would have more questions later.

Gabe followed her into the kitchen where her prep cook,

Kyle, was chopping vegetables, and her pastry chef, Cassie, was working on desserts.

"This is impressive," Gabe said, his gaze sweeping the kitchen.

"Thanks." She was very proud of the kitchen. It had every-thing she had ever wanted: plenty of space for prep work, top-of-the-line cookware, and three stations with stoves, ovens, and other appliances. Larry had been extremely generous in outfit-ting the kitchen of her dreams.

Cassie gave her a brief nod but was clearly focused on the cake she was making. With baking, measurements were precise, and Madison didn't want to distract her.

Kyle came over to help her unload the bags. As his gaze met Gabe's, a smile spread across his face. "Gabe? What are you doing here?"

"I took your chef to my favorite farmers' market," Gabe replied.

"You two know each other?" she asked in surprise.

"Yes. Kyle is friends with my brother, Michael."

She probably shouldn't be surprised that Gabe knew someone on her staff. He seemed to know everyone.

"I'm glad I ran into you, Gabe," Kyle added. "I can't help you Friday morning. I'm going out of town for the weekend, and we're leaving Thursday night. I hope you can find someone else."

"I appreciate the heads-up," Gabe said. "I'll figure something out."

She wondered what Kyle was helping Gabe with, and if it was his food truck, she felt a little odd about that. Kyle was working for her, and while he didn't work Friday mornings, it bothered her that he might also work for Gabe.

Clearing her throat, she gave Kyle some quick instructions on which produce to use for dinner service and then said she'd be back in an hour.

Drea was on the phone when they moved through the dining room, so she gave her a wave and followed Gabe to the car.

"Your restaurant looks great," Gabe said. "Did you pick all the décor?"

"It was a group effort with Larry and a designer, but some choices were mine," she replied as she fastened her seat belt.

"The kitchen is amazing. You must love going to work every day."

His words reminded her of how lucky she was. With the stress of needing to succeed quickly, sometimes she forgot that. But she was grateful for the opportunity, and she would make the most of it. "It is wonderful," she said, not sure what to say without sounding like she was rubbing his nose in how spectacular her restaurant and kitchen were while he was stuck in his food truck.

Changing the subject, she said, "What does Kyle do for you on Friday mornings?"

He shot her a quick look as he stopped at a light. "Afraid he's moonlighting?"

"I'm not afraid; I'm a little curious. Does he work for you, too? Because when I hired him, he mentioned nothing to me about working somewhere else."

"He doesn't work for me. He volunteers. On Fridays, I make lunch for elementary schools in the area. I do a different school each week. I park my truck in the parking lot, and all the kids get free food."

She was surprised and impressed. "That's very generous."

"It's not a big deal. I wish I could feed them every day. These are schools with working families and kids who don't get a lot of special treats, but once a month, they get a fun lunch from me. Kyle helps me cook and goes with me to distribute the food. My other employees work late on Friday night, so I didn't want to have them working in the morning, too." He paused, glancing over at her. "I don't pay Kyle anything. He does it because he used to be one of those kids. We cook in the morning, so I don't think it interferes with his job with you."

"No, it doesn't. I don't have a problem with it."

Gabe glanced over at her, a thoughtful gleam in his gaze. "You sound like you have a problem. I'm not pumping your prep cook for information, Madison. I don't need to. I walk by your place every day. I know how crowded it is...or isn't."

She frowned. "I wasn't thinking that, Gabe." Although, she secretly admitted she had wondered just how much information Kyle had shared with him. But as he'd just said, it didn't matter what Kyle told him. Gabe could see that the restaurant wasn't crowded.

"The only thing Kyle told me about you was that you're a talented chef and he's learning a lot."

"Okay." She felt guilty for even having had the worried thought that somehow Gabe had inside information.

A few minutes later, Gabe pulled into his parking spot at Ocean Shores and turned off the engine. Turning to face her, he said, "I'm not going to be your downfall, Madison. Whatever happens with your restaurant, it's on you. I hope you know that."

"I do know that." She met his gaze. "I'm just under a lot of pressure to make things happen in a short period. And I'm on edge about that."

"I don't think Larry Shaw will pull the restaurant out from under you that fast. He's friends with your father."

"He told me his loyalty to my father only goes so far. He's a businessman. He has to see results."

"Well, you've put together a great restaurant, and you're an excellent chef, so all the building blocks are in place for you to succeed."

"You're right. I'm hoping the competition will get more eyes on me, which will make people more interested in trying my food. Anyway...thanks for today. The market and lunch with your family was fun. I loved meeting everyone, and your grandmother was fun to talk to. She really knows her peppers."

"She does, and she was quite taken with you, too."

"I found her story fascinating, and I understand better why you love to cook with bold flavors."

He tipped his head in acknowledgment. "It has been bred into me. But having tasted your sauce the other day, I'm interested in tasting more of your food. I'm going to get a group together and bring them to La Marée."

She was more than a little surprised to hear that. "Really?"

"Yeah, Max and I were talking about it the other day, and I know some of the women are interested, too."

"Any time. I have plenty of open reservations."

"We'll do it one day next week."

"Okay." She blew out a breath, as she put her hand on the door, then paused. "I guess I'll see you tomorrow at the competition."

"Yes," he said, a mix of emotions in his eyes. "It will be different this round. We won't be working together."

"I never thought I'd be unhappy about that, but I kind of am. Having a partner was better than I thought."

"Working with you was definitely better than I thought it would be. And today was good, too."

"It was." She felt an inexplicably strong and unwelcome emotional pull to him, and she knew she needed to get out of the car, but she couldn't seem to make herself move. "But I might have made a big mistake agreeing to spend all this time with you."

"You haven't made it yet," he said, leaning forward, his brown eyes gleaming with desire and intent.

She licked her lips, wishing she could look away, but she couldn't. "I'm not going to kiss you. That wasn't the mistake I was talking about," she said, feeling a little desperate to make that point.

Disappointment ran through his gaze. "Then what was the mistake?"

"Getting to know you better. Liking your family. It will make it harder to beat you."

"Good. But just because we've become friends doesn't mean

either of us goes easy on the other. Bring your best, Madison, and I'll do the same. May the best chef win."

"I will bring my best," she said with determination.

"Good. Then today you didn't make a mistake." He paused, giving her a pointed look. "But there's still time."

"You..." She gave a helpless shake of her head. "You're way too tempting, Gabe."

"Then give in."

"It feels too...risky."

"All good things in life come with risk. There's a heat between us, and it's not about the competition or our competing dining establishments. It's just about you and me, and the attraction between us. We started something Friday night that we've both been trying to forget. I don't know about you, but I don't seem to be able to do that."

"We have to forget it. Whatever attraction we had started and ended that night."

"It didn't feel like an ending. Just an interruption. If my stupid brother hadn't called, I think we might have ended up together that night."

She didn't want to admit he was right, but as she stared into his deep, brown eyes, an intense desire stirred within her. "Maybe we should give it an ending then. One last kiss." She leaned forward, touching her mouth to his. She didn't know what kind of kiss she'd been looking for, but as soon as their lips met, the kiss took on a life of its own, sparking an instant wave of heat and longing.

She'd spent the last week trying to tell herself he hadn't been that good of a kisser, that whatever she'd felt had been due to too much tequila. But she wasn't drunk now, and her body was on fire. She needed to pull away, but she didn't want to. She wanted to keep kissing him. She wanted to touch him, to take things much further than they should go.

And then the blast of a car horn made them jump apart.

"What the hell?" Gabe asked, looking out the window.

"Looks like someone is getting a ride," she said, following his gaze.

A moment later, a dark-haired woman she'd never seen before came out of the courtyard and got into the car.

"Who's that?" she asked.

"No idea. Never saw her before. She must be visiting someone." He turned back to her as the car pulled away. "Where were we?"

"I have to go," she said quickly. She opened the car door and practically jumped out.

"Madison, wait," Gabe said.

She hesitated, then shook her head and said, "That was the last time. That was the end."

He smiled. "No. That was just another interruption. You and I—we are not done, Madison, not by a long shot."

She turned away and walked quickly into the building, afraid he might be right.

CHAPTER ELEVEN

Monday morning, Gabe headed to the Lazure Hotel just before eleven. He was eager to see what the next challenge would bring. He needed to kill it and get himself one step closer to the grand prize.

As he got out of his car and walked toward the hotel entrance, he was stopped by an attractive brunette, who looked vaguely familiar.

"I'm glad I caught you," she said. "I'm Georgia Marks. I'm a producer on the show *Your Next Great Bite*."

"It's nice to meet you," he said, shaking her hand.

"I was really impressed with your lamb dish and also your presence. You have a look. A charisma." Her gaze swept his face and body before she added, "I think you'd be great on our show. We're scheduling guest chef segments over the next few months. Would you be interested?"

"Sure." He wasn't familiar with the show, but any food show on television couldn't be bad. "What does it entail?"

"We film the show in Los Angeles. You'd be required to be there for two to three days. I'd like to get together with you and explain it in more detail. I'm going to be here for the challenge today, but unfortunately, I have meetings right after that and for the next several days. What about Thursday morning?"

"I can probably make that work."

"Great. I have your phone number and email from the competition entry list, so I will be in touch about a time and a place."

"I look forward to it."

"Good luck today."

As Georgia moved away, he saw Madison approaching, so he waited for her. He'd spent most of the night thinking about her and wondering what would have happened if they hadn't been interrupted again. Every time things got hot between them something came up. But one of these days, they were going to finish what they'd started. He would make sure of that.

As Madison drew near, he saw tension and anger in her face, and he couldn't understand why. He was happy to see her. He'd thought she'd feel the same. But maybe this wasn't about him. "Good morning," he said.

"Hi," she returned without a trace of a smile.

"Everything okay?"

"It's..." She shook her head. "I don't want to talk about it."

"You look like you want to punch someone. It's not me, is it?"

"No. It's a food blogger who came to my restaurant on Saturday night and posted her review today. It was not great."

"Who's the blogger?"

"Felicity Spickler from *Felicity Knows Food*. Have you heard of her?"

"I haven't. She can't be that big."

"Well, her review has already had four hundred views, so she's big enough to hurt me."

"Four hundred views is nothing. Seriously. It's probably trolls or click bots."

"What?" she asked in confusion.

"I'm just saying not every view is real."

"But the blog was only posted an hour ago."

"Well...who cares?" he said with a shrug. "You can't do anything about it. And it's one person's opinion."

"One person with a big, loud voice that will hurt my business."

"Or...it could actually make people look your restaurant up to see what it's all about. Dare I ask what she said?"

"My food is pretty and worth a photo, but it doesn't have soul. It doesn't fill you up. It doesn't warm your heart."

"Ouch," he said as he saw the pain in her eyes. "I'm sorry, Madison, but maybe this Felicity doesn't review high-end restaurants like yours."

"That's all she does."

"Well, you have to stand behind your food. If you know it's good, then you know it. And it doesn't matter what she says or what anyone says."

She stared back at him through troubled eyes. "What if she's right? What if my food doesn't have soul? I know that's important. Food should make you feel good. It can't just be pretty."

"I'm sure your food makes people feel good."

"It didn't make her feel good." She looked down at her phone.

He grabbed it out of her hand.

"What are you doing?" she asked with annoyance.

"Stopping you from driving yourself crazy. You have a competition to focus on. And you can't change what that reviewer said. Move forward. Forget about it. Or it will mess you up for the competition."

"You should be happy if I'm off my game."

"No. I only want to beat you if you're on your game, at your best."

She let out a sigh. "Okay, I won't think about it, but I need my phone."

He handed it back to her. "I doubt you won't think about it, but at least stop reading it over and over again. And if you want to be distracted, maybe think about our kiss yesterday, something I'd really like to do again."

A gleam entered her eyes even as she shook her head. "Not going to happen, Gabe. We both need to focus."

"That's true...for the next few hours anyway. After that..."

"There is no after that." She put her phone in her bag. "We better get inside. We don't want to be disqualified for being late." She gave him a warning look. "And once we're inside, we're nothing but rivals."

"Depending on the challenge, we can still be allies," he reminded her. "There are a lot of people that need to get kicked out of this competition, and if we want to be the last two standing, we should try to make that happen."

"You shouldn't want that to happen because if it came down to just two, I would beat you."

He laughed. "I see you have your confidence back. Let's get to it."

―――――

Madison's confidence dipped once she was standing in the hotel kitchen with eleven other chefs, listening to the rules of their next challenge. They would each conceive and prepare one dish for a panel of six judges. The challenge was complicated and would require several steps. Each step would change the challenge. They would be tested to see how quickly they could adapt the ingredients of their choosing depending on each new blindside.

She didn't like surprises or unpredictability, and anxiety flooded through her at the thought of what might be ahead. But there was no turning back. The lights were on. The cameras were whirring. And she was sweating through her chef's coat.

She'd started out the day feeling ready to take on the world, but the negative blog review had put doubts in her head, and this new, complex challenge was making her want to run again.

Looking across the kitchen to the six chefs on the opposite side of her, she found Gabe, and even though he wasn't gazing at her, she felt better looking at him. He grounded her in a way she couldn't even begin to explain.

As Francine finished her instructions, Madison had another panic attack, as she really hadn't heard the last part, and now the challenge was on. Francine was counting down the time to start. The only thing she knew was that she had to run into the pantry and grab six ingredients.

"Three-two-one-go," Francine said.

She raced into the pantry with the other chefs, her mind spinning with thoughts. There were some basic ingredients that were available to everyone like butter, flour, salt, and oil. Beyond that, she needed to figure out ingredients she could make anything with.

It was hard to decide, and with the time ticking down, she had to pick something if she wanted to make anything. Some of the other chefs were choosing ingredients that would take them in a certain direction, like Asian, rustic, Italian, or French.

It seemed risky. What if she ended up having to make a dessert with asparagus or something like that in her basket, which was why the whole challenge was completely ludicrous. How would anyone produce a spectacular dish under these constraints?

But she couldn't think about all the obstacles. She just had to do it.

Forcing herself to focus, she settled on chicken, butternut squash, honey, almonds, basil, and coconut milk. She could go in different directions with those ingredients as her base.

The clock buzzed just as she returned to her station. She drew in a couple of breaths as the countdown began for round two where they would run to the basket in the middle of the room and pick a card.

When it was time to go, the chefs jostled to pick their cards, not that it really mattered what order they went in, except that they would have ten minutes to start prepping their dish before the next round. And every second counted.

She picked her card and was relieved to see one word on it —savory.

That was better for her than dessert.

She ran back to her station and started taking her chicken apart, having an idea for a coconut milk-based chicken curry. The time went ridiculously fast. Her anxiety soared as the buzzer blared, and she returned to the basket in the middle of the room.

Grabbing another card, her gaze blurred as she saw there were three sentences. With her eyes on the card, she stumbled back to her station, colliding with Gabe along the way.

"Okay?" he asked, steadying her.

She couldn't answer. Her anxiety was raging as she tried to make sense of the words on the card. She stared at it when she got back to her station. She thought there was something about switching ingredients, but was she supposed to put two back and grab two more or just grab two more? And was she supposed to change from savory to sweet or was that optional?

She stood at her station, sweating profusely, paralyzed by her inability to read the card clearly. She felt like she was in second grade again, standing at the chalkboard with everyone staring at her while the teacher told her to read the sentence, but the letters were jumping around like bouncing balls and she couldn't put them together.

Forcing herself to take a breath, she tried to calm down, but everything felt overwhelming. There was chatter and chaos in the kitchen. This wasn't how she cooked. And she was suddenly very sure she wouldn't make it out of this round because she didn't know what to do.

And then Gabe was next to her.

"Get moving, Madison," he said quietly.

"I—I can't. I don't know," she stuttered.

He picked up her card. "You have to switch out two ingredients for two more and change from savory to sweet or sweet to savory. And you only have five more minutes to pick the ingredients, then thirty minutes to cook. You can do this," he added in a forceful voice. "Go."

His command made her move. She grabbed the chicken and basil and ran into the pantry, switching them out for dried cranberries and vanilla extract. She would make a butternut squash coconut pudding with a honey almond crunch and dried cranberries. It wasn't the most sophisticated dish she could make, but at least she would have a dessert.

Thirty minutes later, the buzzer went off again, but they weren't done. There was one more round. She ran back to the basket and picked another card.

When she returned to her station, Gabe was there. He read her card over her shoulder.

"I have to add something on the side that will tie savory and sweet together, right?" She looked to him for confirmation.

"Yes," he said with a nod.

"And I get three more ingredients to do that, plus another thirty minutes."

"You got it."

"Thank you." She ran back into the kitchen, her mind spinning with possibilities. In the end, she picked up caramel, peaches and goat cheese to make a caramelized peach and goat cheese tartlet to go with her pudding. That would add a nice savory-sweet tie-in.

The next half hour passed in a flash, but she managed to get her dish on the counter in front of her when the buzzer went off.

The other chefs were letting out sighs of relief and giving each other high fives, and she joined in, hoping no one else had seen her panic. Although, it seemed doubtful that the cameras had missed her anxiety attack. She had a feeling she was going to be made into some sort of competition storyline, but she couldn't worry about that now. It was time to be judged.

Several other chefs helped her carry her dishes to the panel and then stepped back while she stood in front of a high countertop and watched four women and two men taste her dessert. It was a different group of judges from the previous round, and all of them were acclaimed chefs who knew good food. This wasn't the prettiest thing she'd ever made, but she'd tasted it, and it was good. Would that be enough to keep her in the competition? She had no idea.

The panel asked her a few questions about her dish, and despite the lights and cameras on her, she managed to give them a coherent answer, trying not to analyze their expressions as they ate. They didn't say much, and she was excused.

When she got back to her station, she took a long draught of cold water from a bottle that had been placed at her station by some helpful member of the production crew.

Gabe was the last one to take his dish to the panel, and it sounded great. He'd used chocolate in a mole sauce with rice and vegetables. It seemed like a dish that was right up his alley. He'd managed to follow the challenge but stay true to himself.

As she heard everyone describe their dishes and their individual challenges, she realized all the cards had been different, with one exception. Everyone had had to switch from their original card, savory to sweet or sweet to savory. But there had been other twists.

Some chefs had to use a specific ingredient. Others had to make a cold dish or a hot dish. She was lucky she hadn't had to deal with those extras. But she had been forced to give up ingredients to get new ones, which was a challenge the others had not had to deal with.

Finally, they were asked to line up in front of the judges.

She found herself standing next to Gabe and was happy about that. His solid presence made her feel steadier.

Francine called for their attention. "That was a fun challenge," she said. "For the most part, we really enjoyed the dishes you came up with on the fly and were impressed at how adaptable you all were. The sign of a great chef is being able to make something extraordinary out of something very ordinary. Unfortunately, we will be cutting the competition in half today. Only six of you will go on to participate in round three. If I call your name, please step to the side."

As six names were called, Madison grew more nervous. So far, neither she nor Gabe had been called. She didn't know if that was good or bad, but they were in the same group, so she was hoping for the best.

"If I called your name, thank you for participating, but this will be your last day in the competition." Francine's gaze swung to their group. "The rest of you are in. Congratulations! We'd love for you to stay and talk to our judges and our media guests. And then we'll see you Friday at two for round three."

She felt immense relief she'd made it through the challenge, which made it a little easier to answer questions from the judges and even the media. She made sure to mention her name and her restaurant as often as possible, hoping whatever press she got would balance out the bad review she'd received this morning. She was almost through the gauntlet when one of the judges asked her if she'd had a problem reading her challenge card, and just like that, her relief vanished.

"I noticed you had a quick chat with Gabe Herrera in the middle of the challenge," the female judge said. "What was that about?"

"We were just talking about what we were going to make," she lied, knowing Gabe was only a few feet behind her and could easily negate whatever she said.

Thankfully, the judge moved on with another question about her tartlet. She answered that question and was done. Gabe was coming up behind her, and she had no idea what he would say if he was asked the same question.

She couldn't intercept him, so she headed out to the patio to catch her breath. The ocean view and swaying palm trees under a bright-blue sky were a welcome sight, and she drew in several long breaths before she heard someone behind her.

She turned to see Gabe with a wide smile on his face.

"Congrats," he said, opening his arms.

"You, too," she said as she gave him a hug that felt so good she didn't want to let him go. But there were too many people lurking around, and she didn't want anyone to get the wrong idea, especially since there had already been a question about their conversation.

As she pulled away, she said, "Did the last judge ask you what we were talking about during the challenge?"

"I just said we were discussing food choices." He glanced over his shoulder as two more of their fellow contestants came on to the patio. "Let's get out of here."

"Okay," she agreed, following him through a nearby gate to a grassy area in front of the beach.

They sat down on a nearby bench under the shade of a big elm tree.

"So, are you going to tell me what happened?" he asked, turning to face her.

"I probably owe you that," she said with a sigh.

"It looked like you were having a panic attack."

"I was."

"Why? What happened?"

"My panic was brought on because of an issue I've been dealing with my entire life. I have dyslexia. When I read things, the letters don't always make sense to me. And when I'm super nervous, it gets worse. Everything blurs, and I get very anxious because there's usually somebody watching me, and it's embarrassing that I can't read something simple."

"I had no idea," he murmured. "That sucks."

"I've mostly figured out how to work around it. It doesn't happen as much when I'm calm, and my brain takes a minute to put things in the right order. But that wasn't today. If you hadn't helped me, I'd be out." She paused, giving him a thoughtful look. "Why did you help me?"

"I told you I wanted us to be allies, Madison. I don't want to have to beat you until the end."

"But you could have gotten rid of me early. Or maybe you don't think you need to. You want me at the end because you think I'm weak, and I'll be easy to beat."

His expression hardened. "That's not what I think. That's what you think."

"It's not," she denied.

"Are you sure you're not letting one bad review destroy your confidence? Because you're stronger than that, Madison."

"Maybe I'm not," she murmured.

"Yes, you are. And we did nothing wrong. I didn't help you make your dish. I just helped you understand the instructions. You did the rest on your own. And I'm putting my food against your food, not me against you."

"Can you really separate it like that?"

"I can," he said forcefully. "What about you?"

She hesitated, then said, "I'm not sure. You bailed me out today. It's hard for me to want to beat someone who was very kind to me."

"It really wasn't a big deal."

"It was. No one rescued me in the second grade when I stood at the chalkboard and couldn't read the sentence, and Mr. Dimitry kept telling me that I should know it, that we'd read those words a hundred times already. Kids started laughing. And someone whispered loudly that I was stupid."

"That's terrible. Kids can be cruel."

"It happened in high school, too, when I had to give a speech. I tried to memorize the whole thing, so I wouldn't have to read, but it was too long. The lights were on me, and I started to sweat. My body swayed. I looked at the page, and I couldn't read it. Nor could I remember anything. It was awful. That was the last time I was ever in an event that required public speaking."

He nodded with understanding. "Your anxiety is making more sense now. I'm impressed you had the courage to do this competition."

"I didn't want to, but I have to do something to bring attention to my restaurant. I would rather it be through my winning dishes than fainting in the middle of the competition, but today it could have gone either way."

He smiled. "Don't think about what didn't happen. We both won. We should celebrate. You're not working tonight, are you?"

"No. The restaurant is closed. What about you?"

"I'm free. Let's do something fun."

"Like what?" She felt both tempted and wary to spend more time with Gabe. She was starting to really like him, and he might be able to compartmentalize, but she didn't think she could do that. At some point, she would have to beat him, or he would have to beat her, and that was going to hurt.

On the other hand, she didn't want to think about the review or her lack of reservations for the upcoming week. She didn't want to go to the restaurant and sift through the stack of growing bills and realize how much debt Larry was acquiring. She also didn't want to go home and sit in her apartment, where she'd end up thinking about all that, too.

"How do you feel about roller coasters?" he asked.

"Roller coasters?" she echoed in surprise.

He nodded. "Ferris wheels, spinning rides, throwing darts at balloons."

"You want to go to an amusement park?" She thought for a moment. "I don't know. I feel like I've been on a spinning ride in my head most of the day."

"Then let's get you on an actual ride, one where you can scream your head off, and release all that tension. Unless you don't like rides?"

"Actually, I love roller coasters."

"Really? I would not have guessed that. You don't seem the daredevil type."

"Apparently, you don't know me as well as you think you do."

"Apparently, I don't. Let's go." He got up and held out his hand.

She wrapped her fingers around his as she stood up, feeling a jolt of electricity. She was playing with fire, but she couldn't stop herself. She needed a day off. She needed some fun in her life. And one thing she knew for sure about Gabe was that he was fun. Maybe too much fun.

CHAPTER TWELVE

As Gabe drove Madison to an amusement park next to the beach in San Diego, he thought about what she'd told him. Watching her panic during the cooking competition had made him wonder if she had some kind of deep-rooted anxiety, and now he knew where it came from. He felt bad that she'd had to grow up with that obstacle in her life and that she'd been hurt because of it. He was more than a little happy he'd helped her out. He didn't want her to lose because she had trouble reading the challenge card. Especially not after she'd gotten a bad review of her restaurant. He had a feeling that had started her anxiety, and then the challenge had blown that out of the water.

He was surprised by the review as well. He'd seen the dishes she'd turned out in the competition and had cooked with her during the first round. He knew she was a good chef. What was missing from her food?

A couple of weeks ago, he probably would have rejoiced at her bad review. He'd wanted her restaurant to fail from the moment she'd gotten Larry's backing. But he hadn't known her then. He'd just thought she was some lucky rich girl whose father helped her buy her way into a restaurant. And that had bothered him on many levels. Not just because of the nepotism factor, but because he respected people more who earned their way to the top, and on the surface, it hadn't appeared she'd earned anything.

But that opinion had been wrong. She had been working in restaurants for years. She might have been given an opportunity, but she still had to prove she could make it work, and that wouldn't be easy. While he hadn't eaten at the restaurant, he did know that the high prices would narrow the market regardless of the quality of the food.

She also had no name, especially in this area, and she was competing against a lot of other local chefs who had built their clientele for years.

It was difficult to make any new restaurant a success, but even more so the kind of restaurant she had chosen to open. Because she wasn't from the area, she couldn't even get friends in to fill the tables and advocate for her restaurant. She was starting from ground zero.

And it sounded like there was a chance she might not make it. Larry had set a short time frame for her to sink or swim. If she sank, what would happen then?

He frowned as the question rolled around in his head. He didn't know if Larry would give him another shot at the restaurant if Madison was out. Nor did he know if he would even want to take it if he did. Larry wasn't being realistic about the length of time it took to build a successful business. And knowing how important it was for Madison to succeed, to prove herself, he couldn't root against her. Just like today, when he'd seen her starting to fall apart, he couldn't stand by and let that happen.

She was his friend. Which also felt odd to say, but it was true. And maybe it wasn't that odd.

The first night he'd met her, he'd liked her. He'd been attracted to her immediately, but he'd also been intrigued by her and had wanted to know more. That had all taken a back seat when he'd realized she'd gotten the job he wanted. But a lot had happened in the past two weeks, and while she'd started out as his unknown, unseen enemy, she had become the one person he wanted to talk to more than anyone else.

And he didn't just want to talk. He wanted to explore the attraction between them, the connection that deepened every time they were together. He thought she might feel the same way, but she was afraid of getting too close with everything that was going on. He understood why she felt that way. While he'd refused to see her go down because she couldn't read a card, he still needed to beat her if he wanted the grand prize, and he didn't just want it, he needed it. He couldn't let his feelings for Madison get in the way of that.

But he wasn't going to worry about that now. He'd had enough stress for one day.

He pulled into the parking lot and gave Madison a smile. She hadn't said much on the drive, but that seemed typical. She kept a lot inside.

"Ready to have some fun?" he asked as they got out of the car.

"More than ready."

"What do you want to do first?"

She waved her hand to the towering coaster that was roaring nearby. "The roller coaster of course."

"You're on."

Since it was a Monday afternoon, the park wasn't too crowded, and the line for the roller coaster was fairly short. Within minutes, they were strapped into a car and chugging up the track.

"I love this part," Madison said, giving him an excited look. "It's the quiet before the storm. Everything is going slow. But once we get to the top, we'll fly."

"I prefer the flying to this slow chug-chug up to the top."

"You don't like anticipation? That's a little shortsighted."

He grinned at the teasing look in her eyes. "You make a good point."

"Here we go," she said as they reached the top and then soared down the steep track.

Madison screamed as the wind hit their faces, as they were thrown back and forth against each other. The track went up and down and around, with one final loop sending them completely upside down. They defied gravity for a couple of seconds, before they were turned right side up and flew down the last bit of track, coming to an abrupt stop where they'd started.

He was still catching his breath when she said, "That was amazing. So fun. Didn't you think so?"

He actually thought watching her enjoy the ride had been the most amazing thing about it. But all he said was, "Yes, it was great."

"I kind of want to go again."

"We could."

"No." She shook her head. "There are other rides. Let's try something else."

For the next three hours, they made their way through the park, spinning around on a Tilt-A- Whirl, flying through the air on a giant swing, and going upside down on something called The Hammer. With each ride, Madison let loose a little more, turning into the laughing, funny, bright-eyed woman he'd first met.

She wasn't drunk this time, at least not on tequila. The rides had definitely opened up a new side of her. And she was just as eager to play the games, whether it was throwing a dart into a balloon, a basketball into a hoop, or knocking over heavy milk bottles with a softball. Despite her eagerness, she wasn't particularly good at the games. He was the one to win a giant lion he had no idea what to do with.

"This is for you," he said, trying to hand it to her.

She shook her head with a laugh. "Oh, no. That is yours. You worked hard for it."

"I won it for you."

"Not true. You won it because you didn't want to lose to that teenage boy who was trying to impress his girlfriend."

He frowned. She wasn't completely wrong.

"This has been the best day I've had in a long time," she added.

Her smile was so bright he felt dazzled, which was how he'd been feeling most of the day. "It's not over yet. Let's get a drink and some food. We can watch the sun set over the water."

"That sounds good."

"Although you won't find any Michelin-star food here," he warned.

"I'm actually craving a chili dog with cheese and onions. Do you think they have that here?"

"I can almost guarantee it. You constantly surprise me, Madison."

"In a good way?" she queried.

"In a really good way," he said as their gazes met.

"In that case, I'll take my lion now."

"Your lion?" he asked with a laugh. "I thought it was mine."

"I think she belongs with me. She'll inspire me to be proud and ferocious and the queen of the jungle."

"I think it's a male lion," he said dryly. "And maybe he does belong to me."

"No way. This is Leah, the lioness," she said, giving him a confident smile. "And it's too late for you to claim her. She's mine. As a thank-you, I'll buy you dinner."

"You don't have to do that."

"I want to. And besides, you spent about thirty dollars trying to win Leah, so it's only fair."

"It was closer to forty," he admitted. "I think those bottles were rigged."

"Well, the game of life is rigged, too. You just have to roll with it."

"That's a fairly Zen comment for a woman who was about to have a meltdown a few hours ago."

"Don't remind me," she said. "I feel more Zen now. You were right about a good scream releasing the tension. I have a dry throat, but I feel much better."

"Good. Let's find some chili dogs." He grabbed her hand, and she didn't pull away.

He found himself far happier about that than he should be. He wasn't even a guy who cared much about holding hands. But at this moment, he wasn't sure he'd ever want to let her go. That thought almost made him yank his hand away. He had so much going on in his life, so many people to worry about, that adding one more seemed like a bad idea for many reasons.

He told himself they were just hanging out. She wasn't looking for anything more, and he wasn't, either. They both had their careers on the front burner. He smiled at the cooking reference. It was nice to spend time with a woman who knew exactly what kind of life he led, what kind of pressure he was under. She might not know anything about running a food truck, but she knew what it meant to want to put out good food for paying customers and to build a business. The struggle was real for both of them.

Tonight, however, wasn't about the struggle. It was about the fun, and he wanted to bask in the good times for as long as he could.

———

Madison felt like she was living in a dream she didn't want to end. After picking up chili dogs and fries along with sodas and giant chocolate chip cookies, they went out to the sandy beach next to the park and sat down on the sand to eat.

It was the perfect night, still seventy degrees, as the sun sank toward the horizon. The chili dogs were messy but absolutely delicious, and she licked her fingers as she popped the last bite into her mouth.

Gabe gave her a somewhat confused smile. "I cannot figure you out, Madison."

"What can't you figure out?"

"How you can look so happy eating a hot dog while you spend your days creating complicated dishes for sophisticated palates. Most of your customers wouldn't eat a hot dog if you paid them to do so."

He made a good point. "Chili dogs are a guilty pleasure."

"Why guilty? Why not just a pleasure?"

"Because of what you just said. Hot dogs don't fit with my persona as a chef, the kind of food I want to make and promote. But I still like them, and today was supposed to just be about fun and not work," she reminded him.

"You're right. I wasn't judging you, Madison. You should eat whatever you want, whenever you want. Food is more than just sustenance. My grandmother taught me that. Meals are about connection, people coming together and sharing their day. It's about the experience and the memory a meal might carry as the years pass."

"That's a lovely thought. Your grandmother is very wise. And the chili dogs did make me feel like a kid again and remember a happy day in my life."

"What day was that?"

"I told you about the time I froze in second grade. After I had my meltdown, the school called my mom. When she picked me up, I was sobbing. I wasn't just angry at myself for not being able to read...I was afraid of what my father would say. But my mom was so understanding. She told me it would be fine, that she would get me help and I didn't need to worry about it. Instead of driving me home, she took me to a small amusement park near where we lived. It only had about three rides and some games, but it was a nice escape, and we ate chili dogs even though we were going home to make dinner for my father afterward."

"That is a nice memory. Your mother seems much more fun and easygoing than your dad."

"She is. And my father is not a bad person. He just wants the best for his children. He thinks he can get the best out of us by pushing and pressuring us to work harder. Anyway, we didn't tell him about the amusement park or the hot dogs, and I actually had to force myself to eat a perfectly prepared and healthy meal a few hours later. When I looked at my mom, she just gave me a secret smile, and I never forgot that day." She took a deep breath, feeling far too emotional for this moment in time. "What about you, Gabe? What's your favorite food memory?"

"I'd have to think about that."

"No thinking. Just go with what pops into your head."

"Let's see. My grandparents used to take all of us to a lake in the summer, and we'd put up tents and cook over an open fire. Our meals were always good, but one day we went fishing, and after hours on the lake, we brought home the trout we'd caught. My grandmother grilled it with lemon and some other spices, and it was the best thing I'd ever tasted."

"Because it was so fresh."

"It was perfect. I've never been able to recreate it, either. There was something magical about that fish that night."

"It sounds like a fun trip."

"It was. My brothers and I were crammed into one tent. My sister was just a baby during that trip, so she was with my parents. After we were supposed to go to sleep, my brothers and I turned on the flashlight they'd left with us and told ghost stories." His smile broadened. "I could scare the crap out of my little brothers."

She laughed. "I don't think you should be proud of that."

"Well, I had to take care of them later when they couldn't go to sleep, so it wasn't really a win for me, but in the moment, it was great. Did you ever tell ghost stories with your siblings?"

"No. I'm sure I would have gotten in trouble if I'd tried to scare them, which I wouldn't have done anyway, because I would have scared myself even more. I do not like horror stories."

"And yet you like roller coasters."

"Different kind of thrill." She waved her hand toward the sunset. "The sun has almost disappeared. It will get dark fast."

"Do you want to go?"

She wasn't sure she ever wanted to go. It was one of the best days she'd had in a long time. "Not yet. Let's keep talking. Tell me more about the Herrera family adventures."

"I've got a lot of stories."

"Let's hear 'em," she said with a smile.

It was after nine when they finally left the beach after laughing and talking about everything under the sun. Food often came up in their conversation. She'd never dated another chef, and it was nice to talk about cooking. They'd even argued over whether or not kale should have ever become so popular. She was a big fan. He was not. She'd told him she had a kale salad on her menu that was to die for, and he'd promised to order it when he came in.

Not that she and Gabe were dating, she reminded herself as he drove her back to the hotel to get her car. It was probably good that they weren't heading straight home because that raised all kinds of other possibilities in her mind, like whether or not she wanted to kiss him again or invite him in. But once they were in separate vehicles heading back to Ocean Shores, it would be easier to stay apart.

Not like now when she was itching for him to hit the brake, pull the car over, and kiss her until she was breathless. Just the thought of that made her feel hot and sweaty, and she cracked the window slightly, needing some air.

It was strange how Gabe could steady her but also make her want to jump off a cliff with him. And she should not do that.

It would probably be amazing, but then what? They were still on opposite sides of a cooking battle and a restaurant war. Not that it was much of a war, but it was still there in the background. And what if her restaurant failed? What if she got booted out? There wouldn't be any reason for her to stay in the area.

But that wouldn't happen. She was going to make the restaurant a success.

She frowned. Here she was, ten minutes away from the beach, and she was already starting to worry.

Gabe pulled into the hotel parking lot and stopped his car behind her vehicle. "I'll follow you home."

"Okay." She gave him a smile. "I had a good time, Gabe. Better than good, actually. It was wonderful."

"It doesn't have to be over," he said, a husky note in his voice.

Her heart jumped. "I think it should be."

"I've never been a big fan of the word *should*. I prefer to do things I want to do versus what I should do," he said.

"Doing what I should do usually means fewer problems, less risk."

"Less fun."

"We've had a lot of fun, Gabe."

"You can't have too much," he said. "But I'm not trying to talk you into anything."

"Why not?" she couldn't help asking, even though she should have left it alone.

"I want you, Madison," he said in a voice so direct, so bold, so hot that goose bumps ran down her arms. "But you have to want me, too. And if it's too complicated, then it's too complicated."

She stared back at him, her breath already coming too fast. She didn't want to say no. She didn't want to go back to her apartment alone. But it *was* complicated, and she should stand her ground, stay firm, keep her priorities straight.

"Since you can't seem to come up with a reaction to what I just said, maybe you should get out of the car," he suggested.

She opened the door and said, "I think I'm beginning to dislike the word *should*, too."

"Well, when you're ready to erase it from your head, let me know."

She drew in a breath, then closed the door, and got into her car. Her hands were a little shaky when she started the engine, but she told herself she was making the right decision, the safe choice.

Her mental pep talk continued all the way to Ocean Shores. Gabe pulled into his spot, which was just a short distance from hers. He gave her a brief smile as they walked into the courtyard together. Tonight, the pool area was empty, which was too bad. It would have been nice to have an interruption right about now. But they continued up the steps together.

"Goodnight," he said when they reached the landing.

"Goodnight," she returned, then forced herself to walk down the hall and around the corner to her apartment. She inserted her key into the lock and let herself in.

Flipping on the lights, she took a breath that was filled with regret and flopped down on the couch. She reached for the TV remote but couldn't bring herself to turn it on. She didn't want to watch television. She didn't want to do work. She wanted to be with Gabe.

The strength of her desire propelled her to her feet. She walked to the door, not sure what she was going to do, but she couldn't just stay here and do nothing.

When she opened the door and stepped onto the landing, she ran into Gabe. He caught her by the arms.

"Where are you going?" she asked breathlessly.

"Where are you going?" he returned.

"I was going to knock on your door."

"Why?"

He was going to make her say it.

"Because it's not that complicated," she told him. "It's really pretty simple. I want to be with you, too. I don't want this day to end yet. And I don't care about what I *should* do anymore."

He smiled. "I was going to say the exact same thing."

She grabbed his hands and pulled him into her apartment.

He kicked the door shut behind him.

Then she moved up against him and wrapped her arms around his neck. "Let's keep the fun going."

His gaze was hot and searing. "All night long," he promised.

CHAPTER THIRTEEN

Madison woke up Tuesday morning knowing she hadn't gotten nearly enough sleep, but looking at the man lying next to her in bed made her tiredness more than worth it. Gabe was still asleep and very handsome, with his dark hair falling over his forehead, his lashes insanely long, and the lips of his sexy mouth slightly parted.

Her pulse jumped at the thought of kissing him again. They'd spent half the night exploring each other, but it still hadn't been long enough. She was fast becoming addicted to this man, and that was a little terrifying. She had a lot on her plate. Falling for Gabe definitely wasn't on the agenda. He was her rival.

But her nerves were still humming from the night they'd spent together, and the thought of kicking him out of her life was impossible to consider. She didn't even want to kick him out of her bed.

Gabe shifted and rolled onto his side, facing her. She was sorry to see him waking up, because then she had to stop staring at him, stop remembering how good it had been between them.

As his eyes opened, an intimate smile lifted his lips, and her stomach flipped over. The way he looked at her, like he knew her, really knew her, touched her in a way that made her wonder how it was possible someone she'd only known a few weeks could understand her better than people who'd known her for her entire life. Somehow, Gabe saw the real her, the person she usually hid from everyone, the person she was sometimes ashamed of for being weak or not good enough.

But Gabe made her feel good enough, and that was a power that scared her, too. She had to be the one to make herself feel good. She couldn't let someone else do that. Then she'd be hurt if they pulled their approval away. She knew that to be true from a lifetime of trying to please her father, a man whose love was always conditional.

But last night hadn't been about love. She didn't know why the word had even jumped into her mind.

"Morning," Gabe said, the sleep finally leaving his eyes. "You've been staring at me."

"How would you know? You just opened your eyes."

"I could feel the heat of your gaze."

"You could not."

He laughed. "No, I couldn't, but it was a good guess, wasn't it?"

"Possibly," she conceded.

"It's what I would have been doing if I'd woken up first." He lifted his hand, his fingers running down her bare arm. "Last night was great."

"It was, but I need to get up and go to work."

"I had a feeling you were going to say that." He glanced at the clock on the nightstand. "Damn, it's late, isn't it?"

"Only eight. Is that late for you?"

"It is this morning. I'm meeting Ava in a half hour. She's been going over my books to help me analyze my business."

"She's connected to venture capitalists, isn't she? Are you looking for an investor?"

"Possibly down the road. At the moment, I'm trying to figure out how to keep everything going. I have a lot of expenses. The truck needs repairs. I'm getting a lot of customers, but the food prices have gone up, and I haven't raised my prices. There's a long list of issues and questions and problems."

"I get it. I have a pretty long list myself."

"But you have a financial backer."

"For the time being." She let out a sigh. "It's back to reality, isn't it? Fun and games are over."

"Maybe not quite over. I have to take a shower, and you probably want to take one, too."

She smiled at the wicked look in his eyes. "You know if we shower together, you might be late for your meeting."

"I'll take that risk."

She threw back the covers. "Let's do it."

His eyes lit up as he followed her out of bed and into the shower, which was the longest one she'd ever taken and worth every minute.

———

As Gabe listened to Ava talk about his finances, he had trouble concentrating on the numbers she was showing him on the computer. His mind kept going back to Madison, to the night they'd spent together, and the hottest shower he'd taken in his life.

He hadn't expected to feel such a gut punch when it was time to say goodbye to her. He'd never felt like that before. He'd never had a problem leaving someone after a great night. Sometimes, he'd looked forward to seeing that person again. Sometimes, it had just been what it was.

But this thing with Madison felt different.

When Ava gave him a questioning look with her steel-blue eyes, he realized he hadn't heard anything she'd said in the last several minutes. "Sorry. Did you ask me a question?"

"About ten questions," she said with a smile. "You're not into talking about this today, are you?"

"I'm sorry. I didn't get much sleep last night. I will focus now, I promise."

"Let's do this another time."

"I can do it now. And can I say again how appreciative I am you're taking the time to help me?"

"It's not a big deal. I have the time. My new job doesn't start for a week."

"That's right. Liam said you're joining an investment firm in San Diego."

"Yes, and I'm excited about it. They're promising to give me autonomy from day one, which will be a nice change from the last place I worked."

"That's great."

"It is. As much as I've enjoyed helping Liam build his business, I'm ready to start working with other businesses. I love helping people get their dreams." She paused. "I think your food truck and your culinary skills could be attractive to a number of investors, and I want to put together a package for you. But with the competition going on this week, it's probably best to wait. Not only will you be able to concentrate better when it's over, if you end up with first place, that wouldn't hurt. You'll have media attention, and that will open up more opportunities."

"Good point. But competition and investors aside, I have a lot of expenses coming up, and I need to figure out a way to take care of them all."

She met his gaze head-on. "That won't be easy. What you're doing now is not sustainable, Gabe. The truck will need a major overhaul sooner rather than later. You'll need to adjust your pricing to keep up with inflation, and you may have to make other changes, like limiting the menu to lower-priced items that will give you the most margin."

"I don't want to limit my menu or lower the quality of my food," he argued.

"I'm not talking about quality, just about what you choose to serve. I'm a dollars-and-cents kind of woman. I'm not looking at your numbers with emotion or a dream in my heart." Ava gave him a smile. "Which is why I'm not usually very popular when it comes to these kinds of meetings, especially with friends."

"It's fine. I don't want you to sugarcoat anything."

"You need to improve your cash flow, Gabe. You should also consider pulling back on the free food giveaways, at least until you're in a better financial position. Getting an investor to help you take your business to the next level would probably be the best step you could take. But the trade-off may be giving up control."

"Which I don't want to do."

"There's a lot to think about. But on the positive side, you have a great base of customers, which will make someone interested in bringing you into a restaurant."

"It hasn't worked so far," he said dryly.

"Well, the value of a restaurant often starts with the value of the chef's name. This competition you're in could make the difference. Not only with the cash prize but with the celebrity that comes with it. You should try to win."

"That's my goal, but the competition is fierce."

"And so are you." Pausing, Ava added, "I feel a little guilty saying you should win because I'm sure Madison really wants to win, too, but I don't know her as well as I know you."

"I'm happy to have you on my side. But speaking of Madison, I want to get a group together to dine at her restaurant tomorrow. Would you and Liam like to come? You can experience her food, and I don't think you'll be disappointed."

"That sounds fun. I'll talk to Liam about it." She gathered her things together. "We'll speak again about business matters after the competition is over and plan next steps."

"Perfect." He got up and walked her to the door. "Let me know about tomorrow night. I'll make a reservation once I have a final count."

"I'll call Liam and get back to you."

After Ava left, he sent out a group text to see who else

wanted to go to dinner tomorrow. Hopefully, he could get a big group and fill up Madison's dining room.

He smiled to himself at how much had changed since he'd met her. Before, he'd been rooting every night to see empty tables when he walked by her door. Knowing how much was on the line for her, he definitely didn't want that anymore. He wanted her to succeed. He also wished they could both win the competition, but that wouldn't happen. He just hoped they could make it to the finals, but there was another round with four other chefs to get past, and that would take some work.

So far, the challenges had played into his strengths. But he had weaknesses when it came to plating and fine dining. If the competition went in that direction, Madison would definitely have an edge on him, and not just her. The other chefs left in the competition all had impeccable pedigrees. They'd trained with renowned chefs. He was the odd man out. But he had too much on the line not to fight until the end, so that's what he would do.

———

Before going to work on Tuesday, Madison did a load of laundry in the laundry room downstairs. She was just putting her clothes into the dryer when Emmalyn walked in.

"Good morning," Emmalyn said as she set her basket on top of a washer. "I heard you and Gabe have moved on in the competition. That's exciting."

"It is. Two more rounds to go before the end."

"When is the next round?"

"Friday. And the finals are on Sunday, so it will be a busy weekend."

"It sounds like it. By the way, I just told Gabe I'm in for dinner tomorrow night at your restaurant. He's gathering a big group to come in. I'm very excited about it. I've never eaten in a fine-dining restaurant." She paused. "I hope I won't embarrass myself by using the wrong fork or something."

"Don't worry about that," she said, although she did use between four and six forks depending on the dish that was ordered. But she didn't want Emmalyn to be afraid to eat at her restaurant.

"I'll be among friends, so it will be fine," Emmalyn said. "At least, that's what Kaia told me when I expressed my concern."

She'd been eating in high-end, fine-dining restaurants her entire life and had been instructed in what to do and how to behave from an early age, but clearly Emmalyn's upbringing had been very different from hers. "It will be fine," she assured her. "I want you to be comfortable. If you have any questions, just ask. No one will judge you."

"It's okay if they do. I've been judged a lot in my life." Dark shadows entered her eyes. "But I've learned it only matters what I think, not what anyone else thinks. That's been a big break-through for me."

She could totally relate to that sentiment. "I'm still learning that lesson. I have a very judgmental father."

"I don't know who my father is, but I was raised by people who were not always very nice. Anyway, I'm excited to try something new."

She was more than a little curious about Emmalyn's background, but clearly there was some pain in her past, and she didn't appear to want to talk about it.

"After I get this laundry started," Emmalyn added, "I'm going to head to the beach and work on my tan, although it will probably just look like a sunburn at the end of the day. Want to join me?"

"I wish I could. I'm doing paperwork this morning and then heading to the restaurant around two."

"You work long hours, don't you?"

"It's usually midnight before I get home. That's the restaurant business."

Emmalyn finished loading her clothes into the washer and said, "It sounds hectic. Gabe is always working nights, too."

"That's true," she murmured. "I'm surprised Gabe is organizing a dinner for tomorrow night."

"He said his employees will be running the truck for him." Emmalyn gave her a curious smile. "It seems like two are no longer enemies."

"We never really were." Before Emmalyn could ask her more about that, they were distracted by the sound of an argument going on outside the laundry room.

"I wonder what that's about," she said, following Emmalyn to the door.

She saw Kaia arguing with her brother, who was sitting in a chair at a table by the pool while Kaia cleaned blood off his face.

"What's going on?" Emmalyn asked. "Ben, are you all right?"

"I'm fine," he said shortly.

"You're not fine," Kaia said. "You might need a stitch over your brow."

"Just bandage me up. It's nothing," Ben argued.

"This was not supposed to happen here," Kaia said, worry in her voice. "You're not supposed to be working in vice. You left that behind in LA."

"I'm not working vice. I just got caught up in a bar fight."

"You were in a bar fight this morning?" Madison interjected, before she realized it was really none of her business.

"The fight was about some illegal activities going on at the bar," Ben said. "The good news is that some bad people were put out of business."

"I hate seeing you hurt again," Kaia muttered.

"I should have just gone to the clinic," he said with a sigh. "I don't need a lecture from my little sister. If you don't want to bandage me up, I'll go somewhere else."

"Sit down." Kaia shoved him back in the chair. "I'll do it."

"Do you need anything?" Emmalyn asked.

"No, I have everything this idiot needs," Kaia said. "By the way, Madison, I'm looking forward to dinner tomorrow night. I was able to switch my shift so I can come."

"That's very nice of you."

"Are you kidding? I wouldn't miss it."

"Unfortunately, I won't be able to make it," Ben said. "Sorry, Madison. I have to work. But I'll get there another night."

"It's fine. I'm happy to welcome you any time. I better go. I'll see you all soon." As she hurried up the stairs to her apartment, she felt both excited to welcome her new friends into her restaurant and also a little worried that her food wouldn't measure up. While she'd tried to put the one bad review out of her head, it still stung.

She didn't want her food to be soulless or boring. She wanted it to be the best thing anyone had ever tasted, something they would always remember. Tomorrow night, she would make sure that her friends got the best of everything. Gabe was being very generous to pull everyone together to support her. She knew they were coming as much for him as they were for her because he'd been the one to ask. And she didn't want to let him down. She didn't want to let herself down, either. So, she would cook them a fabulous meal and show Emmalyn she didn't have to be afraid to eat at a fine-dining restaurant.

CHAPTER FOURTEEN

As Madison got ready for dinner service on Wednesday night, she felt a new level of excitement because she was going to cook for her friends. She would also get to see Gabe again, which was thrilling on a different level, because the last time she'd seen him had been in her shower yesterday morning.

She forced that distracting thought out of her head as she got the kitchen and her chefs ready for service. Her team was starting to gel, and she felt more comfortable giving orders than she had when they'd first opened. She needed things to be done her way. At the end of the day, her name and her job were on the line. If she was going to fail, it would be because of her mistake and not someone else's.

Drea came into the kitchen a little before five. "It's looking good for tonight," she said with a smile. "We just got two more reservations for this evening, and one is a producer on *Your Next Great Bite*. She didn't say that when she called, but I recognized her name, Georgia Marks. I told her I would squeeze her in."

"That's exciting. But she might realize you were lying when she sees the empty tables."

"She's coming at the height of the dinner rush. Gabe has a

table of eight, which is amazing. I'm putting your friends right
next to her table so she'll feel the supportive, positive vibe."

"She knows Gabe from the competition."

Drea's expression shifted. "I didn't think about that. Did I
mess up? Should I make sure to separate them? Damn. I probably should have put her at a different time."

"It's totally fine. Gabe and I are rivals in the competition, but
not really anywhere else."

Drea raised a brow in surprise. "You're not still bothered
about his food truck being down the street?"

"No. We have a different customer base, and his line makes
the street look busier."

"That's quite a change of opinion."

"The success of this restaurant is on me, not any other truck
or restaurant stealing my business. I have to be good enough to
make everyone want to come here."

Drea gave her an approving nod. "The competition has been
good for you. You're looking more confident every day. You also
seem to be getting close to Gabe."

She saw the interested gleam in Drea's eyes. "Don't get any
ideas. We're just friends." She stumbled over the word friends,
remembering their night together.

"Sure you are," Drea said with a laugh. "I can't wait to see
where this is going."

"It's going nowhere. That's why we have to just be friends...at
some point." She felt a little desperate to convince herself of
that, much less Drea. "Anyway, let's open the restaurant and get
dinner service started. Nothing else is more important than
tonight's meal. It's not just my friends I need to impress...it's
Georgia Marks, and every other diner in the restaurant."

"Don't worry. We're going to kill it tonight, Madison. And
then tomorrow you can tell me what's really going on with
Gabe."

"I'm a little nervous," Emmalyn told Gabe as they waited in front of La Marée for the second half of their group to park.

He'd met Emmalyn, Kaia, and Lexie out front since he'd be going to his food truck right after dinner. Ava, Liam, Josie, the manager of Ocean Shores, and her friend Maggie would be filling out the table. They were looking for parking, so they'd decided to wait until they got there before going inside.

"I keep telling you it won't matter what fork you use," Kaia said with a hint of exasperation in her voice. "Honestly, it's just a restaurant, Emmalyn. You act like you've never eaten out before."

"I've never eaten in a place like this."

"It's going to be fun, right, Gabe?" Kaia asked.

"Right," he said. "We'll have a good time, and I'm sure Madison will tell us what we should order." He actually felt a little nervous, too, not because of the food or the forks, but because he wanted everyone to like Madison's food.

She'd be destroyed if her friends didn't enjoy themselves. And he worried that this group wasn't her usual customer base. But it would be what it would be. He was getting everyone into the restaurant; the rest was up to her.

He just wished he wasn't seeing her in this group setting for the first time since he'd left her apartment on Tuesday morning, but he'd been so busy yesterday and today that aside from exchanging a few texts with her, he hadn't had a second to see her or talk to her, and he actually missed her. He didn't know when he was going to get her alone, since he'd have to work after dinner, and he had a lot going on this week, but he would have to find the time.

Josie and Maggie came down the sidewalk, followed by Ava and Liam.

"Sorry you had to wait," Liam said. "Parking was brutal. And the line for your truck didn't help."

He smiled without any remorse. "It's doing really well on this street. But let's see what Madison's restaurant has to offer. I'm sure it will be a one-of-a-kind experience." He opened the front door and ushered them inside.

Drea was immediately attentive, getting them seated at a great table by the window overlooking the back garden patio. After handing out menus, she had a busboy fill their water glasses and said their server would be right over.

The restaurant was busier than he'd expected. There were five or six empty tables but there was a nice buzzy atmosphere in the dining room. Maybe the competition was helping Madison draw in more customers.

Taking a look at the menu, he wasn't surprised that the food was sophisticated and complex. He didn't usually eat at restaurants where the portions were small and often put together with tweezers. He liked heartier meals, but maybe it was time he changed that attitude.

He'd thought of Madison as being a food snob, but he had been the same in reverse, and they both needed to expand their horizons. She'd happily tried his fish tacos, and he would do the same.

"Gabe Herrera," a woman said.

He looked up to see Georgia Marks, the producer from the show *Your Next Great Bite,* approaching his table with another man and woman in tow.

He got up to say hello.

"I'm surprised to see you here," Georgia said, giving him a speculative look. "Eating in a competitor's restaurant. That's interesting."

"You know what they say about keeping your enemies close," he joked.

"Good point. I'm sure Madison Baldwin has also tried your food."

"As a matter of fact, she has."

"I'm glad I ran into you, Gabe. I sent you a text earlier today."

"Yes, I'm sorry. I meant to respond. I can do coffee tomorrow if that still works for you."

"Perfect. I'll send you the details. Is eight o'clock too early?"

"That's fine."

"I look forward to our chat," she said, offering him a big smile.

Madison arrived at the table just as Georgia finished speaking.

"Here's the chef now," he said lightly. "Madison, have you met Georgia Marks from the show *Your Next Great Bite?*"

"No, I haven't," she said. "It's a pleasure. Welcome to La Marée."

"I'm looking forward to tasting your food," Georgia said. "I'll let you two enemies talk," she added as she moved away and joined her friends at a nearby table.

"Enemies?" Madison queried.

"I'll explain later," he said.

Madison's gaze turned to their friends as he took his seat.

"I'm so happy to see you all," Madison said. "I really hope you enjoy yourselves. To start things off, I'm sending over two bottles of our best wine. And if some of you would like to order a cocktail, that will also be complimentary."

"That's not necessary," Gabe said.

"I know that. But I love that you've come out to support me." She motioned to a male server dressed in black to come to the table. "This is Ray. He'll make sure you have everything you need. Before I go, can I answer any questions about the menu?"

"What should we order?" Kaia asked.

"Well, if you're looking for fish, the sea bass is really good and very fresh. For meat lovers, I'd recommend the braised short ribs. They're cooked for hours and are fall-off-the-bone tender. The steak is also delicious. Actually, everything is," she added with a helpless shrug. "It's impossible for me to pick a favorite. Anyway, I'll check in with you later. Have fun."

As she left the table, the waiter stepped forward to ask if

they wanted red or white wine or a cocktail. They ordered drinks, chatted more about the menu, and dove into the fresh, hot bread that was placed on each of their plates, accompanied by two kinds of butter, one salty and one sweet.

The service proceeded from there like a well-orchestrated, choreographed routine. Multiple servers attended to their every need. Plates were cleared and courses placed in unison. It was more than a little impressive. And the food was plated spectacularly. He didn't think he'd be that excited about drizzles and dots of flavor, but they were actually very good.

However, a small part of him could see why the negative reviewer had called the food a little soulless. It was all perfect. But perfect wasn't always satisfying. Nor was it particularly unique, and that surprised him, because he'd already seen how creative Madison could be. He wondered if Larry had also had input on the menu.

Madison returned to their table as the dessert came out. Her face was flushed from the heat of the kitchen, her gaze hopeful and a little worried as she asked them if they'd enjoyed their meal.

"It was perfect," Lexie gushed. "The most amazing food I've ever had."

Madison visibly relaxed, then said, "I'm so glad you liked it."

"I had the sea bass, and it was delicious," Emmalyn said. "The service was also just impeccable. If I dropped a crumb, it was immediately wiped away."

As the others added their congratulatory comments, Madison beamed with pride, and he smiled when her gaze finally turned to him.

"What everyone else said," he told her. "It was all good."

"I appreciate you all coming in. It means a lot to me."

"We'll be back," Josie promised. "And I'll tell my friends, too."

"We all will," Kaia said. "We'll get these tables filled in no time."

"Thank you." Her gaze moved toward the table where Georgia had been sitting, but Georgia had left a few minutes earlier. He was actually surprised Madison hadn't made a point to talk to Georgia sooner, but maybe she'd been slammed in the kitchen.

"I better get back to work," Madison said. "I'll see you all at home."

After Madison left, they finished their desserts, paid the check, and then walked outside, saying their goodbyes on the sidewalk.

He headed down the street to his food truck. There was still a good line even though it was after nine on a Wednesday night. He told himself that was good. His business was thriving. It wasn't what he wanted long-term, but it was what he had now, and he should be grateful.

But when he entered the hot, small truck, he couldn't help but compare the difference between his situation and Madison's. They were worlds apart in what they served and the experience they offered. He'd been impressed by her food, by the ambiance in the restaurant, the professionalism of the servers. And he'd been reminded of just how far away he was from his goals. Which was making it difficult to be thankful for what he had because it just wasn't enough.

He had to change his situation. Winning the competition could do that. He could have twenty-five thousand dollars in his pocket and a phone full of new contacts and connections. He already had interest from Georgia for her show. It was just a guest spot, but that could be a launching point for more. And he had to get more. Because he couldn't go on like this. The truck wasn't sustainable long-term, but for now, all he could do was start cooking. He still had customers to feed and that's what he would do until he couldn't do it, or until, hopefully, he found a way to move on.

CHAPTER FIFTEEN

Madison walked down the street around ten o'clock on Wednesday night, eager to talk to Gabe, to find out what he'd thought about her food and the restaurant. And, of course, she wanted to thank him again for organizing their friends to come in for a meal. Everyone had seemed to enjoy themselves, although she doubted they would have told her if they hadn't had a good time.

The truck was shut down, but she could see Gabe in the window. There was no sign of any other employees; they must have already gone home. She was happy about that. It felt like forever since they'd been alone.

She peeked her head in the back door. "Hello? Can I come in?"

"I'll come out," he said quickly, barely giving her time to see the inside of the truck before he came through the door. "It's hot in there."

She nodded, seeing the sweat on his forehead, the heat in his face. She meant to start by asking him how his night had gone, but instead she said, "What did you think of my restaurant?"

Before he could answer, his phone rang. "Sorry, I have to get this. Michael," he said quickly. "What's happening?"

Her brows drew together as she heard the tension in his voice. Michael was his brother. She hoped nothing was seriously wrong, but there was a lot of stress in Gabe's face.

"Okay," he said finally. "I guess that's the best of the worst news. I'll check in with you tomorrow but call me if you need anything tonight."

"What's wrong?" she asked as he ended the call.

"My grandmother slipped in the kitchen. They took her to the hospital. Fortunately, she didn't break anything. But she bruised her hip, and she's in some pain."

"Oh, no. Poor Ana. Is she home now?"

"Yes. Michael was at the house when it happened, so he was able to get her to the hospital quickly."

"I'm so sorry."

"She has pain medication, and she's going to sleep now." He blew out a breath. "She was just starting to feel better after dealing with cancer the last two years. I hate that this happened."

She moved forward and put her arms around him, knowing how much he loved his grandmother, and how important Ana was to their family. "It sounds like she's going to be okay."

"Maybe for tonight. I feel like I should go over there, but it's late, and everyone will be going to bed."

"Is your brother spending the night?"

"Yes."

"Then he'll let you know if there's a problem."

"You're right." Gabe paused as he looked down at her. "How are you doing?"

"Better now," she said, pressing herself to her toes, so she could kiss him.

He was so tense he didn't respond as fast as he normally did, but as their mouths moved together, she could feel his body relax as desire flared between them.

"I missed that," she said as the kiss ended. "I know it's only been two days, but it feels like a year since we were together."

"It does," he agreed.

"I was thinking maybe tonight..." Her voice trailed away as she saw the expression on his face. "Or another time."

He stared down at her. "It's not that I don't want to. I'm just worried...about a lot of things."

She nodded in understanding, feeling stupid for having even suggested they get together when he was clearly upset about his grandmother. "Of course. It's been a long day anyway."

"I'll say," he said, a heavy note in his voice, as he moved away from her to shut the door to his truck.

She wrapped her arms around her body, feeling an unexpected chill despite the warm evening.

When he turned back to her, she gave him a questioning look. "Did you like your dinner tonight? Which entrée was yours?"

"I went with the sea bass. It was excellent. You're a very talented chef, Madison. Every time I taste your food, I'm more impressed."

She was touched by his words, but she couldn't shake the feeling he wasn't being completely truthful. There was something a little off between them. Maybe he was just worried about his grandmother, and she was reading too much into his tense look.

"I'm glad you enjoyed it," she said.

"Your plates were very artistic," he added.

"I've always believed people eat with their eyes before they open their mouth."

"I hope that's not true," he said tersely. "No one would ever eat my food if it was."

"Your plating isn't bad, at least not what I've seen so far in the competition. And here, you're operating out of truck. It's a different experience. It's not a lesser experience; it's just different."

"Having eaten in your restaurant, I think I was giving my experience here too much credit." He ran a hand through his hair. "Who am I kidding? I'm selling tacos out of a truck. And I'm one of many people in this area to do that. There is absolutely nothing unique or special about what I'm doing."

She hated the sour note in his voice and was beginning to realize that dining in her restaurant had made him feel bad about his food truck. "You're selling yourself short, Gabe."

"I'm not. And you know that, better than anyone, Madison. Your restaurant ran like a well-oiled machine. The only thing missing was white gloves."

"That's too pretentious for me." She paused, giving him a wary look. "It feels like we're about to fight, and I didn't come here to fight with you. I also didn't want you to come to my restaurant and feel bad about your truck afterward. I wanted you to have a good time."

He frowned at her words, then blew out a breath. "I'm stressed out about things that have nothing to do with you, and I don't want to fight with you either, so why don't I walk you back to your car?"

She didn't know this Gabe. He was angry and frustrated and worried. She suspected some of it had to do with his grandmother. Maybe even more than some of it. He just couldn't express his fear about that situation, so he was focusing on his food truck, which was not where he wanted to serve his food, and she couldn't blame him.

"You don't have to walk me back," she said.

"I do. It's late."

She didn't want to waste her breath arguing, so she headed down the street, and he fell into step alongside her. When they got to her car, she said, "I hope your grandmother is all right."

"Me, too." He let out a sigh. "I'm sorry, Madison."

"For what?"

"For not telling you how great everyone thought their food was tonight. You blew our friends away. It was an experience they won't forget. And I'm sure they'll tell their friends."

"Thank you for saying that, but we don't have to talk about my food. You have a lot on your mind."

"I do. I want to spend more time with you, Madison, but this probably isn't the best week for that."

"It probably isn't," she agreed, but she was disappointed. "By the way, did you talk to that producer again before she left the restaurant? She was gone when I came out to say hello."

"I didn't talk to her again tonight, but I'm seeing her tomorrow morning, so I can ask her what she thought about your restaurant."

She was surprised by his answer. "You're seeing her tomorrow? Why?"

"She actually spoke to me the other day before round two. She might have an opportunity for me to appear as a guest chef on her show. I think it may depend on how well I do in the competition, but she asked me to meet her for coffee tomorrow."

"That's great. Why didn't you mention it before?"

He shrugged. "I talked to her right before you told me about your negative review. It didn't seem like the right time. And then I got busy with other things."

"You don't have to hide your good fortune from me. I can be happy for you and sad for myself at the same time. Two things can be true."

"There's not anything to be happy about yet."

"Anything on TV would be good."

"She's probably interested in you, too. That's why she came to your restaurant tonight. She wasn't at my truck."

"Maybe. I guess I'll see."

He smiled, and it felt like the sun had just come out from behind the clouds. "You did good tonight, Madison. I don't want my mood to bring you down."

"You're worried about Ana and your business. I completely understand. And, honestly, Gabe, I owe you a big thank-you for organizing the dinner tonight. I know people said they wanted to try my restaurant, but you're the one who made it happen, and I appreciate that more than I can say."

"It was nothing."

"It was a lot more than nothing. Maybe one day soon, I can show you how much your effort meant to me."

He smiled again. "I'm going to hold you to that."

She gave him a quick kiss and then got into her car. He waited for her to drive out of the lot before he left, and she was reminded again of how hard he tried to protect people, which was why his grandmother's fall had upset him so much. Thank goodness, Ana would be all right, but she felt bad that the woman was in pain. Maybe tomorrow she'd make her something special to eat and have Gabe drop it off. Or if he was busy, she could do it herself.

A voice inside her head questioned whether she wasn't getting a little too involved with Gabe and his family, but she shut those questions down. Not everything needed to be overanalyzed. Ana had been so sweet to her. She could do something in return without it having to mean something.

As she drove home, her mind shifted to Gabe's meeting with Georgia Marks. She was a little surprised he hadn't told her about it, but she could appreciate that he hadn't wanted to rub the opportunity in her face. A guest spot on a cooking show could be great for Gabe.

It wouldn't be bad for her, either. She really hoped her food had impressed Georgia. But she'd done all she could do. She'd have to wait and see. And a part of her wasn't sure she'd even want to do a TV spot. More lights, more cameras, more stress. None of that was exciting, but the idea of building her brand was, so she'd do whatever she had to do to make that happen.

———

"We're very interested in having you on our show," Georgia Marks told Gabe over coffee and pastry Thursday morning.

"Why me?" he asked curiously. He'd been feeling off ever since he'd seen Madison's restaurant and realized the level at which she was working compared to how he was working. And Madison wasn't the only one. Every other chef left in the competition was running their own restaurant, so he couldn't quite understand Georgia's interest in him.

"You're self-made. You don't have a traditional cooking school background, and I think our avid home chefs will be able to relate to your story." She gave him a smile. "You also have flair and charisma. And you look great on camera. I think you're going to be a very popular addition to our guest chef lineup. We'll start with one segment and see how it goes. If it does well, you'll be invited back for more. There's really no downside, Gabe."

"Except the travel to LA and the time away from my business," he said.

"You'll be well-compensated."

"How well?" he asked bluntly.

"If you're interested, I'll send you more information this afternoon. You can look at the time commitment and the numbers and let me know." She paused. "Our show is growing in popularity. It may not be at the top of the network yet, but it soon will be, and, frankly, some of the top shows wouldn't give you this opportunity."

"I appreciate your directness."

"Only way I know how to be," she replied with a confident smile.

"Are you inviting any other chefs from the competition to participate on your show?"

"We haven't decided yet. We know we want you. The others we're thinking about."

"Madison is a hell of a chef," he said. "You must have seen that last night."

"Our meal was very good," she agreed. "But the chef herself is a little bland. There's also nothing particularly unique about her story. But it's still a possibility." She gave him a thoughtful look. "Is there something between you two? You're pitching her now. You were in her restaurant last night. Am I missing something?"

"No. She's a friend. She actually moved into my apartment building last week, so I've gotten to know her outside the competition, and I'm impressed with her talent."

"But you can beat her, right?"

"Of course," he said with a laugh.

She nodded approvingly. "That's what I thought. We like winners, Gabe. Bring home the trophy, and you'll be even more attractive to the network."

"That's my plan."

"Good. Now that business is done, tell me more about yourself. Are you single?"

"I am," he said, as images of Madison flashed through his head.

"Have you ever thought about moving to LA? There might be more opportunities for you there."

"My family is here, so I haven't considered that."

"Maybe you'll change your mind. I can show you around when you come up to do your guest segment...if that works out, of course."

"That would be great."

"I'm going to be in town until Monday. Maybe you could show me some of the sights around here," she said with a suggestive and flirty smile.

"I wish I could, but this week is packed."

"Too bad. I have to get going now; I have another meeting. If you change your mind and have time to get a drink one night, let me know."

"I will. Thanks again." He rose as she got to her feet. He was going to shake her hand, but she leaned in for a hug that felt more personal than professional.

And then she said, "Good luck in the competition. I'll be

there for the last two rounds. I hope you'll still be competing at the end."

"So do I."

After Georgia left, he sat back down and finished his coffee. The opportunity she was offering was very interesting. While he'd never thought about being a television chef, it would certainly give him more credibility than he had now. Any step he could take that would get him to his ultimate goal of running a restaurant, calling his own shots, was a step he needed to take. But before he could do anything on Georgia's show, he needed to win the competition. And that's really all he should be thinking about.

CHAPTER SIXTEEN

Madison knew she was probably overstepping, but after thinking about Gabe and his grandmother all night, she'd been unable to let go of the need to do something for the sweet, kind woman who had made her feel so welcome in a houseful of strangers, and who had been eager to hear about her restaurant and her dreams. Gabe's grandmother had shown more interest and expressed more support in her goals than anyone in her family. And she wanted to do something to make her feel better.

So, she did what she always did: she cooked. She made her favorite soup for when someone was feeling under the weather, a butternut squash and carrot ginger soup. The squash was high in vitamins A and C. The carrots were rich in beta-carotene, the ginger would act as an anti-inflammatory, and the garlic would boost the immune system. Plus, it tasted absolutely delicious.

When the soup was ready, she put it into a container and headed to Ana's house, happy that she was good with directions and remembered how to get there. A man, who looked like a younger, leaner version of Gabe, opened the door.

"Hello," she said. "I'm guessing you're Michael."

"I am. And you are?"

"Madison Baldwin. I'm a friend of Gabe's. He told me about

your grandmother's fall, and I made her some soup. I thought it might make her feel better. Would you give it to her?"

"I could, but I'm sure she'd rather see you than me. She's annoyed that I keep asking her how she's feeling. In fact, she told me to go home, so I'm on my way out. She's in her room, watching her stories. You can go on back. It's the first door on the right. My cousin, Laura, is putting her kids down for a nap, and my mother is out in the garden on a call." He waved her into the house. "See you later."

"Okay, thanks."

She felt awkward entering the house without Gabe, but she didn't want to bother anyone, so she walked down the hall to the open door and the sound of a television soap opera. Ana was reclining on the bed, but she had her glasses on and was looking at a crossword puzzle book, a pencil in her hand.

She knocked on the door.

Ana's head popped up and a smile spread across her face. "Madison. What a nice surprise."

"Can I come in?"

"Of course." Ana took off her glasses and set down her book and her pencil. "Is Gabe with you?"

"No. But I heard about your fall, and I brought you some soup I made this morning. It's my special cure-what-ails-you soup, otherwise known as butternut squash with carrots and ginger."

"It smells like heaven," Ana said.

"Would you like me to pour some in a bowl for you and heat it up, or shall I put it in the fridge for later?"

"Right now, you can set it down over there and come sit next to me." Ana waved her hand toward the desk and then patted the bed next to her.

She did as she was told and perched on the side of the mattress. "How are you feeling?"

"I'm beginning to hate that question."

"Sorry."

"I'm all right. Just feeling silly for slipping on some water. I actually knew it was there because I spilled it. But I turned around to get a towel and then I realized my pasta water was boiling and I got distracted, and down I went. Thankfully, I didn't break my hip, just bruised it."

"I'm glad to hear that."

"Me, too. I've been pretty tired of my bed this year. And just when I was getting out of it, I'm back in it. But you don't need to hear about my problems. Let's talk about you. Gabe was going to take me to your restaurant tonight, but I'll have to postpone that until next week."

"I'd love to have you any time," she said, surprised Gabe had been planning to bring his grandmother to dinner. He really was going out of his way to get her some business.

"It will be such a treat. I haven't eaten at a fancy restaurant in years. I can't wait."

"I'll make sure you get the best dishes in the house."

"I'm betting all your food is good. I heard you and Gabe made it to the next round. That's very exciting. I'm hoping to make it to the finals on Sunday if you and Gabe are still in it."

"Well, there are four other chefs we have to beat tomorrow, so we'll see."

"Will your family be coming to the finals?"

She'd texted her mom about the competition, but aside from a good luck text in return, she hadn't talked to either of her parents. There would be nothing to report unless she won. Her father would not be impressed with anything less.

"No, they won't be coming," she said belatedly, realizing Ana was still waiting for an answer. "I'm not very close to my family."

"That's a shame. Why is that?"

"My father is a difficult man to talk to and very judgmental. My mom is lovely but always in his shadow."

"What about siblings?"

"My brother and sister and I were raised to compete with

each other. We were always being compared, and I think it put a wedge between us."

"I don't understand why parents do that," she said with a bewildered look. "Families should be about love, not competition."

"I agree with you. I've never liked competition, especially with family or friends."

Ana gave her a thoughtful look. "Is it difficult competing against Gabe?"

"It's starting to be," she admitted. "I know how much he wants to win, but I also need to win. I don't know if Gabe told you, but my father's friend is the owner of my restaurant, and they're both concerned I won't be able to cut it as the manager and the head chef. They've only given me a few more weeks to prove myself."

"A few more weeks? That's not very long. Restaurants can take years to build."

"They will definitely not give me years. Things are getting better because I'm getting some press from the competition, and that's creating interest in the restaurant. But I don't know if it's enough, or if it will last past Sunday."

"If you can get them in the door, you can keep them coming back."

"I hope so. And I'm sorry. I don't know why we're talking about me."

"Because I'm tired of talking about my woes. I'd much rather hear about your life." A sparkle entered her gaze. "Now, tell me the truth. Are you sweet on my Gabe? Is that why you brought me soup?"

She licked her lips, knowing it would be impossible to lie to this woman. "I brought you soup because you were so welcoming the other day. It was really nice. I grew up in a cold house, and this house, your family, felt like how a real home should feel."

"I'm glad you felt that way. But you didn't answer my first question."

"I like Gabe," she admitted. "But there's a lot going on with the competition between us. I guess if it's meant to be, it will be."

Ana immediately shook her head. "No. I hate that expression. You should not be a woman who waits for things to be handed to her. If you want something, go get it."

"I don't think that necessarily works when another person is involved."

"Oh, believe me, it does. It's how I got my husband. We came from families that didn't get along."

"Like Romeo and Juliet?"

"Yes, but we didn't drink poison and die together," Ana said with a laugh. "I had to convince him our families were not as important as we were. And he finally gave in. We got together and our families had to learn how to coexist. It took some time, but eventually, everyone came around." She paused. "I know Gabe can be stubborn. And he wants a bigger life than he has. But he's a good man, and if you like him, you should tell him."

"I think he knows I like him."

"I wouldn't count on that, Madison. From my experience, when it comes to love, men can be idiots."

"You're not calling me an idiot, are you, Abuela?" Gabe said from the doorway.

Madison jumped up from the bed, wondering what else he'd heard. "Hi," she said with a breathless smile.

"Hi," he returned, his gaze meeting hers with a shared intimacy that probably wasn't lost on his grandmother. Then he turned to Ana. "Who were you calling an idiot?"

"All men," Ana said with a laugh. "I suppose that includes you."

"What did my gender do?" he asked.

"Nothing you need to know about," Ana replied. "Madison brought me some soup."

"Is that what smells so good?" His gaze moved back to her. "That was thoughtful of you."

She hoped he meant that, and he didn't think she was out of line bringing soup to his grandmother. "I was just telling Ana that she was so kind to me when I came for lunch last Sunday that I wanted to make her something that would warm her heart."

"I can't wait to try it," Ana interjected. "Maybe you could heat up a bowl for me now, Madison."

"Of course," she said, moving toward the desk to get the container. "You visit with Gabe, and I'll bring it to you when it's ready."

"Actually, it will go faster if Gabe shows you where everything is in the kitchen," Ana said. "Then you can both come back and keep me company while I eat."

She had a feeling Ana was doing a little matchmaking, but she actually felt more comfortable going into the kitchen with Gabe, considering neither Laura nor his mother even knew she was in the house. When they got into the kitchen, she could see his mom was still out on the patio talking on the phone, so it was just the two of them.

"I hope you're okay that I brought this," she said, turning back to him.

"You could have told me about it, and I would have been happy to drive you over," he returned. He pulled out a pot from the cabinet under the stove. "I'm assuming you want to heat this on the stove and not in the microwave."

"It would be better that way," she agreed as she opened her container and poured soup into the pot. Then she turned the heat on low. "How was your meeting this morning?" she asked as the soup began to heat.

"It was interesting." He crossed his arms as he leaned back against the counter. "Georgia wants to book me for a guest chef spot on her show. She's sending me some paperwork this afternoon."

"That sounds exciting. Are you going to do it?"

"Maybe. I haven't decided."

"Why wouldn't you do it?" she asked in surprise.

"I'd have to be in LA for several days, maybe a week. I have a lot of responsibilities here."

"I'm sure you could take a week off for something that could prove very lucrative."

"Maybe. But I've also never thought of myself as a television chef. It's not my goal."

"I know it's not, but maybe it helps you get to your goal. It's a lot of visibility, and I'm beginning to realize how important that is. I naively thought it was just going to be about my food. But my name is a factor, and it's not big enough."

"Not yet," he said with a smile that made her feel like she was seeing the old Gabe.

"You're back," she murmured.

He gave her a questioning look. "What do you mean?"

"You were strange last night...standoffish, distracted. It felt like you wanted to put some distance between us."

"I was just thrown by hearing about my grandmother's fall."

"I don't think it was just that. It had something to do with my restaurant, didn't it?" She could see by the shift in his expression that she was right. "I thought so. What? You didn't like my food and were afraid to tell me? Is that why you didn't want to talk to me? Was it bad? Did the others hate their meals, too?"

He put up a hand. "Stop. You're putting words in my mouth and expressing feelings that aren't true. Your food was great, and everyone thought so."

"Then what? Did you have regrets that we got together a few nights ago? Did you want to make it clear it was a one-night thing? I don't like to play games, Gabe, so I'd rather you just tell me up front what you want or don't want."

He stared back at her. "Okay. I did pull away last night, and it was partly because of the restaurant. But not because I didn't like the food or the ambiance. It was because I did. I liked it a lot. I was impressed by everything. The service was impeccable, and you were running the whole thing from your gourmet kitchen. When I got to the truck, and I squeezed into that small space with my two employees, I realized how far apart we were. We're not competing on the same level. I'm not even in the same game with you. It's like I'm in T-ball and you're in the Majors. The difference between us is staggering. But that isn't your problem, it's mine. And I'm over it now."

"Just like that?" she questioned.

"Well, I'm getting over it," he conceded.

"Six months ago, I was looking at restaurants and chefs with the same exact feeling of envy and yearning, Gabe. I'd been employed by five different restaurants in the past ten years. Nothing was working out for me. It was why I felt desperate enough to accept a favor from my father. I know what you were feeling because I've felt it, too. I also know you're eventually going to have your own place."

"You don't know that, because it might not happen. It takes money, connections, luck..."

"You just need to find the right opportunity, the right partner to back you." She paused. "There's still a chance that three weeks from now, Larry will be looking for a new chef. That's how much longer I have to prove myself."

"That's ridiculous. Nobody proves themselves that fast. And I'm not interested in taking over your restaurant. La Marée is you, and it's awesome, but it's not me."

"You could change it to be you."

He shook his head. "You're not going to lose the restaurant, Madison. Larry probably just wanted to light a fire in you. But he's not going to pull it out from under you that fast."

"I'm not so sure about that. Larry likes winners."

"And that's what you are."

She appreciated the pep talk even though she wasn't as confident as he was that Larry wouldn't give her the boot. "We both have a lot on the line with this competition. I wish we didn't have to go against each other."

"Well, the next round tomorrow is not just about us. We

have to get rid of the other four chefs so we can both make it to the finals. I think there will be a lot of attention and opportunity given to the finalists and the winner."

She nodded. "I agree. You know, I felt a little jealous, too, last night when you told me you had a meeting with Georgia this morning. She was in my restaurant, and if she really liked my food, it seemed like she would have called me for a guest spot. Did she say anything about her meal?"

"She said your food was excellent."

"And?"

He hesitated, then said, "Frankly, Madison, I don't think it's my food that got me the meeting with Georgia. She likes my story of being self-made and not classically trained, and she thinks I have charisma."

She smiled. "You do have that." She saw his somewhat awkward expression and knew what he wasn't saying. "Did she want to offer you more than a guest spot on her show? As in maybe a date?"

"She did suggest we get drinks, but I told her I didn't have any time between now and the finals on Sunday. She goes back to LA after that."

"Was that wise? Maybe you should have flirted back."

"No," he said flatly. "I couldn't do that. I'm not interested in her." He moved away from the counter and put his hands on her waist. "I'm interested in you."

"Even though a part of you is jealous of me?"

He grinned. "Well, you just admitted that a part of you is jealous of me, too. So we're even. And there's a much, much bigger part of me that really likes you." He pressed his lips against hers.

She lingered in the kiss, loving the feel of his mouth on hers, happy to have the connection back between them. She didn't know how long it would last, but maybe now was all that mattered.

But when she heard Gabe's mother's voice getting louder, she pulled away. She stepped out of his arms just as Theresa came through the door. She gave them a surprised look as she finished up her phone conversation.

Then she said, "Gabe, Madison—I didn't know you were here."

"Madison brought Abuela soup," Gabe said. "We're heating it up. She said she was hungry."

"That's good to hear. I'd love to see Ana eat something. She had no appetite this morning. Thank you, Madison. It was very sweet of you."

"It was nothing."

Theresa gave her a thoughtful look. "I'm sorry we won't be able to come to your restaurant tonight. We were excited about it."

"I'll look forward to seeing you another night."

"We can't wait. Are you going to be here for a few minutes, Gabe?" his mother asked.

"Yes. What do you need?"

"I want to run to the store, but I don't want to leave Ana alone, and Laura is busy with her kids."

"I'll be here," he replied. "Take your time."

"Thanks."

As his mother left the kitchen, she realized her soup was simmering. She turned off the heat and poured it into a bowl. Gabe grabbed a spoon, a napkin, and a plate to put the bowl on, and they moved down the hall.

"It smells so good," Ana said, when they entered her room. She put down her crossword book once again. "I can't wait to try it." She tipped her head to Gabe. "There's a tray by the desk from my chemo days."

Gabe grabbed the tray, set it on her lap, and then put down the plate. Madison carefully placed the bowl on top of the plate. "I wish I'd brought you some bread," she said.

"Oh, no, this is perfect. I love a good soup more than anything else in the world." Ana dipped her spoon into the soup, blew on it for a few seconds, and then put it into her mouth. A moment later, she said, "Wonderful. So flavorful. I love it." She went back in for another spoonful. "Tell me what you'll be doing next in the competition," she said.

Gabe pulled over the desk chair while she sat on the side of the bed.

"We don't know yet," she told Ana. "They don't tell us the challenge until we're ready to do it."

"Are you worried about anything?" Ana asked.

"I'm not great at dessert, so a dessert challenge would be concerning for me. I also don't have a lot of experience with Asian flavors." She turned to Gabe. "What are you worried about?"

"Plating," he replied. "I know I'm weak there, especially after I saw your plates last night. They were works of art."

"I could show you some plating techniques."

"Why would you want to help me?" he questioned.

"You helped me the other day."

"What happened the other day?" Ana asked with interest.

The way she was watching them made Madison feel like Ana thought they were better than an episode of her favorite soap opera.

"I have a learning disability that makes reading difficult, especially in stressful situations," she said. "The last challenge involved reading instructions off cards. Gabe helped me understand what the competition required."

Ana nodded approvingly. "That's my Gabe. He's always been generous. I'm glad you two are getting along. I don't want you to let this competition come between your...friendship."

Madison didn't care for the pointed pause before the word friendship, but she wasn't going to argue with Gabe's grandmother, and it was up to him to correct her if he wanted to, which he didn't seem inclined to do.

Gabe was happy to change the subject, though, asking his

grandmother to tell her about growing up in Venezuela and her journey to becoming a chef.

Ana finished her soup while she talked about the past, and there was a sparkle in her eyes and color in her cheeks that hadn't been there when Madison first arrived. She loved hearing Ana's stories and while Ana downplayed the struggle of coming from a poor town in Venezuela to opening a restaurant in San Diego with her husband, Madison knew that it had to have been a very high mountain she'd had to climb.

It made her feel a little guilty for taking the easier way to the top by accepting a favor from Larry. She'd told herself she'd put ten years into her dream already, so it wasn't like she was skipping a lot of steps, but she'd definitely skipped some.

She would have liked to talk to Ana longer, but a quick glance at her watch told her she needed to be on her way. "I'm sorry, I have to go," she said. "I have deliveries coming to the restaurant at two and I need to be there."

"Of course. I'm sorry I kept you so long," Ana said.

"I enjoyed every minute," she said, getting to her feet. "I hope you feel better soon."

"I already do. Your soup did the trick. It is the magic cure-all soup."

She smiled. "It always works for me."

Gabe followed her down the hall, carrying the empty plate and bowl. "I'll walk you out," he said.

"There's no need."

He paused as they heard a crash and a muttered swear from the kitchen. "Sounds like my mother is back. Let me put this in the kitchen and check to make sure she doesn't need anything else."

"I don't have a lot of time, Gabe."

"Two seconds," he promised.

"All right." She waited by the door as Gabe went into the kitchen, not sure why she was willing to delay her life for him, except that it was getting harder to say goodbye to him.

As he spoke to his mother, she took a moment to peruse the rows of family photos on the walls. There were many pictures of Gabe and his siblings as kids, with their parents, their grandparents, and their cousins. It looked like he'd had a very joyous childhood, and it was no wonder he was so close to everyone. There was a lot of love in every photograph.

He came out of the kitchen giving her an apologetic smile. "Sorry, I didn't mean to take that long. My mother always has a few things to say."

"No worries. I was looking at your photos. You were a good-looking kid."

"Better than now?" he teased.

"You know you look good," she said, unable to resist smiling back at him. "And I have to go."

"I know." He opened the door for her, and they headed outside. Her car was parked in front of the house, and his vehicle was right behind hers. "My grandmother was thrilled with your soup and also with your presence," he said. "Thank you for taking the time out of your busy day."

"I really like her. And I can understand how she inspired you to become a chef. I know I only heard a little of her story, but it was amazing."

"My grandparents had courage and grit. They didn't quit on their dreams or on their family."

"You don't quit, either." She let out a sigh, wanting to say so many more things to him, and wanting to do so many more things with him. "I wish I didn't have to go to work. It would be fun to play hooky again."

"I agree. I wish I didn't have to go to work, either. I also have a problem on my hands that I need to solve this afternoon."

"What's the problem?"

"I haven't found anyone to replace Kyle tomorrow for the school lunch, and it's impossible to do it by myself, so I need to get on my phone and make more calls. I can't disappoint the kids."

"But you have the competition tomorrow. How can you do both?"

"Food prep for lunch starts at nine and service is from eleven thirty to twelve thirty. The competition doesn't start until two."

"Oh. Well, if that's the case, I could help you," she said impulsively.

He gave her a doubtful look. "You want to serve tacos with me at an elementary school?"

"Yes. Why not?"

"It's a lot of work right before the competition, as you just mentioned. You don't want to go into it tired."

"I won't be that tired, and I want to help you, Gabe, to say thanks for bringing in our friends, and for trying to bring your family into my restaurant as well. You also came to my aid when I couldn't read the challenge cards. Let me do this."

"Okay. You're in. But cooking in a food truck is a lot different than what you're used to."

"I'm excited to try it out."

He grinned. "That excitement will last about ten minutes."

She smiled back at him. "With you around, my excitement usually lasts a lot longer than that."

His gaze darkened, and he let out a little groan. "You really shouldn't say that right before we both have to go to work."

"Something to think about," she said, feeling sexy and mischievous.

"I haven't been thinking about much else," he said. "Maybe later tonight..."

She hesitated. "I want to say yes, but there's too much going on today and tomorrow."

"Okay." He put his hands on her hips and pulled her in for a kiss. "But I'm going to miss you, so let's make a plan for tomorrow night."

"That sounds good. But what if..." She didn't want to say the rest, but she knew he could finish her sentence, and he did.

"If one or both of us loses?" he asked. "Let's deal with that if and when it happens. I don't want to think about losing and you don't want to, either."

At some point, at least one of them would have to confront a loss. At the end of the day only one person would come out on top, but hopefully tomorrow they'd prove themselves worthy enough to make the final two.

CHAPTER SEVENTEEN

Friday morning, Madison met Gabe in the elementary school parking lot where he had parked his truck in a reserved space. Like her, he was dressed in dark jeans and a T-shirt.

"I'm ready," she said eagerly, as he opened the door. "Put me to work."

"It's not going to be like cooking in your kitchen," he warned.

"Of course it won't be like that, but obviously you can make great food in the truck. You have a never-ending line of customers. Right?"

"True." He stepped back and waved her inside. "We'll start with prep. We'll need to begin grilling by eleven, ready to serve at eleven thirty."

"Yes, Chef," she said with a smart-ass smile that seemed to relax him.

"It's good you know your place," he returned with a grin.

"You're so tense, Gabe. I feel like you're more nervous now than you are in the competitions. Why? Do you think I'm judging you?"

"Maybe not me, but the truck needs upgrades."

"You know what I see?" she asked as she waved her hand

around the interior of the truck. "Perfectly organized spices, labeled and organized drawers, a refrigerator filled to the brim with high-quality ingredients, as well as a super clean workspace and grill. I can't wait to start cooking. Just tell me what you want done, and I will do it. I'm pretty good, you know."

"Better than anyone who has ever been in this truck, I'm sure."

"Besides you," she said, meeting his gaze. "Where do you want me to start?"

He pointed to the cutting board. "Onions and tomatoes."

"Got it."

For the next two hours, they worked in surprising harmony. It was close quarters, and they bumped into each other on more than a few occasions, which was distracting because she was so attracted to him.

She wanted to sneak a kiss or a touch, but this was his business, and she wouldn't take it less seriously than he did. So, she kept her hands to herself, even though it was much more difficult than she would have thought.

When the bell rang for lunch, they were ready. Because the truck window was higher than the height of most of the kids, they'd set up a table in front of the truck, and Gabe sent her out to serve the food.

It was a relief to be out of the hot kitchen. Seeing the kids' happy faces and their big smiles made all the work worth it. The joy with which they received their tacos and quesadillas touched her heart. The kids could choose between a chicken taco, beef taco, or cheese quesadilla. Their choice of entrée was accompanied by a cup of sliced apples and berries, along with four baby carrots and a homemade dressing dip.

When every kid had been served, Gabe came out of the truck to speak with the principal, a middle-aged Hispanic woman who had nothing but complimentary and grateful things to say.

Madison was reminded then that Gabe did all this for free.

He bought the food. He gave up his time. And he did this every Friday for a different school. That had to add up.

"Thanks for your help, Madison," he said, when all the kids, teachers, and staff had gone back into the building, and it was time to clean up.

"I should be thanking you. That was the most fun I've had cooking in a while."

"I find that hard to believe," he said dryly. "But you were an enthusiastic chef, I'll say that. I do pay my assistant chefs. It's not a lot—"

"Stop." She put up her hand. "You're not paying me anything. I wanted to volunteer. And seeing those kids so happy to get your food, it was worth every minute of my time. You didn't just fill their stomachs; you filled their hearts with your generosity. I could see some of them were overwhelmed that they were getting something special." She felt a little emotional as she finished speaking, and she thought Gabe might feel the same, because he was suddenly looking away from her.

Then he cleared his throat and said, "We better pack up. We have a competition to get to."

She let out a little sigh. "You had to remind me. That won't be nearly as much fun as this was."

"What if they ask you to make the perfect roast chicken?" he teased. "I bet you'd find that fun."

"Good point. Wouldn't it be wonderful if that were the challenge?"

"Not for me."

"Well, I don't think they're going to have us make hallacas, so I doubt either of us will be making our last meal."

"Hopefully, it's not our last meal in the competition. Whatever the challenge is, we have to crush it."

"Agreed. One last thing, Gabe. I told you I don't want money for this, but I want something else."

"What's that?"

She grabbed his hand, pulled him into the truck, and took the kiss she'd been craving for the last few hours.

Gabe kicked the door shut, as he backed her up against the counter and kissed her until she was breathless, and every nerve in her body was tingling.

"Damn," he muttered as he gazed into her eyes. "We shouldn't have started this now."

"I know. I should say I'm sorry, but I'm not."

He shook his head, gave her one last kiss, and then stepped as far away from her as he could, which wasn't that far, considering how little space they had. "We're going to finish this later."

The promise in his eyes sent another shiver down her spine.

No matter how much she wanted to finish things now, they had to clean up and get to the competition. Everything else would have to wait.

———

It was one thirty when Gabe arrived at the Lazure Hotel. He'd sent Madison off earlier as he had to drive the truck back to his parking spot and then pick up his car and get to the competition. He needed to get his head in the game and stop thinking about Madison and all the things he wanted to do with her. This round would be tough, and he couldn't go into it distracted.

After leaving his car in the lot, he headed into the hotel and saw Madison in the lobby. She was off to one side and reading something on her phone. Her stance was tense and so was her expression. He hoped that didn't mean she'd gotten another bad review.

They'd agreed to keep things strictly professional once they arrived at the hotel, but the competition hadn't started yet, and he didn't like what he was seeing. Instead of heading into the ballroom kitchen where they'd get their challenge, he moved toward her, very aware that there were members of the media in the lobby as well as judges and food magazine columnists. Any

interaction between him and Madison would be noted, so he had
to be careful. He shouldn't be talking to her at all, but he had a
feeling she was so distracted by what was on her phone that she
was unaware of the people looking at her.

"Hey," he said quietly, as he drew near.

She glanced up from her phone, a stressed look in her eyes.
"Is it time?"

"Almost. There are people looking at you right now, so whatever is going on, you should hide it with a smile and follow me to
the ballroom as if you don't have a care in the world."

Her gaze darted past him. "I didn't realize," she muttered,
forcing a smile on her stiff face. "Let's go."

They walked toward the ballroom but instead of heading
inside, he led her out a side door to a small empty patio.

"What's wrong?" he asked when they were alone.

"Nothing."

"Doesn't look like nothing."

"My parents are coming to town tomorrow night for dinner.
They'll be meeting Larry at La Marée. They want to celebrate
me making it into the finals, so I better not let them down today
and make their trip a waste of time."

"I'm sure they didn't say that."

"My father did." She turned her phone on and handed it
to him.

As he read the text, he realized the message from her father
was even more harsh than she'd said. Madison's father obviously
believed that a tough, shaming pep talk would somehow inspire
greatness, but he didn't know Madison at all if he believed that
would work.

She wasn't someone to respond to negativity, to do better if
she was reminded of how many times she'd failed in the past and
how this was an opportunity she could not screw up, that it
wasn't just her neck on the line, but also his. He'd gone out on a
limb for her and with the restaurant yet to take off, she needed
to win to give Larry confidence in her.

He handed back the phone, looking at her watery blue eyes and feeling like he wanted to kick her father's ass. "You can't let him get in your head."

"He's always in my head. Every time I try to succeed at something, his voice is there, telling me I better do it this time because I've messed up before, and his children don't screw up."

"I'm sorry," he said. He couldn't, and shouldn't, say what he really thought. "Look, this is nothing new, right?"

"No, it's not new. But this time it isn't just about me losing; it's about his friend not being impressed by his daughter. And that friend is my boss. If I don't give Larry a reason to keep believing in me, he may not even give me another three weeks."

He could see the pressure mounting in her gaze, in the pitch of her voice. "You can't think about any of that right now."

"How can I not?" she asked, a desperate note in her voice. "I don't care about disappointing my father, but I do care about the restaurant. I can't lose it."

He was beginning to realize how much of her identity was tied up in the restaurant. "You can't think about everything that might happen if you lose. You have to focus on the challenge, whatever it is. Today is just about cooking, and you can cook with the best of them. That's all that matters. You can't control the judging."

"I know that." She took a deep breath and let it out. "I can do this."

"Of course you can. Instead of making everything big and overwhelming, keep your focus narrow, stay in the moment," he advised. "Whatever happens, win or lose, you're still going to be a talented chef. That's all today is about—showing off your cooking skills."

A small smile lifted her lips. "That's a much better pep talk than my dad delivered."

"That text sounded more like a threat than a pep talk."

"That's his style. He believes tough love takes a kid further than coddling and handholding."

"Well, I don't agree with him. He's also not a chef, and he has no idea what he's talking about. I doubt he knows anything about the restaurant business."

"He eats at a lot of award-winning restaurants."

"So what? Just because you eat good food doesn't mean you know anything about making it or running the restaurant that makes it." He checked his watch. "We better get in there."

"Thanks, Gabe." She gave him a quick kiss. "You need to win, too."

"Let's both come out on top," he said as he opened the door, and they headed into the ballroom.

———

Madison tried to erase her father's troubling message out of her mind once she donned her chef's coat and got into line with the five other chefs competing to make it to the finals. She was actually starting to get used to the lights and the cameras and wasn't nearly as aware of them as she had been the previous rounds. She was more concerned with the challenge.

"Today, you'll be serving a meal to a panel of twelve judges, representing media, food critics, and award-winning chefs," Francine said. "All twelve judges will rank the dishes from one to six, with six being the best. Today's challenge will be two-fold: the food and the plate. Both have to tell the same story. It can be any story you want to tell, but there has to be a narrative that is represented by the ingredients and the way they are placed on the plate. The chefs with the top two dishes will move on to the final round on Sunday."

It was a broad challenge, which in some ways made it more difficult. Being able to do anything was almost worse than having rigid parameters.

Gabe was standing next to her, and for the first time, she could feel his tension. Being judged on his plating was his biggest concern. And she doubted he'd ever told a story with his food on a plate. She'd only done it a few times during some of her cooking classes. It was a tough challenge because it wasn't just about the food.

They would have two hours to prepare and plate their dishes and would be serving them to the judges at four o'clock. Two hours wasn't much time to not only come up with the idea for a dish and a story as well as make it happen. But the countdown was on, and they were sent to the kitchen where they would have to choose from the available ingredients.

She decided to pick her protein first and build her plate around that. There was a lot of bumping between the chefs as they ran to the fridge to grab what they wanted to cook. She was thrilled to get halibut as she envisioned a sea theme for her plate.

Gabe seemed unfocused, looking at various proteins, not settling on anything, and they only had a limited amount of time to figure out their dish.

As she moved through the produce section, picking out the rest of her ingredients, she saw Gabe continue to pick out proteins and then put them back. She made her way back to the fridge.

"Go with what you love to cook," she said.

"Whatever the hell that is," he muttered. "I'm not a theme-oriented cook. I don't know how to tie the food in with the plate and tell a story."

"Tell your story, your grandparents' story...the humble ingredients, the struggle, the restaurant, the legacy," she said, the words flying out of her lips. "And cook the food that inspired you."

He straightened, gave her a sharp look, then said, "You're right. That's my story."

She gave him a smile and moved away, knowing she needed to focus on her own story, which now didn't seem as good as the one she'd given to Gabe. But she didn't have family inspiration or a legacy. She just had herself. She was going to do her own version of a surf and turf, combining the sea and the land with fish and the most perfect vegetables.

The time flew by. Before she knew it, she was fifteen minutes away from her service and starting to plate. She'd chosen a light-blue plate with ridges to reflect waves. She wanted the plate to portray a journey from the ocean to the earth with balance and harmony.

She started with a generous dollop of cauliflower purée and spread it in an elegant swoosh. Then she placed a halibut fillet, crispy skin side up, slightly overlapping the purée. After that, she arranged baby carrots and asparagus spears around the halibut, intertwining zucchini and yellow squash ribbons into delicate nests that she placed among the other vegetables. She scattered fresh peas around for a burst of color and freshness and then finally drizzled an herb oil to add a vibrant green hue and aromatic lift to connect the land with the sea.

It was one of the prettiest plates she'd ever done and maybe one of her best dishes ever. She didn't know if the story was as good as anyone else might tell, but she felt confident she'd expressed the vision in her head. Hopefully, that vision was good enough.

She had no idea what Gabe had pulled together. He was plating on the other side of the kitchen and would go in front of the judges after her.

With the assistance of several servers, she made her way out to the long table that was the focus of the cameras and the lights. She was presenting with Chef Art, whose pork loin looked monochromatic to her, but she had no idea how it would go over taste-wise.

Francine asked them each to tell their story, and she got a little nervous and sweaty when it was time to talk. But when she looked at her dish sitting so beautifully on the table, she was able to compose her thoughts.

"My idea came from the belief that we're all interconnected, and that starts with the world we live in," she said. "My dish will take you on a journey from the sea to the land and show how the elements of nature flow together in a perfect harmonious balance that nurtures all of us." She blew out a breath at the end, barely hearing what Art had to say about his dish. She was more focused on seeing some of the judges studying her plate with interest. Hopefully, she'd pulled it off.

They were excused and made their way back into the kitchen.

"How did it go?" Gabe asked.

"Okay, I think." She looked at his plate, surprised by how good it was. "Wow, that's amazing."

"It's an arepa with beef medallions. From humble to sophisti-cated...I hope."

"Good luck," she said as he headed into the dining room.

She hadn't been lying when she'd said his plate was really good, and she thought his story would be intriguing. He'd taken a humble ingredient in Venezuelan culture, an arepa, made from ground maize dough and paired with the highest quality beef, surrounding it with microgreens and even a drizzle of something. The colors were bright and vibrant, and she was quite sure the flavors would be the same. Most importantly, it was his story on a plate, and he'd not only taken his food to a new level, but he'd also taken his plating skills in the same direction. She really hoped the judges would like it. And they would like hers, too...

CHAPTER EIGHTEEN

An hour later, they were called back into the dining room. The judges remained seated at their table while the six of them huddled at the end of it, and the lights and cameras were bright and whirring.

"We want to thank you for a fantastic meal," Francine said. "All six dishes and stories were incredible. Frankly, we were blown away, and this was our most difficult judging yet. But as you know, only two of you will go on to compete in the finals on Sunday."

Madison wished she was standing next to Gabe, but Art was in between them, and she felt a little adrift without Gabe's solid body next to hers. But she just had to keep it together for the next few minutes.

She wanted to win the round, but she also wanted Gabe to win, too. And there were four chefs standing in the way of that happening.

"I know it's been a long day," Francine said. "So, I'll get straight to the results and announce our top two chefs. The first chef moving on to the finals gave us a dish that was strikingly beautiful and, in her words, completely balanced and harmonious. We agreed with her assessment. And that chef is Madison Baldwin."

The crowd broke into applause, and she was almost afraid to believe it was true. But her fellow chefs were congratulating her, and then Francine asked her to step to the side.

She wanted to give Gabe an encouraging smile, but he wasn't looking in her direction, and she felt a chill run down her spine. She didn't want this competition to come between them. He had to have made it to the finals with her.

Francine seemed to take forever to collect her thoughts. Finally, she said, "The next chef moving on told us a very personal story, one that resonated with many of us, especially those of us who grew up cooking with our families."

Madison's heart sped up, and her hands clenched into fists. She held her breath, praying it was Gabe's story Francine was talking about.

"And that chef is..." Francine paused again, then smiled. "Gabe Herrera."

Madison had to hold back a cheer as she clapped as hard as she could, feeling an overwhelming sense of relief that they'd both made it to the finals. It almost seemed unbelievable.

But Gabe was walking toward her, and since all the other chefs had hugged him, she did the same, whispering, "We did it."

He gave her a wide, beaming smile as they separated and faced the judges once more.

"We're excited to have two very different and very talented chefs in the finals," Francine said. "For the next round, you will each cook a four-course meal that must include a dessert. You'll have from ten a.m. on Sunday morning until five p.m. when you'll serve dinner to a very elite group of judges, who you will meet on Sunday. For the competition, you'll also be able to select one additional chef from your fellow contestants to help you win the title. Madison, you will be selecting first."

She looked at the other contestants, who had varying degrees of disappointment and anger on their faces. She was pretty sure none of them wanted to help her or Gabe. But she decided to pick Lyssa. Since their first team challenge together, she'd appreciated Lyssa's plating skills and her background in fine dining would go well with hers. "I'll take Lyssa," she said, giving the other woman a hug as she came forward to join her team.

"Gabe?" Francine asked.

"Jacob," he replied.

"Any particular reason?" Francine asked.

"He's fast and likes hot flavors," Gabe returned.

"Well, it looks like we'll have the men against the women, both in individuals and teams," Francine said with a laugh. "Get some rest and good luck. And for those of you not moving on, we appreciate your time and your effort and hope you enjoyed participating in the competition. We wish you luck in your future endeavors."

As Francine finished speaking, the cameras and lights went off, and Madison turned to Lyssa. "I hope you don't mind helping me."

"Of course not," Lyssa said. "I'm disappointed I'm not moving on, but you're a fantastic chef, Madison, and we'll work well together. Plus, I'd like to see a woman win. And if it can't be me, I'd like it to be you."

As the judges got up from the tables, many of them came over to express their appreciation for her dish, and she felt a little overwhelmed by all the positive comments. She could see Gabe getting the same attention, and she had a feeling it would be a very close race to the end. But this was what they'd both wanted. And she didn't want to think about Sunday yet. It would be here soon enough.

When she finished her last interview, she wanted to talk to Gabe, but he was caught up in conversation with the beautiful Georgia Marks, the producer who was interested in having him on her show. Georgia had her hand on Gabe's arm and was whispering something in his ear. Clearly, she had picked her favorite. Madison could only hope Georgia wouldn't be judging the finals.

Feeling awkward now that she was on her own, she decided to leave. She'd wanted to celebrate with Gabe, but he was busy, and she couldn't just hang around like a third wheel, hoping to be noticed by the producer.

When she got to her car, she texted Drea with the good news that she'd made the finals and asked her how things were going at the restaurant.

The text she got back was filled with celebratory emojis and praise. Drea told her dinner service was going well, but reservations were down a little, which was not what she wanted to hear. She asked her how tomorrow looked and warned her that Larry would be coming in for dinner along with her parents.

Drea replied that tomorrow's reservations were better, so the restaurant should look busier when they arrived.

She told her she'd check in later but was going to take a minute to catch her breath since everything was under control there.

As she sent that text, she looked back at her messages to see the one from her father.

She didn't really want to answer him. But she did want him to know she'd won. She decided to send a group text to her mother, her father, and her siblings to let them know she was in the finals. She then sent a separate text to Larry.

Her mother got back to her immediately, telling her how happy she was for her and how she couldn't wait to celebrate tomorrow night. Her father said he'd expected nothing less. Neither of her siblings immediately replied. Larry came in next, saying he was thrilled and hoped the result would bring more people into the restaurant. He then added he'd seen a less-than-stellar review, and he wanted to talk to her about that tomorrow. They would have a chat before dinner service started.

A less-than-stellar review was the last thing she wanted to discuss. She wanted to bask in her glory, but the competition was just one piece she needed to increase her chances for success. She couldn't forget that. Which meant, she should go to work.

She was just about to start the car when a text came in from Gabe, telling her he was going to get drinks and probably dinner with Georgia. He didn't think he should refuse because she wanted him to meet some other members of her team. He'd check in with her later, but he didn't know how long it would go.

She was more than a little disappointed they couldn't celebrate together now, but he had an opportunity that could be good for his career, and she couldn't blame him for taking it. She also needed to realize that from here on out, they would be going against each other, and maybe putting a little space between them wasn't the worst idea.

Ignoring her mixed emotions, she sent a simple, happy text. *Have fun! Congrats again. We did it!*

He replied with a thumbs-up, which didn't say nearly enough, but for now, it was all she was going to get.

———

Madison thought about going into the restaurant, but she'd been working all day, and as much as she loved La Marée, she needed a break. Between working in Gabe's food truck and the Lazure Hotel kitchen, she'd been sweating all day over a hot stove. She needed to cool off. Maybe she'd go for a swim when she got back to Ocean Shores. That might clear her head.

After parking in her spot, she got out of the car and heard music playing in the courtyard. When she entered, she found a dozen people around the pool, having drinks. There were balloons attached to one chair, along with two bottles of champagne. It must be someone's birthday.

"There she is," Kaia declared. "The champion. We didn't think you'd be back until eleven. We were going to put these in front of your door." She got up from the table to give her a hug. "Congratulations."

"This is for me?" she asked in shock.

"You and Gabe," Emmalyn said, hugging her next.

Lexie followed. "We're so proud of you both."

"I can't believe you already heard," she muttered.

"It was posted on the website," Lexie said. "We were keeping an eye on it. Let's get you a drink, Madison. We have wine, beer, or tequila."

"I'll have a glass of wine," she said.

"Red or white?" Ava asked.

"Red would be great." She'd only met Ava and her boyfriend, Liam, briefly, so she didn't know them well, but she was looking forward to getting better acquainted.

"Is Gabe on his way?" Ava asked as she poured Madison a glass of wine.

"No. He's meeting with someone from the Culinary Network."

"That sounds great," Liam said with excitement. "I could see Gabe on TV."

"He's very charismatic," Emmalyn agreed.

She sipped her wine as she nodded in agreement. "He is that," she murmured.

"Do you think you can beat him?" Kaia asked, giving her a speculative look.

"Yes," she said with a smile. "And I'm pretty sure he thinks he can beat me, so we'll have to leave it to the judges."

"Won't it be difficult to go against someone who is a friend?" Emmalyn asked.

She shrugged. "It is what it is."

"I've competed against my friends in surfing," Liam said. "I would just tell myself that they want to win as much as I do, and whoever is better that day deserves it."

She liked that approach. "That's what I have to do. I can't make it personal."

"Well, you are a fabulous chef," Lexie put in. "We all saw that the other night. It was one of the best meals I've ever had."

There was a chorus of agreement, and she felt touched to have such supportive neighbors, who were quickly becoming friends. As everyone sat down, she took a chair next to Kaia. "How's your brother?" she asked.

"He's fine. He's back at work," Kaia said, an annoyed glint in her eyes.

"You worry about him, don't you?"

"My brother is a magnet for trouble. I thought moving here to Oceanside would make him safer, but he finds danger wherever he goes."

"It sounds like he's a good cop."

"He's certainly willing to do whatever it takes," Kaia said. "Ben is a lot like our father, who was a Navy SEAL."

"That's impressive."

"My dad was and still is the ultimate tough guy. Ben follows in his footsteps."

"Don't you as well? As a paramedic, you're out on the street saving lives."

"That's true, but my job is not usually dangerous."

"Don't listen to her," Lexie put in. "Kaia had someone pull a knife on her a few weeks ago."

"The individual was having a mental health episode," Kaia said. "But I was able to calm him down."

"Sounds like you and Ben have more in common than you're saying," she said dryly.

Kaia made a little face. "Well, don't tell him that. Do you have siblings?"

"An older brother and a younger sister."

"Are they also chefs?"

"No. I don't think either one of them could even make a grilled cheese sandwich," she said with a laugh. "We have very little in common and aren't close."

"Well, you can't pick your family," Lexie interjected, a shadow in her gaze, making Madison wonder what Lexie's family was like.

Lexie and her Aunt Josie seemed to be very close, but maybe she was referring to her parents. Thinking about Lexie's parents made her think about her own. They'd be in town tomorrow, and while she was happy to see her mom, her father was another story. At least she'd made it into the finals, and they could celebrate that. That would hopefully take some of the focus off the restaurant numbers.

She sipped her wine, listening to various conversations going on around the pool. She loved how friendly everyone was. They were like a family, teasing each other and telling stories, but there was an underlying thread of caring and acceptance, and that felt rare to her.

By ten o'clock, the exhaustion of the day caught up to her. Gabe hadn't come back, nor had he texted, so she grabbed her bottle of champagne and one of the balloons and headed upstairs. She was disappointed she hadn't heard from him, but drinks must have turned into dinner. She felt a little jealous of the beautiful woman he was spending time with. Not that he couldn't flirt with whoever he wanted to. They weren't exclusive. She didn't really know what they were. Except that she liked him...probably too much.

CHAPTER NINETEEN

Gabe woke up Saturday morning with a throbbing headache and a lot of regrets, not just for the amount he'd had to drink the night before, but because he hadn't made good on his promise to see Madison after the competition was over. He hadn't even texted her because his phone had died halfway through the night, and by the time he got back to Ocean Shores, her lights were out. Hopefully, he could make things right with her today. He wanted to talk to her more than he wanted to do anything else.

After showering and dressing, he left the apartment and went to see her. He knocked, hoping she was home. It was ten o'clock in the morning, so he didn't think she'd be at the restaurant yet, but with her parents and her boss coming to the restaurant tonight, she could be doing any number of things.

Fortunately, a moment later, she opened the door. She was in shorts and a T-shirt, her hair in a messy ponytail. She had no makeup on and had never looked more beautiful. There was a purity about her, an authenticity that was more than a little attractive.

"Hi," he said, a million other thoughts running through his mind, but that was all that came out. "Can I come in?"

She gave him a somewhat wary smile. "Sure. How was your night?"

"It was long," he said as he stepped into her apartment. "I was going to text you, but my phone died."

She gave a nod. "It doesn't matter."

"It does. I'm sorry. I wanted to see you last night. I wanted to celebrate with you, but when I got back, your lights were out."

"I hung out by the pool for a while, but I was so tired, I had to go to bed early. Did you see the champagne and balloons they got for us?"

"I did. It was very thoughtful." He drew in a breath, hating the cool politeness between them. "Could you just tell me I'm an asshole for bailing on you after the competition, for not texting you last night, and for not keeping my promise to see you later? Tell me you're pissed at me. But don't tell me it was unforgiveable."

"You told me not to put words in your mouth. Don't do the same to me," she said sharply.

"You're right. I just feel like we're standing in a block of ice, and I want to crack it. I want to get back to where we were."

"I'm not as angry as you seem to think I am," she said. "I was disappointed we didn't get to celebrate, but you had an opportunity to meet with people who could help your career. I couldn't blame you for that. I would have done the same."

"Then why does it feel like you're distant?"

She let out a breath. "I'm not trying to be distant, just realistic. It's probably better we didn't spend the night together, because tomorrow we're going to be trying to beat each other. You want to win, and you need to win, and I feel the same way. One of us will be disappointed. I don't want to hurt you. I don't want you to hurt me. But it's inevitable."

"We can't make it personal, Madison. We're not trying to beat each other. We're just trying to do our best and whatever happens, happens."

"I know we'll both try to keep it professional, but I'm not

sure we'll succeed. Anyway, tell me what happened with your meeting last night. It must have gone well."

"It started out with drinks with Georgia and her partner, Brian Cobbs. But then two other executives from the Culinary Network invited us to dinner, and we went to Rosea. That took forever."

"Are you going to do a guest spot on Georgia's show?"

"Maybe. But it turns out the other executives also really liked my story, and they think I could do my own show."

Her brows shot up in surprise. "That's amazing. Your own show on the Culinary Network? That's great, Gabe."

"It's exciting, but it would involve moving to LA, and I'm not sure I want to do that."

"But you'd be on television, and you'd be cooking your food, and people would know you."

"I'd be cooking my food for television. No one would be eating it except people in the audience, or maybe some guests. I don't know." He ran a hand through his hair, feeling his head beginning to ache again. "Being on TV hasn't been my dream. I want to cook for people in my own restaurant, not on a television set."

"Think of it as a step toward that. If you get notoriety from a show, you're going to find an investor really quick."

He nodded. "So, you think it's a good idea?"

She hesitated. "I do. I know it would be difficult for you to leave your family."

"I love my life here."

"You might love your life even better in LA. It's a fantastic opportunity. I'm sure you'll be paid well, too."

"There are a lot of details to be worked out. They gave me the general pitch, but there will need to be more meetings before anything happens." He paused. "You're partly responsible for their interest. You told me to tell my story on the plate."

"It was still your story and your food," she said, dismissing his comment.

"But I was stuck. As soon as Francine talked about plating, all I could see in my mind was a blank white plate with no ideas on it."

"It was the first time I saw fear in your eyes," she said with a nod. "But you conquered it. You won."

"I think you won, Madison, and I came in second."

"I'm not sure it mattered what order they called our names in. Your dish looked great, and everyone said it tasted incredible. You deserve to be in the finals."

"As do you. Without a speck of help from me. You created a sophisticated and harmonious plate filled with the richness of the sea and the bounty of the land."

"I should have said it that way," she said with a smile. "I don't even remember how I explained it, but it wasn't that pretty."

"Your plate of food spoke for itself."

"It was nice to put out something I really liked. If I lost with that dish, I was okay with it."

"That's the right way to think."

She shook her head. "My father would say that's the worst way to think, that you can never have doubts in your head. You have to go into whatever you're doing with absolute belief you're the best."

"Well, after seeing your father's text yesterday, I don't think much of his wisdom."

"He's a very successful man."

"Maybe in his field, but that's not your field, and you're not him. If you had lost yesterday, it wouldn't make you any less of a chef today."

"No, but it would have made dinner tonight a lot more uncomfortable. I'm dreading their arrival. And Larry wants to meet beforehand to talk about the restaurant and some bad review he read. I don't know if it's the one from Felicity that I saw or another."

"He's not going to shut things down with you moving on to

the finals. You're on a roll. You're getting good press. You should be confident going into dinner service tonight."

"I want to be, but I have to admit that since I opened the restaurant, I've learned a truth I thought I knew but really didn't."

"What truth is that?"

"That having my own restaurant would give me freedom, but that doesn't happen when you have an investor. Larry has a big say in what's on the menu, the pricing, and the décor. Since it's his money on the line, I can't overrule him."

"You can if you believe what you're doing will make his investment stronger. He's not the chef; you are. You need to remember that."

"You're right. Anyway, I need to take a shower and get on with the day. Sorry I can't spend more time with you."

"I understand. I missed my chance last night."

"You did. I had some very exciting things planned for you."

He was happy to see the teasing light back in her eyes. "Damn. Now I really feel bad about bailing on you."

"You should."

"Can I get a raincheck?"

"We'll see. After tomorrow, we may be going in very different directions."

She was right, but he didn't like her answer. And he liked the idea of never being with her again even less.

CHAPTER TWENTY

As she drove to her restaurant, Madison was glad she and Gabe had had a chance to talk. But his exciting news had only made her realize their futures could be veering away from each other very soon. Gabe could be moving to LA to start a new life. And she loved being in Oceanside.

Although, her future was up in the air, too. Even if she won everything tomorrow, if the restaurant didn't turn a profit at some point, she would be out, and she'd have to start over again. Who knew where that start might take her? There were simply too many variables in both their lives to even be thinking about a relationship.

But she couldn't stop thinking about Gabe. He was the first person she wanted to talk to in the morning and the last person she wanted to talk to at night. He understood her, sometimes almost better than she understood herself. He'd inspired her to be true to herself, and that had made her cooking better. And even though they were rivals, he'd somehow become her best friend. She couldn't imagine not talking to him every day, not seeing him, not kissing him again. The physical attraction was just as strong as the mental and emotional connection.

But that connection might, and probably would, be broken

by their career directions, by their work aspirations. How could he not go to LA and become a celebrity television chef? It was too great of an opportunity for him to get out of his truck and get the fame and acclaim he deserved.

And she was building her brand in Oceanside. She had to focus on her restaurant, on this huge chance she'd been given to prove herself as a chef who could also run a restaurant.

As she parked in the lot behind the restaurant, she reminded herself this was her dream, what she'd always wanted, but it didn't ring all the way true because it wasn't truly hers; it was Larry who'd rented the space, who'd put his money on the line, and it was Larry who had the power to change anything about La Marée, including the chef.

It also bothered her that it might not just be Larry. Her father could not keep his mouth shut if he had an opinion, and as Larry's friend and her father, he was far more invested in her business than he should be. But her dad was the reason she was here, so she had to suck it up and get ready to welcome them all in for dinner.

They'd told her they wanted to celebrate, but it didn't feel like a celebration. It felt like another competition, one she wasn't sure she could win.

———

Three hours later, her kitchen was humming. Everything smelled delicious. Her cooks were working in harmony, and she felt ready for dinner service. But first she had to get through her meeting with Larry.

He arrived a little after four o'clock and spoke to each of the chefs, as well as Drea and the bartending staff, before calling her into the office fifteen minutes before they opened the door for dinner service.

It felt strange to see Larry's big, stocky body filling her chair, to be the one sitting in the hardback chair in front of the desk, as if she had no higher position than anyone else in the restaurant who had been called in to see him.

"Congratulations on your win," he began.

"Thank you. One more round to go."

"Yes, and I'm expecting you to take the trophy home. We need that for this restaurant to succeed. Second place won't be good enough."

He sounded exactly like her father, which wasn't surprising, since they were very much alike.

"I'll try my best."

"It's not the effort I'm looking for; it's the result. I've been going over the financials, and while I've seen positive, upward growth the last two weeks, it's still not enough. I'm sure you would agree."

"I believe the trajectory is headed in the right direction," she said.

"Yes, but I need the trajectory to move faster. I applaud your efforts to increase business by participating in this local contest. I can see that you have had a jump in reservations after every round, including tonight. Drea told me that you had six new bookings today, many of whom mentioned the competition."

"That was why I entered," she said. "I'm making my name locally, and that's where our customers are."

"What are your marketing plans for next week, after this competition is over?"

"I'll continue to post on social media, and I believe word of mouth will increase business."

"What about other competitions?"

"I don't know if there are any other competitions that are local."

"Perhaps you should travel."

"But then I would be away from the restaurant," she protested.

"Elliott is an accomplished executive chef. He can execute the menu in your absence. I had my assistant do some research.

There is an audition for a nationally televised competition next week in Los Angeles. I'd like you to try out. I think if you're coming off a win here, that will make it easier to get selected. Although..." He paused, his gaze sweeping her face. "I spoke to a media consultant, and she believes you need to work on your image."

"What does that mean?" she asked, her alarm growing with every word that came out of his mouth.

"The consultant thinks you come across as quiet and a little boring. She wants to have you see a stylist, work on your wardrobe, and also polish your interviewing skills. She said you seem to get tongue-tied in front of an audience and that won't get you on national television, no matter how good of a chef you are."

"I'm not really interested in being on television," she said, surprised at the direction of this entire conversation. "I want to run this restaurant and make it a success. I can't do that if I'm going to compete in Los Angeles."

"I'm not sure you can do that if you stay here. Social media posts won't get us where we need to go. You're the face of this brand. You have to sell it everywhere, and this is a tourist desti-nation. We want visitors to Southern California to drive to Oceanside to eat at the restaurant run by their favorite TV chef. Why do you think so many Michelin-starred chefs are going on television? It's a way to stand out."

He wasn't completely wrong, but she didn't want to do anything he'd suggested.

"Think about it," Larry added, as he got to his feet. "I'll be back at six thirty with your parents. After dinner, we'd like to take you out for drinks to celebrate. Can you make that happen?"

"Of course."

He came around the desk. "I'm looking forward to seeing this restaurant full tonight."

"Me, too," she said as he left the room.

But she wasn't looking forward to seeing her parents and spending time with them after dinner, when she was sure the conversation would push her in a direction she didn't want to go.

———

Dinner service went well. The restaurant was busier than it had ever been, which put more pressure on her team to get the food out not only fast but also perfectly. There were a few glitches here and there, but for the most part Madison was happy. When her parents and Larry had finished their meal, they'd told her they'd meet her in the bar at the hotel where they were staying.

She changed out of her chef's clothes and put on a dress and heels before going to meet them.

The bar was as swanky as the beachfront hotel in San Diego. The drinks were even pricier than the ones she served at her restaurant, but since her father was paying, she ordered a very expensive glass of wine, knowing she would need it to get through the celebration, which she suspected would soon turn into an interrogation.

Her mother gave her a warm smile when she got to the table. "Dinner was delicious, honey. Every dish was perfect, and the plates were so pretty. I'm so proud of you."

"Thanks," she said, knowing her mom tried to be supportive. She was just often overrun by her father.

"Are you nervous about tomorrow?" her mother asked.

"A little. But I'm excited to make my own menu. No crazy challenges to complete. I just have to cook my food really well."

"The food of La Marée," Larry said. "I would assume you are making dishes from our menu."

"I was going to do one of the appetizers, yes," she said.

"What about one of the main courses?" her father asked in surprise. "You need to make a dish people will want to come in and try. Isn't that the point of this competition?"

"Well, uh..." She hesitated, wondering why she hadn't chosen

SUMMER LOVING 213

to make one of her dishes, except that she made them every
night, and it felt a little repetitive. "I'm going to do a new take
on our chicken dish. It won't be exact, but it will be close, and it
will be good."

"That's ridiculous," her father said shortly. "You should make
the exact same dish. It's crazy that you wouldn't do that."

"I don't want to make something I make all the time. The
judges said they wanted a one-of-a-kind meal, not something
they could come into the restaurant and order tomorrow."

"If the dish you make isn't one-of-a-kind, then you're not
doing it right," her father said.

"I agree with Philip," Larry said. "I want to see at least two
of the four courses coming off our menu. That's how we get
diners into the restaurant. They'll want to taste the dish that
won you the title."

"If I win," she muttered.

"None of that. You will win," her father said confidently.

"You're so talented," her mother added. "You can make any
dish special, Madison. And I know when I watch those cooking
competitions, I can't wait to go to that chef's restaurant and try
their signature dish."

"Okay," she said, desperate to change the subject. "Those are
all good points."

"It's going to be so fun to see you compete tomorrow," her
mother said.

She didn't think it would be fun at all, but she was going to
try not to think about them being in the audience. "So, tell me
what's happening with Carter and Vivienne."

As her parents started bragging about her siblings, she sipped
her wine and tried to relax, but her mind was spinning in a dozen
different directions. She was starting to feel like winning was
only going to send her down a road she wasn't sure she wanted to
take.

———

After finishing up his food service on Saturday night, Gabe settled on the couch in his living room to work on his menu for Sunday. Max was at the table on his computer, and they both had their headphones on, so as not to disturb each other.

Max was definitely working harder than he was, his fingers flying across the keyboard, while his pad was mostly blank. He felt a little like he had yesterday when he'd been unable to think of a story or a way to plate that story. Then he'd gotten a little nudge from Madison, but that wasn't happening now. It was every man or woman for themselves.

He needed to come up with four perfect dishes, but every choice he made, he second-guessed. He'd never felt so indecisive in his life. And it wasn't just about the menu; it was about his career. He had some big decisions coming up, and he wasn't going to have a lot of time to think about his choices before he had to say yes or no.

He was relieved when he got a text from Madison a little before eleven.

I just got back and saw your light was on. Do you want to talk for a few minutes?

His pulse jumped, and he sent an immediate reply. *Yes. I'll come to you. Max is working here.*

He grabbed his pad and pen and headed out of the apartment. Her door was open, and she was waiting for him. She looked beautiful and tired at the same time. He wanted to wrap his arms around her, but he wasn't quite sure of her mood or what she wanted to talk about.

"How's it going?" he asked as she invited him inside, and they sat down on her couch together.

"It's been such a long day," she said. "I had a meeting with Larry, then served him and my parents dinner, and then met them all for drinks at their hotel after."

"That explains the pretty dress," he said with a smile.

"It was a swanky bar at a five-star hotel."

"Your parents are rich, aren't they?"

"Yes," she said. "But that's them, not me. As you might guess, my father thinks it's important for his children to make their own money."

"On that point, I might agree with him. Don't kill me."

She smiled. "I don't disagree it's important for kids to make their own way. That's not my problem with him."

"I know."

She kicked off her high heels and tucked her legs underneath her. "Have you been working on your menu?" She tipped her head toward the pad in his hand.

"Yes. And you can see I've gotten nowhere." He turned the pad to face her.

"You just have four headings," she said with a smile.

"I can't seem to commit to an idea. What about you? Do you have every dish plotted out to the last detail?"

"I thought I did, but Larry and my father told me I'd be a fool not to make dishes from my menu. I wasn't going to do that because it didn't feel like it was in the spirit of the competition, which was to push ourselves and come up with something new and exciting. But they feel that customers will want to come to the restaurant to try a winning dish, and I can't say they're wrong."

"It's a solid point," he agreed. "One I don't have to worry about."

"You're not making an upscale version of anything you sell on the truck?"

"No. I'm going to cook a meal that reflects the kind of restaurant I want to have one day."

"That sounds nice."

"It's not really different than cooking the dishes you've built your restaurant around. My menu is an aspiration. Yours is a reality."

"But it's not completely my menu. Larry had input."

He was surprised by that. "I didn't know he helped you create the menu."

"It was more that he edited or took things off he didn't find appealing, so I did come up with the menu. But there were dishes he didn't go for, and I wanted to make one of those dishes tomorrow."

"Then do it. If it wins, he'll probably be happy to put it on the menu."

"If it doesn't win, he'll be convinced he was right."

He could see the troubled conflict in her eyes. "Here's what I think. You can't cook with anyone looking over your shoulder. At the end of the day, it's you who wins or loses, no one else. It's what you said yesterday. You should make something you'll be proud of, whether you beat me or not."

She smiled. "You're right. With such good advice for me, why are you stumped about your menu?"

"I'm making the same mistake, considering other people. I want to honor my grandparents, my heritage, but I also want to be myself."

"Then make something you'll be proud of, whether you beat me or not," she repeated.

"You're so wise," he said dryly.

She laughed. "I know." She paused, a lot of emotions moving through her gaze. "I kind of wish it wasn't all happening tomorrow. I want more time before..."

"Before what?" he asked.

"Before everything changes. You could be moving to LA. I could be entering another cooking competition. Although, that might also be in LA."

"What? When did you decide that?" he asked in surprise.

"I didn't decide. Larry is pushing me to audition next week. He thinks the only way I can make my restaurant successful is to become a celebrity chef."

"Is that what you want to do?"

"Not really. It's nothing I ever considered, and I don't know if I'd be good at it. I don't have your natural charisma. In fact, Larry already has a media consultant lined up to teach me how to talk in front of the camera. Apparently, neither Larry nor the consultant have been impressed with the online interviews they've seen."

"Screw them," Gabe said forcefully. "You're not a puppet. You don't have to jump when he says jump."

"I think I do. If I don't go along with him, he might kick me out of the restaurant."

"You can be successful without doing more competitions. If you want to do it, that's great. More power to you, but if you don't want to do it, you won't be happy, and you won't win because your unhappiness will be reflected in your cooking."

"Yes, but how do I convince Larry of that? If I just say no, he'll probably fire me. I really thought I'd finally be calling my own shots when I got this restaurant, that my time of dancing to someone else's tune was over, but that's not what happened."

"You still have a lot of control, just not all."

"I know I shouldn't be complaining. I'm super lucky to be where I am. Anyway, that's enough about me. Have you thought any further about your options?"

"I've been thinking about them all day, but I haven't come to any conclusions. I'll decide after the competition."

She nodded, then yawned. "Sorry. It's been a long day."

"It has. I should go. I just don't want to." He slid his hand behind her neck and brought her face to his. Then he kissed her, closing his eyes as he savored the taste of her mouth. He felt a deep hunger for this woman, a desire so strong it made him want to forget everything else.

Madison broke the kiss and gave him a breathless and emotional look. "We can't keep going tonight. We both need to sleep, and being together now will make tomorrow harder."

"You're right," he muttered. "I wish you weren't."

She stood up, and he had no choice but to get up and follow her to the door. He paused in the doorway and said, "Good luck in the finals."

"You, too. I mean that, Gabe. If I can't win, I'll be happy you're the one who beat me."

"I'll feel the same." He took a breath. "Tomorrow won't be the end of everything for us, just the competition." He said the words as forcefully as he could, but he wasn't sure he believed them any more than she did.

CHAPTER TWENTY-ONE

Madison arrived at the hotel at eight forty-five Sunday morning and met Gabe and their sous chefs in the ballroom. She and Gabe wished each other luck. Then they filmed a short segment with Francine welcoming them to the final round.

When that was done, they were sent to the market with a generous budget to pick up their ingredients. They had only thirty minutes at the store, and it was a challenge to get every-thing she needed in that amount of time, but she was happy she'd spent so much time on her grocery list, because she didn't want to get back to the kitchen and discover she'd forgotten something important.

She didn't speak to Gabe at the market, and once they returned to the hotel kitchen, it was down to business. As soon as she started to prep, her nerves eased. There were cameras around, but she forgot about them as she concentrated on what she was doing.

When they started cooking in earnest, more cameras arrived, and the last thirty minutes of cooking were being livestreamed into the ballroom for an audience of fifty plus people as well as the five judges who would determine the winner.

As time was winding down, several judges made their way

through the kitchen, asking them each about their menus. She hated having to take time to speak to them, but thankfully they kept their questions to a minimum, and she hoped she didn't sound completely incoherent in her answers.

Some of their questions made her doubt her choices, but it was too late to make any changes. While she hadn't caved completely to Larry's request that she replicate the dishes on her menu at La Marée, she had decided to make one of the most popular entrées, a roasted duck, as well as a dessert featuring a fresh berry crumble.

She had no other real ideas for dessert, anyway, and she thought the crumble would be delicious and something she wouldn't screw up. The appetizer would be something she didn't serve at the restaurant, but she thought would be a great starter for the duck, and her other main dish would be the perfect roast chicken with vegetables. It was risky to make something so traditional and so simple, but she knew if she could pull it off, it would be a winner.

As the kitchen heated up, she could smell the peppers Gabe was roasting and knew that his menu would be very different from hers. But different didn't mean bad or good. It would just depend on what the judges preferred.

Gabe also seemed to be working in a rhythm with Jacob. They didn't talk a lot, but when they did, they seemed to be on the same page. She was in sync with Lyssa as well and was feeling pretty good about where they were. But the last twenty minutes, her hands started to shake as everything she did was being filmed. She had to start over on the plating of her appetizer because the plates weren't good enough. But she finally got it done and was happy enough with the result.

When the buzzer went off for the first course, she and Gabe met at the doorway.

"Good luck," he said again, giving her a warm smile.

"You, too."

They headed into the ballroom to cheers and applause. Larry

and her parents were in the front row. Gabe's family was seated just a few seats away from them. She was happy to see Gabe's grandmother and mother, as well as his sister and brother. They were all cheering wildly for Gabe, while her family was politely clapping.

She was happy to turn away from the audience and walk up to the table where the five judges would taste their food. In addition to Francine and two judges from the other rounds, there were two new, highly renowned, award-winning chefs on the panel that she would have to impress.

After they each described their dish, they returned to the kitchen to cook their first entrée. The duck was a dish she made every single night at the restaurant, so she could do it in her sleep, but small things kept going wrong. She burned her sauce and had to remake it, very aware again that every little mistake was being caught on camera, and her boss was watching her screw up.

Finally, she pulled it together and headed back into the ballroom to present her dish.

As she walked out with Gabe, she caught a glimpse of his plate, which smelled amazing and was very colorful. His beef was served with a bright-yellow Aji Amarillo sauce, over a sweet plantain purée and an array of colorful roasted vegetables.

While her plate was sophisticated, his was more rustic, but maybe slightly more appealing than hers. She hoped her flavors were more on point than his, but she wasn't sure.

"Looks good," he murmured.

"Yours looks even better," she said.

"We'll see what the judges have to say."

They entered the dining room to more applause, and she felt even less confident talking about her duck dish, knowing what Gabe had put out for this course.

Then it was time to move on to the third course, which was her roast chicken with truffle potato purée and fragrant, earthy vegetables. She'd never been able to make this dish the way her mentor in Paris had made it, but hopefully tonight she would come closer than she ever had. Either way, it was her personal obsession, and if she could do it well, she could at least be proud of the dish, no matter what happened.

Thirty minutes later, they delivered their third course to the judges. This time she spoke with passion and confidence because the chicken was exactly as she'd imagined it.

Gabe had made pan-seared seabass on a coconut-based polenta, with a mango papaya salsa garnished with bright bell peppers. It looked good, and she had a feeling the taste would match the appearance. She had never seen him cook like this, but he was pulling out all the stops, swinging for the fences, and so was she.

Their final course was dessert, and she thought her berry crumble with freshly made ice cream was good, but she didn't think it would knock anyone's socks off. Gabe offered a tres leches cake with a guava sauce, and she was shocked he'd actually had time and the skills to make a cake. The man was full of surprises.

When they'd delivered their final plates to the judges, they went back into the kitchen and celebrated the finish with their sous chefs and a glass of champagne.

After their sous chefs left to change clothes for the final judgment, she tasted some of Gabe's food, and he tasted some of hers.

"We both killed it," Gabe said with a smile. "Especially you with the roast chicken. Wow. I couldn't see how that was going to be as good as it is."

She gave him a happy grin. "I'm glad I made you a believer. You outdid yourself, Gabe. I had no idea you could cook like this, and your plates were magnificent."

"They were better than I thought they might be. I have to admit Jacob helped with that."

"Well, I had help, too, so that's fair. And the plate is not the food."

"I think it's going to be close," he said. "Are you nervous?"

"Not anymore. I feel relieved it's over...whatever happens."

"I saw your boss out there. I assume the man next to him was your father."

"And my mother was on my father's other side. I saw your family, too. They must be so proud of you."

"I'm sure they are, but I think we should be proud of ourselves." He raised his glass. "Let's drink to us, to one hell of a day of good cooking."

She clinked her glass against his. "I have to admit you inspired me, Gabe. You made me better."

"Same here," he said, meeting her gaze. "You pushed me to go big, Madison. I knew that was the only way I'd have a chance against you."

She was moved by his belief in her, and there were so many things she wanted to say to him, but the production coordinator came into the kitchen and told them the judges had made their decision. It was time to find out who was the winner.

When they reentered the ballroom, everyone was on their feet clapping, and it felt amazing and overwhelming.

As soon as they faced the judges, her nerves tightened. This was it. The end of a long competition, and it would only be worth it for one of them.

Francine gave them a beaming smile. "I think all of us would agree that was one of the best meals we've ever had. Truly exceptional work. Gabe, you took us to Venezuela. You showed us where you come from and how special and wonderful the food from that region is. But more than that, you made it your own."

Applause followed her words. Then she turned to Madison. "Madison, your menu was sophisticated and complex, but you also showed us how to take something classic and simple like a roast chicken and make it exceptional. I have never tasted a roasted chicken that good in my life, and I know that opinion is shared by my fellow judges."

She swelled with pride that at least they'd liked the chicken.

"It was a very difficult decision," Francine added. "It really came down to one course by a very small margin. You both made our job extremely difficult."

She held her breath as Francine paused for what felt like an eternity. Then she said, "The winner of the *San Diego Cook-Off* is Gabe Herrera."

Applause and cries of joy followed the announcement. She turned to Gabe, seeing the shock and happiness in his dark-brown eyes. "Congratulations," she said, giving him a hug.

He whispered in her ear, "I thought it was going to be you."

"I didn't," she whispered back as they pulled apart.

The judges came to congratulate Gabe as well as her. She was touched by how much they'd liked her chicken and also her appetizer, but Gabe had won the dessert round and also the second round with his beef. The only reason he'd taken it all was because her duck was a little underdone, and she'd known that. She'd messed up her timing, and she'd screwed up the one dish she made every single day, her restaurant dish. She had no idea what the judges had told the audience while they were eating her duck, but it probably hadn't been good.

When the judges and her fellow chefs, who had all come back for the finals, finished congratulating her, she made her way to her parents and to Larry.

"You did good," her mom said, giving her a hug.

"I'm sorry I didn't win."

"Your duck was underdone," her father said shortly, disbelief in his gaze. "If it had been cooked properly, you would have won. I don't know how you screwed that up."

"I messed up the timing."

"You were so busy in the kitchen," her mom said. "It's no wonder you made a tiny mistake, but it was still good. And the judges loved your chicken. You always wanted to make that the way your teacher made it in Paris. I think you did that."

"I think so, too," she said, exchanging a smile with her mom.

Her smile faded with her father's next words.

"Why would you make a dish that's not on your menu?" he asked in bewilderment. "And how can you mess up the one dish you actually make every night?"

"It was disappointing that your mistake was with the duck," Larry agreed.

"I regret that, but mistakes happen," she said evenly.

"They can be costly," Larry said heavily.

"I'd like to put the roast chicken on the menu," she said. "After this, I know we'll get customers asking for it."

"Well, they certainly won't be asking for the duck. But the chicken doesn't really fit our menu."

"It fits perfectly," she argued. "And I've wanted to put it on the menu from the beginning."

"Why don't we talk about this later?" her mother suggested. "I know you've been cooking all day, Madison, but we have reservations for dinner at the Terrace in an hour. Why don't you come?"

Going out with the three of them was the last thing she wanted to do, especially after seeing how disappointed both Larry and her father were. She could see Gabe being hugged and kissed by his family and knew that even if he hadn't won, that would have still been their response. But that was his life, and this was hers.

"I'm exhausted," she said. "I'm sorry, but I just need to go home."

"We hardly ever see you anymore," her mother said with disappointment. "We leave tomorrow morning. Please come, at least for a drink. I won't take no for an answer."

"All right," she said, knowing it meant a lot to her mother. "I'll come for a drink."

"Perfect. Do you want to come with us? We have a car."

"No. I'll drive myself. I just need to say a few goodbyes, and then I'll join you."

As they walked away, she was surprised to see Lexie and Emmalyn walking toward her. They each gave her a big hug of congratulations.

"I didn't know you were here," she said.

"We were in the back. It was a nail-biting few hours wondering which one of you was going to win. Sorry it wasn't you," Lexie said with compassion in her gaze.

"If it couldn't be me, I'm glad it was Gabe," she replied.

"Watching you and Gabe work in the kitchen was fun," Emmalyn said. "We just wished we could have tasted all the dishes, especially your roast chicken. The judges raved about that."

"I'm happy to make it for you sometime."

"I'm sure the last thing you want to do right now is cook," Lexie said.

"You're right about that," she said with a laugh. "I'm actually meeting my parents and my boss for dinner."

"I hope they're taking you somewhere great. But I can't imagine you getting better food than what you served," Emmalyn said.

"That's sweet of you to say. I feel so lucky to have moved into Ocean Shores. Everyone is so supportive. And while I know you probably came to support Gabe—"

"Not true," Lexie interrupted. "We came to support both of you."

"I appreciate that."

"Where did Gabe go?" Emmalyn asked, looking around the room. "We were going to say congratulations, but I don't see him anymore."

She pointed to the far side of the room where Gabe and his family were talking to Georgia Marks and some other individuals who were probably with the Culinary Network. "He's over there, but I think he's busy."

"We'll catch him at home," Lexie said. "I need to get back."

"Congrats again," Emmalyn said.

As they left, she debated whether she wanted to go over and say hello to Gabe's family, but with the television producers there, she didn't want anyone to think she was trying to get in on Gabe's win, so she headed into the kitchen to get her things. She'd just packed up her knives and exchanged her flats for heels when Gabe came running into the kitchen.

"Thank God you're still here," he said, throwing his arms around her. "I'm so sorry, Madison."

"Don't be sorry, be happy. You won. You deserved it," she said as she gave him a hug. "You did a fantastic job, Gabe. Every course was perfect."

"They had to be to win. Listen I want to celebrate with you. Georgia and some others from the Culinary Network are taking me out, and I want you to come with us. I want them to meet you."

She immediately shook her head. "No. This is your night, Gabe. They want the winner, and that's you."

"We're both winners."

He was trying to make her feel better, and she appreciated the gesture, but there was only one winner, and it wasn't her. "I can't come. I have to meet my parents and Larry. Go have fun. I'm really happy for you." She didn't know why her eyes suddenly teared up, but she didn't want him to think she was sad, so she forced a bright smile on her face. "But since you won all the cash, I expect you to take me out to dinner one night very soon so I can help you spend it."

"You're on."

"I need to go."

"Me, too." He hugged her again and gave her a kiss. "This is the end of the competition, but it's not the end of us."

She wasn't sure that was true. It looked like Gabe would get all kinds of offers after this. She had no idea where his life would go or where he would end up. Nor did she have any idea where her life would go if Larry decided to fire her. But she wasn't going to think about that now.

———

When she got to the Terrace Bar and Restaurant, which was a stunning property right on the ocean in San Diego, she found her mother seated alone at a table in the bar, sipping a glass of wine.

"Hi, Mom." She took a seat at the table, noting the empty chairs. "Where's Dad and Larry?"

"They ran into some business acquaintances." She tipped her head to the right of the bar where Larry and her father were talking to two other men.

"I'm surprised they left you here all alone."

"I told them I was fine, and I'm glad I have a minute to speak with you. I'm so proud of you, Madison. I've seen you cook before but watching you do it in that kitchen under all that pressure, with those cameras on you, was mind-boggling. Then you had to talk in front of the judges, and that went well, too."

"I've come a long way since the second grade," she said lightly.

"I was hoping that memory would have faded by now."

"It's dimmer. And I really appreciate your support, Mom."

"I know your father is always hard on you."

"He hates losers," she said pragmatically. "And that's what I was today."

"He doesn't hate you; he loves you. You're his daughter."

"It's okay, Mom. You don't have to try to make it better. I know I disappoint him."

"Everyone disappoints him. He disappoints himself. Your father wants so badly for everyone he loves to succeed, and he thinks that tough love is the way to make that happen."

She gave her mother a smile. "I think you've given me this same speech at least ten times in my life."

"Maybe you still need to hear it."

"I'm an adult. I don't need Dad's approval anymore. I made myself proud tonight, and I feel good about what I did. I made one mistake and that was enough to give Gabe the win, but he deserved it. He cooked a fantastic meal."

"The two of you seemed very friendly."

"We've gotten to know each other during the competition, and also outside of it. He lives in my apartment building."

"I had no idea. What a coincidence." Her mother paused. "Larry said he almost hired Gabe when he first decided to open a restaurant in Oceanside."

"I heard that, too. Maybe he should have hired Gabe."

"Don't say that. You're so talented."

"I am talented, but I'm tired of trying to convince people to believe in me. If Larry gave me the job because he wanted to do a favor for Dad, and he's disappointed now, then he should make a change."

Her mother frowned at her words. "You can't quit, Madison."

"I'm not quitting. But I won't live in fear. I can't run a restaurant with threats of being fired hanging over my head. Maybe that inspires some people to work harder, but it doesn't do that for me."

"Well, don't get ahead of yourself. I think Larry and your dad were a little disappointed you came in second, but you still made it to the final two. You're getting tons of press. The episodes will be on television and the Internet. You're making a name for yourself. And I have no doubt about your ability to get to the top of your field."

Her mother's words meant a lot, and she was beginning to wonder why she'd always given her mother's opinions less weight than those of her father. "Thank you," she said. "I mean that. You've always been my cheerleader."

"Sometimes, I cheered too softly," her mother said with a guilty gleam in her eyes. "I've always been someone who wanted to keep the peace. I don't think that was good for you."

It hadn't been good for her, but now that she was an adult it was easier to understand and forgive.

"You did your best, Mom. And I'm glad you came down this weekend." She let out a tired sigh. "Would you mind very much if I left? I don't think I can take any more constructive criticism from Dad or Larry. I'm exhausted. I just want to go home and put on my sweats and sit on the couch."

"That doesn't sound like much of a celebration."

"It's what I need right now."

"Then you should go. But don't be a stranger, okay? I know the restaurant keeps you busy but come home once in a while. Or maybe we could meet somewhere for a spa day sometime. We can get your sister to join us."

"Sure," she said, not as excited about having her sister come along.

"You know, Madison, life isn't that much easier for your siblings," her mother said. "I've had to give them the same talk about your dad that I've given you."

She gave her mother a doubtful look. "But they always win. They're super successful. And they achieve in areas that Dad respects."

"They don't always win, and they feel pressure, too. Sometimes, they're jealous of you. Out of the three of you, you're the one who is really living out her passion."

She was shocked by her mother's words. "Really?"

"Yes."

"Well, I guess I never saw it that way. But I do want to cook with joy and passion. This competition made me realize a lot of things about myself and my goals. Meeting the other chefs, seeing them cook, hearing them talk about food, what it means to them, what it means to me...it's given me a perspective I didn't have before."

"Even when you lose, you can learn," her mother said.

"I've done a lot of losing and a lot of learning," she said. "But having won a few rounds in this competition, I'm starting to understand what it feels like to win, and I don't just mean a trophy. I need to figure out how to be successful and true to myself." She leaned over and hugged her mom, then got to her feet. "Say goodbye to Dad for me. I'm sure I'll be hearing from Larry soon."

"Love you, Madison."

"Love you, too."

As she left the restaurant, she felt lighter than when she'd gone in. It had been nice to have such a good talk with her mom. It made her feel like she'd finally expressed thoughts she'd needed to say for a long time. And moving forward, she was going to stop letting other people define her. She knew who she was now and what she wanted.

CHAPTER TWENTY-TWO

Gabe spent Sunday night and all of Monday in a whirlwind of celebrations and business meetings. Many people who were in town just until Tuesday wanted to grab time with him, and he wanted to accommodate as many of them as he possibly could.

He kept trying to find a time to talk to Madison, but beyond a few texts, there hadn't been a free minute in the day. She'd been understanding, encouraging him to revel in his victory and explore every opportunity. He deserved it.

She deserved it, too, and he knew it was only the slightest of differences that had put him in the position he was in. He wished that winning hadn't come at her expense. But that was the essence of competition: only one person came out on top.

He was happy the competition was over because he didn't want to compete with her. He didn't want them to be rivals. He wanted a much different kind of relationship. What that relationship could be, however, got more complicated with every potential offer, some of which could take him out of the city, out of the state, even out of the country.

Tuesday morning, he woke up determined to talk to her before he spoke to anyone else, but that plan was derailed by a surprising call from Larry Shaw.

After that conversation, he left his apartment and walked down the hall to ring her bell. He waited a long minute, then rang the bell again, feeling a crushing wave of disappointment that she might not be home.

Then the door flew open, and Madison gave him a breathless smile. She wore a tank top and shorts. Her blonde hair was damp, her cheeks flushed, as if she'd just gotten out of the shower. Every time he saw her beautiful face, he felt like he'd been punched in the stomach, and today was no different.

"I wasn't sure if I heard the doorbell ring or not," she said. "I was blow-drying my hair."

"Can I come in?"

"Sure." She let him in, and they sat down on the sofa in her living room. "You've been a busy guy."

"I have. My head is literally spinning."

"What's going on? From your texts, it sounded like you were having a lot of meetings."

"I've had some very interesting offers floated by me," he admitted.

"Like?"

He hesitated. "We don't have to talk about me. I want to know how you're doing."

She shook her head. "I want to talk about you, Gabe. I'm not a sore loser. You beat me fair and square."

"I think you beat yourself with one tiny mistake."

"One big mistake, and one I don't usually make. But that was on me, and I want to know about the offers. Please share. You don't have to feel bad because good things are happening for you. I want good things to happen for you."

"You're a very generous person, Madison."

"So are you. Tell me the good news."

"Well, Georgia still wants me for her show, but they have a chef under contract, so she can only offer me the fill-in guest spot. She thinks that could lead to a full-time gig as soon as the other contract is up, which is in about two months. However, she introduced me to some other producers, and one of them wants me to host my own show. Apparently, people seem to think I have a face and personality for TV."

"I think they're right," she said with a warm smile. "You do have a good-looking face, Gabe. And a lot of charm. What kind of show would that be?"

"I'm not entirely sure. I also got a call from a documentary filmmaker, who is making a movie about food in different parts of the world and wants me to lead a tour through Venezuela, using my heritage and my cooking knowledge to find other great cooks from that area and introduce the world to them."

"That sounds interesting, too."

"My grandmother would love it," he said. "But that's more of a temporary gig. It would take a month to film, and that's a lot of time depending on what else I'm doing."

"Maybe you can be a guest chef on Georgia's show and do the documentary when you're not doing that."

"That's a possibility. I don't really know what to do. One minute, I'm this guy who makes tacos in a food truck and the next minute, I'm supposed to be a celebrity television chef?" He shook his head in bewilderment. "It's hard to wrap my head around that."

"You have never been just a guy who makes tacos in a truck," she said. "You've always been more than that. I'm so glad the world sees your talent."

"It feels good to have offers, but they're taking me far away from my original dream of owning my own restaurant, Madison. That's what I've always wanted."

"All these could just be steps to get to that place, Gabe. Also, it's only been a day, so you may get offers from restaurant owners, too. This is just the beginning for you."

"What about for you?" he asked, his recent call with Larry ringing through his head.

She gave him a speculative look. "Did you speak to Larry?"

"Why would you think that?" he countered.

"Because he told me yesterday that he should have hired you instead of me. I thought he might get in touch with you."

"Larry called me this morning," he admitted. "He said he might be making some changes and wanted to know if I'd consider taking over La Marée."

"I'm not surprised," she said, her expression dimming.

"I'm sorry, Madison."

"This is what you always wanted, Gabe. You parked your truck down the street from La Marée to prove to Larry he made a mistake, and now he's looking to you to save the restaurant."

"I did all that before I met you," he said, needing her to really know how much his feelings had changed. "That was before I knew how good you were. I hope you don't still believe I want you to fail."

She met his gaze. "I don't believe that."

"Good," he said with relief.

"This isn't on you, Gabe. Larry is disappointed in me for many reasons. I lost the competition by undercooking one of our signature dishes. The roast chicken dish I got the most praise for isn't even on our menu. Besides all that, he doesn't think the numbers are growing fast enough. The only way he'll consider keeping me on is if I continue to compete in cooking competitions to build a name for myself that will draw people in and create positive publicity for the restaurant."

"He's an idiot. You need to be cooking at your restaurant, consistently bringing people back for your incredible food. That's what will build your business. And that roast chicken dish should definitely be on your menu."

"I told him that, but he doesn't agree. He's worried about his investment. He gave me a chance because of my father, but now he wants to take more control."

"What are you going to do?" he asked, realizing what a difficult position she was in. "You could compete again. You could look at the competitions as a way to build your restaurant. You almost won this last one. You could do it all again."

She nodded. "I've thought about it. But I wouldn't be building my restaurant anymore; I'd be building his. There would be another chef making the food while I was out making my name. Larry told me in the beginning I'd have autonomy, that I knew the restaurant world, and he didn't. But that changed almost right away. He wanted input on the menu. He chose some of the décor. He was very particular about pricing and what kind of food he wanted to serve. I was on board for most of it because I did come into it wanting to run a fine-dining restaurant, and he was, for the most part, giving me a lot of say. But now he's lost faith in me, and once that happens, it's difficult to get it back."

He frowned at her words. "I don't know how Larry could lose faith in you. You barely lost the competition and look how many chefs you beat along the way."

She shrugged. "It is what it is. What did you tell him? Are you interested in taking over La Marée?"

"No. I told him he's being too impatient. Restaurants take time to grow. You've only been open six weeks, and you haven't even had a chance to see the bump in revenue from being in the finals. A lot of people in that audience will come to your restaurant, Madison. They'll want to meet you and taste your food. He should give you time to prove that."

"He thinks I've had enough time."

"Well, he's wrong. And I told him I'm not interested in running La Marée. It's not the kind of restaurant that would showcase my talents. But it is the kind of restaurant that will showcase yours."

"I don't think so, Gabe."

There was a finality in her voice that surprised him. "What does that mean?"

"I'm going to tell Larry today that I'll run the restaurant for another month. I appreciate the opportunity he gave me, and I don't want to leave him in the lurch. But we are not on the same page, and I think we'll both be happier if we part ways."

He was shocked by her words. "Are you sure you want to

quit your dream, Madison? I know you said he had more input than you wanted, but it's still your restaurant. And the kitchen is amazing. It's a dream to cook in. You need to think about this. Give yourself some time to recover from the competition and to show Larry that what you did the past two weeks is already paying off. This is too big of a decision to make so fast."

"I've actually been wondering if I'm in the right place for some time now. The past few weeks I have learned so much Gabe. Not just about running a restaurant, but about myself, how I want to cook, what I want to cook, and who I want my customers to be. I've been trying to be the chef my father could be proud of, that he could talk about to his friends. It's so ridiculous that I'm thirty years old and still trying to make that man respect me. I'm done."

"He wasn't happy that you lost, was he?"

"I knew he wouldn't be. But I had a good talk with my mom after the finals. She has always supported me, and I realized I never gave her credit for that. All I could focus on was my father's disappointment, instead of her joy and encouragement. Why did I give him so much power over me?" she asked in bemusement.

"Because he's your dad."

"My mother says he drives himself just as hard as he pushes the rest of us. He hates the feeling of being a loser, and that's why he's so tough on us, because he doesn't want us to feel like failures. She might be right. I know he loves us. He just doesn't know how to be a parent who doesn't criticize. Anyway, it doesn't matter anymore. I'm not him. I'm not my siblings, and I'm not my mom. I'm me."

"That's more than good enough, Madison," he said, liking the new strength and confidence he saw in her beautiful green eyes.

"I'm beginning to think so, too," she said. "You've always built me up, Gabe. Even when we were trying to beat each other, you were there for me. You pushed me in a good way."

"You did the same for me. But that said, let's just admit we were the two best chefs in the competition."

She laughed. "Well, it's probably good if we only say that to each other."

He grinned. "I agree. What are you going to do if you quit La Marée?"

"I don't know." She paused. "I did get a call this morning from a restaurant group in San Diego. They want to talk to me about running a restaurant for them."

"What?" he asked, shocked by her casual statement. "Why didn't you say that before now? That's huge."

"I'm not sure how real it is. It was just a message from an admin. I'm sure they're talking to a lot of people. They'll probably call you, too, Gabe."

"Don't downplay it, Madison. This is a good thing, and I'm very sure it's real."

"I'll call them back and find out. Anyway, I don't know what the future holds. But I don't think it will be in fine dining. It struck me when you brought our friends to the restaurant how nervous some of them were about eating there, and that's not the feeling I want to create. I don't want to be exclusive or elitist. I don't want to just serve people like my father and Larry. I had more fun cooking in your truck for those kids than I've had in a long time. And making that roast chicken, that's my style. Rustic, classic but elevated, beautiful, cooked with love and respect for every ingredient. That's who I am," she said passionately. "I know I've made good food at La Marée, but the whole scene: the pricing, the way the menu is written, the formal service... It's not accessible to everyone, and that bothers me. I want to be authentic from now on. I want to be me, faults and all." She blew out a breath. "Sorry. That was a long speech."

"That was amazing," he said, impressed by her words. "You've gained a lot of clarity and confidence."

"I have," she said with a nod. "That reviewer was right. My

food is good, but it doesn't have enough soul, and I need to fix that. I can't do that at La Marée."

"Maybe you can. Tell Larry what you just told me."

"I did. Not in exactly the same way but close enough. He said he wants his original vision of the restaurant. He wants the chef who told him she could make that happen. But I'm not that chef anymore. And he has changed, too. I understand it's his money on the line. The risk is great for him. He should have absolute confidence in who runs his restaurant, and he does not have confidence in me."

"Someone else will," he said with certainty.

She met his gaze head-on. "I think so, too. Anyway, it sounds like we both have changes coming up."

"Changes, opportunities, and possible moves. But that's our professional lives. Let's get personal," he said, feeling suddenly nervous because there was a lot on the line.

"Considering what you just said, this is probably the wrong time to even attempt to figure out our personal lives," she said slowly, her gaze a mix of emotions.

"I disagree," he said strongly.

His words brought a helpless smile to her face. "Why am I not surprised you disagree, Gabe?"

"Because you know there's something happening between us, and I don't want it to stop happening," he said. "Do you?"

"You might be moving away, and I might be as well. Starting something now seems foolish. Who knows where we'll be in three months? We could be miles apart. We could be countries apart."

"We already started something, Madison," he argued. "The first night we met, I couldn't take my eyes off you. And while you might have been a little drunk, I was completely sober, and I didn't want to stop talking to you or kissing you after we left the bar. When my idiot brother's call interrupted us and you took off, I was afraid I wouldn't see you again, and I was incredibly disappointed. I'd never had such an interesting and odd conversation with a woman. Certainly no one had ever asked me what I wanted my last meal to be. I was intrigued."

"That was the tequila talking."

"But then we started discussing food, and you were as interested in the subject as I was, and that almost never happens."

"Not for me, either. I have bored a number of men with my roast chicken story."

"If only they had realized just how good that chicken was you were talking about."

She smiled. "You were skeptical, too."

"I was, until I tasted it. You did your mentor proud."

"I think so, too. I finally got it right because I was cooking with love and passion, not just precision and perfection."

"It needed all of that to be as great as it was."

She nodded. "I kind of wish you'd made your hallacas for the final round."

"I thought about it, but that's my grandmother's dish, and her recipe, one she hasn't chosen to share with me, although I basically know it just from having watched her all these years. But I felt like I needed to make the menu mine."

"That was a good decision." She took a breath and let it out. "I liked you that night at Maverick's, too, but then I hated you the next day when I realized you were responsible for the line blocking my door, making a mockery out of my restaurant being half-empty every night."

"I wasn't a big fan of yours, either, until I realized my impression of you was completely wrong. You weren't just playing at being a chef. Your father didn't buy you the job."

"He did connect me with Larry."

"But you had been cooking in the trenches for years. You were well-trained and well-suited for that job. And you were trying so hard to make things work. That's when I realized how petty I was being. You weren't my enemy. My lack of vision and obsession with Larry's rejection of my offer to work for him were the things that were holding me back, not you." He took her hand and wrapped his fingers around hers. "That's all in the past. I want you to be in my life going forward."

"I want you to be in mine," she admitted. "I just don't know if we can both get what we want and make that happen, too, Gabe."

"We can if we try. We can have it all."

"I'm not sure that's true."

"We'll make it true. You should go for what you want, and I should go for what I want, but we're chefs, and we can cook anywhere, right?" He took a breath, wanting her to understand the depth of his feelings for her. "You've got my heart, Madison, and I can't live without my heart or without you. So, wherever you go, I'm going. I'll find an opportunity here if you want to stay in Oceanside. And if you want to leave, I'll look for something to do somewhere else."

Her eyes grew teary. "That's the sweetest thing anyone has ever said to me. But I can't let you give up opportunities for me. You'd end up resenting me."

"I wouldn't. Because I know what my priorities are. I didn't just learn how to cook from my grandmother. I learned that love means putting someone else first. And I want to put you first."

"Did you just say you love me?" A tear slipped from her eye, and he wiped it away with his finger.

"I think I did, and I didn't mean to make you cry."

"They're happy tears. No one has ever wanted to put me first, Gabe."

"Thank God, because then I wouldn't be here with you."

She gazed into his eyes. "You have my heart, too. So, wherever you're going, I'm going. You're right. I can cook anywhere. And I'll cook a hell of a lot better if I'm with you. We can argue all night about kale."

"I have better ideas for our nights than arguing about kale. But I do like that we can do that, too."

"So do I."

He felt a wave of relief at her words. "Then we'll figure it out.

We'll factor each other into any decision we make. What do you think about that?"

"I think you're going to be stuck with me."

He smiled. "I sure as hell hope so."

She cupped his face and gazed into his eyes. "We may not know where we're going eventually, but I'm thinking we should start now by going into the bedroom. Didn't we agree that whoever won would comfort the loser?"

"I don't remember that deal," he said with a laugh. "But what we found together, Madison, that's the real prize, so we both won. That deserves celebration more than comfort. And we've delayed our celebration far too long." He pulled her into his arms for a kiss...that was once again interrupted by the buzzing of his phone. "Damn," he muttered in annoyance.

"You should get that," she said. "It might be important."

He checked his phone. The number did not belong to anyone in his family. "Not as important as you." He shut off his phone, then pushed her back against the sofa cushions with a smile. "No more interruptions. I want to show you how much you mean to me, Madison."

"I want to show you the same. And by the way, I'm falling in love with you, too."

"Good. So, kiss me already."

"Okay, but just to warn you...I'm never going to want to stop, Gabe."

He smiled. "I'm counting on that."

EPILOGUE

One Month Later

Madison looked around the kitchen of La Marée with mixed feelings. This had been her dream kitchen, her dream job, but the dream had changed when she'd finally figured out who she was and what she really wanted.

Tomorrow, the restaurant would close for a month. During that time, a new chef would come in and make changes to the décor, the menu, and hire his own staff. The name of the restaurant would change. None of the cooks who had worked for her would be staying. They were all moving on to other jobs. In fact, two of them had left in the last week, and she'd spent the final three days with a skeleton crew.

Drea came into the kitchen with a somber expression on her face. "It's kind of sad to say goodbye to this place. I really thought it was going to work, Madison."

"Me, too. I'm sorry I made you quit your other job to come work for me."

"Are you kidding? I don't regret a second of it, and Larry was a fool to replace you with some guy from New York City."

"He's won several cooking competitions and is supposed to be very good," she said. "He's also opened three other restaurants, so Larry is getting someone experienced to take over this place. Which is what he probably wanted in the first place until he decided to do my father a favor."

"I still say it's his loss. You're an amazing chef. Even though you lost to Gabe, the business went off the charts the week after the final round. I was really hoping both you and Larry would reconsider, but you seemed determined to move forward, and he seemed to think the frenzy would die out quickly, which it didn't."

She had been happy that the restaurant had been fully booked the last several weeks. And many of her customers had become regulars. Some of them had expressed disappointment that she was leaving but had promised to follow her wherever she went.

"Do you have any regrets?" Drea asked curiously.

"Only that you'll be unemployed for a few months."

"I could use a vacation before you rehire me," she said with a smile. "Marcus is taking me to Europe for three weeks. I can't wait."

"I'm so glad it's working out for you two."

"And I'm happy you and Gabe figured out you were better lovers than enemies."

"We are definitely better at love than hate," she agreed. "I just hope we're not making a mistake, mixing business with pleasure. We make a good team in the kitchen, but now we'll be running a restaurant together."

"It's going to be amazing. Do you have a name yet?"

"Still working on that." She and Gabe had just signed a deal with a local restaurant group to open their own restaurant in a beautiful space in San Diego, about twenty minutes from Ocean Shores. It was currently under construction, so they wouldn't be opening for another three months, but it was going to be an exciting time of planning their joint venture. "We have to figure out how to mesh our food and our styles."

"I have no doubt that what you come up with will be fantastic." Drea paused, giving her a questioning look. "I thought Gabe might be here tonight for your swan song."

"He got delayed in LA. But it's fine. I'll see him later." She'd missed Gabe the last week as he'd been filming a guest spot on Georgia's show. While their restaurant was being built, Gabe had accepted several of his other offers and was quickly building a name for himself.

"Well, I guess it's time to turn off the lights," Drea said. "Can I buy you a drink?"

"I'm not in the mood. Rain check?"

"Of course."

"Thanks. But if you don't mind, I will take a ride home. My car is in the shop, and when I came to work, I thought Gabe would be driving me back to the apartment."

"No problem. I moved my car out front earlier."

"Okay." She grabbed her bag, having removed all of her personal items from the restaurant earlier in the week. At the door, she took one last look at her kitchen, waiting for the rush of sadness, but instead she felt excitement about the future. She'd made the right decision. And knowing that her future wouldn't be tied to her father or to Larry made it even easier to turn off the lights.

She followed Drea through the dining room to the front door where they turned the sign one last time to Closed and walked out of the building. She locked the door and stepped onto the sidewalk. Since Larry would be changing the locks tomorrow and start remodeling soon after that, she didn't need to worry about returning the key. Maybe she'd keep it as a reminder of where she'd been. Or maybe she'd throw it away because it didn't matter where she'd been, only where she was going.

She was about to follow Drea to her car when she saw the

bright lights of a truck coming down the street, and then a loud horn went off. She smiled as Gabe stopped his food truck in front of the restaurant.

As he got out, she said, "Hey, you're blocking my door."

He laughed as he came over to join her and Drea. "It doesn't matter anymore, does it?"

"It actually never mattered," she said as she gave him a hug. "But what are you doing in the truck? And I thought you were stuck in LA."

"A white lie," he said. "I've actually been busy cooking. My truck has one last party to cater before I put it into retirement. And our friends thought that Ocean Shores would be the perfect place to sign off."

"We're having a party?" she asked in surprise and delight.

"Yes." He turned to Drea. "We'd love for you to come. I sent you a text earlier."

"I know. I meant to reply. I appreciate the invitation, but it's Marcus's brother's birthday, and I told him I'd meet him when I got off work. You two go and have fun. The work will start sooner than you think."

"I can't wait," Gabe told Drea. "And I'm glad you're going to join us in our venture."

"Me, too," she said. "I'll see you soon."

After Drea left, Madison got into the truck with Gabe. "It smells good in here," she said.

"I've been cooking for the past hour."

"I can't believe you did this. You've been so busy. When did you have time to plan a party?"

"I didn't plan it. Lexie, Kaia, and Emmalyn led the charge. I'm just bringing the food. They wanted to celebrate our last nights with your restaurant and my truck and toast to our new venture."

"We have great friends. We are so lucky to live at Ocean Shores." The more she'd gotten to know the other tenants in her apartment building, the more she loved them, and the happier she was they'd been able to find a restaurant space not too far from home.

While they'd spent a week exploring all kinds of opportunities, in the end what they both wanted to do was open a local restaurant so they could stay close to their friends and to Gabe's family. Plus, they both had reputations here, and their romantic relationship and new business venture was already building interest in a restaurant that didn't exist yet.

"We are lucky to live at Ocean Shores," he agreed. "But I might need to make a change."

She looked at him in surprise. "What do you mean?"

"I told you Max went to LA with me."

"Yes. And..."

"The movie is a go."

"That's wonderful. I'm so happy for him."

"I am, too. Filming starts in six weeks. Max needs to be in LA for casting and then filming. He figures he'll be out of town at least three months, maybe longer. He wants to sublet our apartment, and it would be easier if he did the entire place, not just one bedroom." He gave her a quick look. "What do you think about us living together?"

"Well, we're basically doing that already," she said.

"Yeah, but it's different when you can't kick me out."

She grinned. "I haven't wanted to kick you out so far. And I haven't noticed you being too eager to leave."

"I never want to leave you, Madison. And I would like to live with you, if you're ready."

"I'm ready, Gabe. Living together and working together...it's a lot of together, but I'm here for all of it."

He nodded with happy approval. "Me, too."

"And I'm very happy for Max."

"You can tell him that tonight. We drove down from LA together. He needs to pack, and he wanted to see everyone before he leaves again."

"The party should be a celebration for him, too."

"We'll definitely raise a glass to Max," he said as he pulled into the parking lot at Ocean Shores. "Do you want to help me serve?"

"Of course."

Their friends must have been watching for them because the truck was almost instantly swarmed with people. Before she and Gabe could start serving food, Kaia pulled them both out of the truck for a toast.

Emmalyn handed her and Gabe two plastic flutes of champagne while everyone else gathered around. Besides Kaia and Emmalyn, she could see Ben, Lexie, Max, Ava and Liam, Brad and Serena, Josie, Maggie, Frank, and two women she'd recently met at Kaia's book and wine club, Skye and Paige.

"To our two favorite chefs," Kaia began. "This is the beginning of a beautiful future. Cheers."

They lifted their glasses and echoed "Cheers" as they took a sip of their champagne.

"We need to toast to Max, too," Gabe said, lifting his glass. "To his first but not last blockbuster movie."

"This is your night," Max protested.

"We're sharing it with you," Gabe said. "You're on your way, Max."

"This place has a lot of high achievers," Ben commented.

Madison laughed. No one in her life had ever thought she was a high achiever until now.

"I want to say one thing," she interjected, no longer hesitant to speak her mind in public or private. "When I moved in here, I had no idea I would find not just friends but family. Your support of me and my restaurant has been so touching, and I can't thank you enough. I want to toast to all of you."

They lifted their glasses once more, and then Gabe said, "We better start serving these hungry people some food."

They went back into the truck and started putting together the tacos that Gabe had already prepped. As they bumped into each other, she laughed. "This really is a small space."

"Tell me about it," he murmured. "But I like small spaces when you're in them." He gave her a kiss. "I missed you."

"Not as much as I missed you."

"Hey, hey," Kaia said, ringing the bell on the shelf by the window. "None of that. We're hungry."

They both laughed, and then Gabe said, "We better get to work. One last service for the truck and my old life."

She'd finished her last service a few hours ago, so she knew exactly how he felt. As he started to move away, she put her hand on his arm and drew his gaze to hers. "The best is yet to come, Gabe."

A happy grin spread across his face. "I know that, Madison. And I'm not just talking about our restaurant. I'm talking about us."

"Me, too." She gave him another quick kiss, and then they got to work treating their friends to one last taco truck dinner.

WHAT TO READ NEXT...

Are you excited to go back to Ocean Shores?

Don't miss the next book in the series,

Moonlight Feels Right

Emmalyn McGuire has finally found her rhythm as a kindergarten teacher, but she's still searching for that special someone and the kind of love she has only read about in books. Enter Hunter Kane, a brooding military pilot recovering from a life-altering accident. Struggling with grief and his new reality, Hunter hides away at Ocean Shores, only to have his world upended when his late buddy's ex leaves her spirited daughter in his care.

Overwhelmed and out of his depth, the usually guarded and cynical Hunter turns to the sweet and generous Emmalyn for help. Despite her initial nerves around the sexy, injured pilot, Emmalyn's heart goes out to the little girl who needs them both.

As they stumble through the chaos of makeshift parenthood—pancake explosions, petting zoo pandemonium, and hide-and-seek mishaps— their bond deepens. Hunter's darkness is brightened by Emmalyn's happy glow, and she finds a man with whom she can lighten the heavy load of secrets she has carried too long.

Amidst laughter and tender moments, they discover that love isn't just about romance—it's about finding someone who stands by you through the mess of life. Don't miss this charming and irresistibly heartwarming romance from #1 New York Times Bestselling Author, Barbara Freethy!

For a complete list of books, visit www.barbarafreethy.com

ABOUT THE AUTHOR

Barbara Freethy is a #1 New York Times Bestselling Author of 93 novels ranging from contemporary romance to romantic suspense and women's fiction. With over 13 million copies sold, thirty-three of Barbara's books have appeared on the New York Times and USA Today Bestseller Lists, including SUMMER SECRETS which hit #1 on the New York Times!

Known for her emotional and compelling stories of love, family, mystery and romance, Barbara enjoys writing about ordinary people caught up in extraordinary adventures. Library Journal says, "Freethy has a gift for creating unforgettable characters."

For additional information, please visit Barbara's website at www.barbarafreethy.com.

Made in the USA
Columbia, SC
22 July 2024